LISA HELEN GRAY

AIDEN

A NEXT GENERATION CARTER BROTHER NOVEL
BOOK TWO

FAMILY TREE

(AGES ARE SUBJECTED TO CHANGE THROUGHOUT BOOKS)

Maverick & Teagan

- Faith engaged to Beau

-Lily

-Mark

-Aiden

Mason & Denny

-Hope

-Ciara

-Ashton

Malik & Harlow

-Maddison (Twin 1)

-Maddox (Twin 2)

-Trent

Max & Lake

-Landon (M) (Triplet 1)

-Hayden (F) (Triplet 2)

-Liam (M) (Triplet 3)

Myles & Kayla

-Charlotte

-Jacob

Evan (Denny's brother) & Kennedy

-Imogen

-Joshua

AIDEN

ONE

AIDEN

L IFE HAS A WAY OF KNOCKING YOU down and making sure you hit every branch on the way.

A few hours ago, my biggest dilemma was getting my neighbour's builders to stop working and give my hangover a chance to recover.

But then one phone call changed my life forever. Nothing would ever be the same.

Why?

Because I'm a father.

Something I didn't know about until the doctor called me and told me I have a daughter, that the mother died during childbirth, and that I needed to head over to the hospital to collect her. Like he was asking me to do nothing more than pick up a parcel.

All this led me to the present, where I've lost track of how long I've been sitting on my front lawn—well, my neighbour's—wondering what I'm going to do with a baby.

A baby.

I don't know the first thing about raising a baby. I'm way out of my depth. My sisters could help me, both babysat when they were teenagers, and Lily— she's a school teacher.

A throat clears, but I don't turn my head. "Excuse me, but are you okay?"

The voice is soft, almost angelic, and I wonder if I'm dreaming. This has to be a dream because I can't be a father. I've been nineteen for barely five minutes. I had so much to do before I even thought of kids. There is no way I'm capable of looking after one, let alone raising one.

The angelic voice whispers through my head once again. "You're sitting in stingers."

I want to grunt, to snap and tell her I have bigger problems to worry about, but I can't make myself turn around, can't bring myself to speak.

"Please… Are you okay? Can you look at me?"

Tyres crunch the gravel before the sound comes to a stop. A door opening then slamming shut echoes over the garden, over the birds tweeting in their nests.

I hadn't wanted this. All I'd wanted when I woke up this morning was the chick in my bed to leave, followed by some peace and quiet so I could go back to sleep.

"Aiden." Hearing my mum's voice, I look up. She rushes over to me, her face pinched with concern and her eyes glassy. "It's okay, we've got him."

My neighbour must walk off because a few moments later I hear her door shut. I look up at my dad and flinch at his expression. Instead of showing the same concern my mum is feeling, his expression is murderous, and I know I'm about to get a lecture on how stupid and immature I am.

There's nothing he can say that could make me feel any worse.

"Aiden, come on; we need to get to the hospital."

I stand on shaky legs and turn to look my mum in the eye. "I'm a dad. I can't be a dad. What am I supposed to do?"

Before she can open her mouth, my dad is shaking me, looking ready to land a punch to my face. I can't blame him; I messed up. And when a Carter messes up, they mess up fucking good.

"You'll go to the hospital, get your daughter, and bring her home. You'll fucking raise her, care for her, love her, and make sure she wants for nothing. You got yourself into this, boy; you're sure as hell going to do right by her. She's a fucking baby."

He shoves me back a step and I blink, noticing for the first time that I'm crying. "I know she is. I know I messed up, but I don't know the first thing about babies. Can't you have her?"

Mum gasps, but my dad? Yeah, he looks pissed, and I don't bother ducking when his fist lands on the side of my jaw. I deserve it.

"You're a grown-ass fucking man, Aiden. We won't be cleaning up your mistakes anymore. You're on your own with this one. We will help you the best we can, but you're responsible for a tiny human now." He runs his fingers through his hair, looking skyward as if searching for answers.

"I know," I whisper, rubbing my eyes. I never cry—and Landon putting chilli in my drink doesn't count. That shit was hot.

"Let's get to the hospital. Afterwards, we can go from there," Mum says.

I nod, moving until I'm by her side. "I don't even have anything for her."

My dad hears me and sighs. "We can hit Mother Care on the way home. I'll call Maddox and ask him to bring his truck."

I groan, running a hand through my hair. "What am I supposed to tell them?"

My dad gives me a dry look. "That you fucked up and that this is what happens when you don't wrap it up. I'm sure after they hear this, they'll think twice before jumping into bed with a stranger."

Mum gives Dad a warning look before turning to me. Her expression softens as she rubs my shoulder. "Why don't you go get a top on and meet us in the car?"

I look down at my bare chest. Fuck, I'm so glad the chick from this morning already left. There would have been no way for Mum to talk Dad out of beating some sense into me.

Nodding again, I step towards the stairs leading to my flat, when my dad's hand stops me. He looks torn up, hurt. "I'm sorry for laying a hand on you,

Aiden. I just didn't want this for you. I wanted you all to work on getting your careers, to travel a little. I didn't want this for you, but it's happened."

I pat his shoulder, giving him a small smile. My dad has never laid a hand on any of us, not even when we got into trouble doing stupid shit that could have killed us. Yeah, we got a slap around the head a few times—Maddox more than most from his parents, which is why he doesn't have two braincells to put together. Our dad shouting at us was enough for us to listen and obey. Most of the time.

So, I know when he hit me, it was out of fear, not hate. Plus, I've seen him hit, and I know he held back. The last time he punched someone, he knocked them clean out. The guy deserved it for pinching my mum's arse. But that's another story.

"It's fine, Dad. I knew this wouldn't be the easiest news for you to hear. I'll be back down in a minute."

My words leave my mouth in a gasp at the end when he pulls me in for a hug, slapping my back. "You can do this. We will help, but she's your daughter, not ours."

I nod again, still feeling numb from the revelation, and head up the stairs.

———————————————

THE SOUND OF screaming newborn babies echoes down the hallway as the doctor leads us to a private room.

My parents stay with me, but it feels like a blur. If it wasn't for my pounding headache and churning stomach, I would think I was in bed, at home, dreaming.

"Take a seat."

We do, the chair squeaking under my weight. When I'm down, I look straight at the balding doctor and get to the point.

"How do you know she's mine? I never went and got a DNA done."

Pity fills his eyes as he clicks on his computer. "I've known Miss Giles since the beginning of her pregnancy. She knew there could be several complications during the delivery, so she planned ahead—to make sure her baby had a home. She informed me she took a toothbrush of yours, which is on file. In the test that followed, the DNA on that toothbrush revealed a positive match. If you would like another DNA test, we can do that today. However, you are listed as her emergency contact and as the baby's father."

I scrub my face, feeling the rough hairs on my jaw from not shaving this morning. My mind tunes out the sound of my mum and dad asking questions, and travels back to when Casey showed up at my door. I remember losing my toothbrush that night and thinking I'd just misplaced it. I have a tendency to walk around while brushing my teeth if I'm in a rush, and then dropping it wherever.

"Son?"

I shake my head and look to my dad, tears brimming my eyes. I can't let them fall—not now, not in front of a stranger. "Sorry, what?"

He rests his hand on my shoulder, squeezing gently. "He's going to take us to the baby and have someone come in to take a DNA test. It's just a swab."

I nod, getting to my feet and rubbing my sweaty hand down my leg. My mum takes my other hand as we walk out of the room.

I know should ask what I missed, what they spoke of, but at the moment, I'm doing everything I can not to hyperventilate. I'm about to meet my kid. My baby.

The doctor throws back a curtain, and the second he does, my eyes zero in on the screaming baby kicking her feet in a tiny bed. She's dressed in a pink polka dot all-in-one and a pink beanie that looks far too big for her head.

I'm taking one step in front of the other, towards her, and before I know it, I'm standing above her crib. The second I look down at her, I know she's mine.

She has my nose, the same colour and shape of my eyes, and even has a head of dark brown hair.

She's beautiful, and for a few moments I can't breathe. She's mine. Really mine. My heart bursts, overwhelmed with emotion. This beautiful baby girl is mine.

It's all too much, and I nearly collapse to my knees when they give way, but thankfully my father is there to catch me. He picks me up, resting me against his chest as tears spill down my cheeks.

"She's so tiny," I croak out, looking back down at my daughter.

My dad chuckles, patting my back. "She's got a set of lungs on her, that's for sure."

"She's due a feed. Would you like to do it?"

I turn to the nurse I hadn't realised was there and nod, my throat swelling.

"Take a seat and I'll get her out for you."

My arse lands in the only chair in the tiny cubicle, and without taking my eyes off her, I watch the nurse carry her over.

I hold my arms out like I've seen done in movies. I'm shaking badly, scared I'm going to hurt her, but the minute she's in my arms, nothing matters but her. I'd do anything to protect her, to keep her safe.

She looks lost, so small and pink against my tanned arms. She quietens down and her eyes open in wonder, her body settling against mine with a few sniffles. The love I feel for her already is overwhelming. I've known her for two minutes and already she owns me.

The nurse hands me a small glass bottle, the top looking far too big for my baby. "That will choke her," I tell her.

The nurse laughs, but I narrow my eyes on her and she sobers. "It will be fine, I promise. Just rub the teat against her bottom lip and she'll do the rest."

Not taking her word for it, I look to my mum. She's crying silently, and when she notices I'm watching her, waiting for her approval, she nods. "It's fine, Aiden. I promise."

There's no one I trust more than my family, so I do as the nurse instructed and watch as my little girl sucks on it like she hasn't been fed before.

Dad laughs, standing next to me to get a better look. "She sure is hungry."

"Takes after her dad," I whisper, still amazed this tiny human is mine.

"And her granddad," Mum adds, before giggling.

Dad gasps. "Oh, God, I'm a granddad. I'm too young to be a granddad."

"Shut up." Mum stands closer, her voice quiet so she doesn't disturb her. "She's so beautiful, Aiden. And you're a natural."

I look back down at my girl, smiling. "I don't know about that; she seems to be doing this all on her own."

"I'm going to step outside and see where Mason is on the car seat and stuff."

My head snaps up at that. "Can you get him to pick her up a blanket? Maybe a pink one? Her hands are a little cold."

"I can do that."

"And maybe a fresh set of clothes. She has a stain on her chest."

Dad chuckles, his eyes warm and no longer filled with anger like they were earlier. "I'll do that, too. We can get the rest tomorrow. Today, we can just get essentials, okay?"

"Yeah."

"What's her name?" Mum asks the nurse, who is still moving around the room.

She looks up at Mum's question, sadness filling her eyes. "Her mum passed away before we could get a name. She never mentioned one before, either, so we left it blank."

"Have her family been informed?"

Before I can tell my mum, the nurse fills her in. "Sadly, she doesn't have any next of kin."

Mum's eyes water again as she looks down at the baby. "Can you give the morgue my name, number and address? We will arrange her funeral. She should have someone who cares what happens."

"I'll go get a form for you to fill out and I'll personally take it down myself. It broke my heart to know she had no one."

"She has us," I pipe in, saddened. Casey may not have been for me, girlfriend wise, but she wasn't a bad person—from what I remember of that night. She just seemed a little lost, looking for a good time.

Another nurse walks in, bringing Mum a chair, as the other one leaves. She pulls it closer to me and runs her finger down my daughter's cheek. "She really is beautiful. What will you name her?"

I hadn't even thought of that. I don't know why, but I presumed she would already have one. "Tequila?" I offer.

Mum looks at me in horror, and I grin. "You cannot call your baby that."

"Relax, I'm joking."

"You need to wind her."

"Do what to her?" I ask, horrified by the sound of it.

She laughs at my expression. "Rest her face like this," she says, then places her hand under my daughter's chin. I almost push Mum away when it looks like she's grabbing her face, but I look closer and notice she's not using pressure. "If you hold her like this as you sit her on your lap, you can rub her back and tap it."

I do as she says, fingers trembling through my fear of dropping her. "This okay?"

"Yes, though maybe try tapping a little harder. You need to get her wind up, otherwise it will cause her severe pain in her belly."

Jesus fucking Christ. I'll break her back if I tap her harder. She's delicate, but I also don't like the thought of her being in pain either, so I listen to my mum.

"What about Sunday?"

"What about Sunday?" Mum asks.

I chuckle. "Her name. What about Sunday? It's Sunday." I shrug. Plus, the only name I would want to use is my Nan's, Mary's, but I know Faith has always wanted to name her first baby after her.

Mum's expression softens. "I think it's perfect. I love it."

"Sunday Carter," I murmur.

"What about her middle name?"

I give her a dry look. "Do I look like Google? I don't know. What about Casey, so she has something from her mother?"

Mum's eyes glisten with more tears. "Perfect. Sunday Casey Carter."

I look down at Sunday, knowing, without a doubt, I'll never love anyone or anything more. No matter what life throws at us from here on out, I promise to do everything to make her happy.

TWO

AIDEN

MY SMALL FLAT IS CRAMMED WITH my family. We've only been back an hour and already they have a cot set up, a basket until she's big enough to go into the cot, a changing unit, and a plastic mat that I won't be using. Mum said it was to change her on, but looking at it, there is no way I'm putting Sunday on it. It's plastic and cold. I'm not letting her go through that shit.

I'll just put her on a blanket. I don't care if she pisses or throws up on it. I know how to use the washing machine now.

I'm glad to have her home, where she belongs. The hospital wanted to keep her in for the day to monitor her and run an emergency DNA test, since I wasn't aware of the first one being conducted. It has been a long day.

Maddox, my eldest cousin, walks over, taking a seat next to me while everyone unpacks the bags they brought.

As soon as word got out, they all went out and bought Sunday things she will need. I won't even need to go out tomorrow, thanks to my family.

I'm lucky to have each and every one of them. We've always stuck together, but what they've done for me and my daughter tonight, accepting her without meeting her… goes above and beyond.

"So…you've got a daughter."

I chuckle at his expression, watching her like he doesn't know what to think. "I do."

"You look natural. When your dad called, I thought for sure you would be a panicked mess."

I shrug, not meeting his eyes. "I've got this. I was fine. Made of rock, me."

Mum giggles behind me, tapping Maddox on the shoulders. "Don't listen to him. He completely lost his shit."

Maddox laughs, fist bumping the air. "I knew it."

"Fuck! Here," Liam groans, handing him a twenty.

"You bet on me?" I ask, jokingly appalled. Well, kind of. I'd have done the same if it was one of them, but it kind of rubs me the wrong way hearing they bet on me.

Maddox gives me a dry look. "Of course, I did. What kind of family would we be if we didn't?"

A sour feeling enters my stomach. "Have you bet on me failing her?"

Mum gasps and Maddox looks taken aback. "Of course not. We might have made up a few bets, but, Aiden, you've got this. You have too much support to fail. Plus, we wouldn't let you."

"But you think I would?" I ask, feeling my eyes burn as I hold my daughter closer.

"No, we don't," Faith says, stepping closer with her boyfriend, Beau. "If anyone can do this, it's you. Look at how great you're doing already. Me? I would be losing my mind."

I smile at my sister's lie. She'd already know what to do. I love her for trying to make me feel better though. "Thank you. But I'm still figuring it out. It's only been four hours."

"Son, you are doing incredibly well. Don't let worry and panic eat at you. If you have any concerns, we're here."

"I need to get going. I've got work in the morning," Charlotte explains, moving towards our huddle. "Can I hold her before I go?"

My arms instantly flex. "Not right now. She's just gone to sleep."

Charlotte pouts. "Can I come by tomorrow after work?"

I nod. "Sure."

"We should get going too," Mum announces, and a little panic fills me.

"Now?" I ask.

She chuckles, running her fingers over my head. "Yes. You're going to be fine, but I'll leave my phone on loud, just in case."

"Okay."

"Wait!" Uncle Max shouts, and I glare at him when Sunday stirs.

"Seriously?" I growl.

He rolls his eyes. "She'll get used to it, trust me. Hayden didn't sleep unless there *was* noise."

"Whatever!" I snap.

"Anyway, I want you all to take a look at baby Sunday. I want you to know this is what happens when you have sex. Hayden, this is why *you* can't have sex. I'm too young and sexy to be called Granddad."

"Oh, my God," Hayden growls, grabbing Maddison's arm. "Come on, let's go before he starts drawing diagrams."

"I'm serious. I don't want any grandbabies."

My mum just shakes her head at him before turning to address me. "I'll be by tomorrow. I've left instructions on the kitchen side on how to make a bottle."

I stand up, securing Sunday in my arms. "Thank you for everything, Mum. I don't know what I would have done if you hadn't come. And thank you, guys, for all the stuff you've bought us. I really appreciate it."

Mum hugs me, careful of Sunday. When she pulls back, her eyes are tearing up again, causing me to chuckle. "I love you. Take care of her." She faces the room, clapping her hands. "Okay, people, let's go."

I say my goodbyes as I walk everyone out. Once they're gone, I make my way to the kitchen, grabbing the instructions for the steriliser and for the monitor they've attached to the cot and basket that checks a baby's heartrate or something.

As if having a child wasn't scary enough, they then throw all this at you, which is enough to give me an aneurism.

A knock on the door startles me. I groan, looking down at my sleeping daughter. "Bet it's Nanny coming for another kiss."

Moving towards the door, I don't bother checking the peephole. I'm surprised to find Maggie, my landlady, on the threshold.

"Hey, Maggie, what brings you here at this time of night?"

She stares at me with wide eyes. "Is that a baby?"

My eyes flick down to Sunday, whose face is scrunched up, her mouth in a cute, little pout with a bubble blowing out. "Yeah."

"Who in the hell left you to care for a baby?" she says, wisps of her grey hair pulling free from her high bun in the breeze.

Not taking any offence, I gesture for her to come in. I can understand her reservations. Just last week I killed her fish that I was meant to keep fed. I felt bad, but out of sight, out of mind. I forgot all about them.

"She's mine."

"What do you mean, she's yours? When on earth did you get a baby?" she asks, her voice high-pitched.

I beam. "I got her today."

"Well, you didn't buy her from a shop, so I ask again: where did you get her?"

I chuckle, bending down a little so the small woman can take a closer look. Maggie's face softens as she reaches out and runs a finger down her cheek. "Apparently, I knocked a girl up." I pause, my throat closing. "She died during birth. From what the doctors were able to tell me, she knew it was a high possibility."

She gasps, her hand going to her throat. "Oh, that poor girl. What did you call this little treasure?"

My chest swells with pride. "I've named her Sunday, because it was the day she was born. Between me and you, I felt a little rushed in naming her. But I really love it. It fits her. And then I used her mother's name, Casey, as her middle name."

She smiles. "That is a beautiful, strong name. At least you didn't call her Gaga or Britany."

I scrunch my face up in disgust. "Yeah, I don't want my daughter getting picked on at school."

She giggles. "Like anyone would put a hair out of place with you as her father."

"Darn straight."

"It's late and I need to go feed my kitties. I was just worried when I saw all the cars outside. I didn't want to intrude, so I waited for everyone to leave."

"I'm sorry if they parked in your space again. They had to unload loads of stuff and wanted to be closer to the doors."

She waves me off. "I've parked my car in the garage. I'm too old to be driving. I'd rather walk or get a taxi anyway. Before I go though, Bailey, our neighbour, came to visit when I was out. She left a note, asking if you were okay. She mentioned stinging nettles? I was going to bring it over but when I saw all the cars outside, I thought I should wait. And you know me; I'm getting old."

I scoff. "Maggie, don't talk daft. You're still in your prime. If I was ten years younger, I'd totally snatch you up."

She giggles, slapping my arm lightly. "Oh, you."

I shrug. "Just telling the truth," I flirt, winking.

"I'll let you get this little one to bed. Enjoy the peace while you can."

"What do you mean?" I ask, a little panicked.

She looks at me, then huffs, shaking her head. "Boy, babies cry. They keep you up all night. Hell, if you can pee in peace, I will give you a medal."

A little out of my depth, I shrug, playing it off. "It will be fine."

"Since I only just found out about Sunday, I haven't got you anything. I'll grab Miss Sunday something when I go into town next, but you, boy, can have three months' rent free."

Surprised, I can only shake my head. "You can't do that, Maggie. It's very kind and generous of you, but it's too much."

She gives me a stern look, which has me stepping back. "Don't be rude. It's a gift, and you don't return gifts. Unless it's an ugly-arse jumper. Then you throw that shit away. I'll pop in tomorrow to see if you need anything. Put me down for babysitting duty, too, please. I love babies."

Still too stunned and a little scared of the woman, I nod. "Okay, thank you—for this and for checking in on me."

"Always. You're like family now. Take care of each other," she tells me, before leaving, closing the door quietly behind her.

Alone again, I move to my sofa, keeping Sunday in my arms. Mum warned me not to hold her when she's sleeping but I can't put her down. It killed me to let her go when I had to put her in her car seat. I wanted to keep her in my arms, too scared that if I let go, something bad would happen.

After reading through the instructions, I'm confident enough I'll be able to sterilise her bottles in the morning. I'm glad I had Mum today, she pretty much helped me do everything.

She's always been my rock though; my whole family have. I'd be lost if I never had them in my life.

Sunday stirs in my arms. I look down and begin to rock her. "Hey, sleepyhead. You missed your aunts and uncles. You have a lot of them." My cousins have even declared themselves uncles and aunties, not wanting the title of second cousin. I wouldn't have it any other way. They're going to be a big part of her life.

She starts to cry. Feeling a little overwhelmed, I get up, rocking her back and forth as I head to the kitchen.

I grab the bottle Mum made off the side and flip the lid off, before giving my girl what she wants. She settles down instantly, guzzling her food. I chuckle, moving back to the living area to take a seat.

I go through the motions, burping her then feeding her until she finishes the bottle. I'm just getting the last of her wind up when she's sick all down herself and my leg.

"Well, shit," I mutter, heaving a little at the sight. Everyone in our family has a problem when it comes to sick. Seeing it, hearing it, even smelling it has our gag reflexes working overtime. I've lost count of the number of times one of us have watched the other be sick and then ended up throwing up ourselves.

I walk into my room, where they've set up her stuff, and take her over to the changing unit. She starts screaming, and panic consumes me. I want to hold her to me, but I want to get her out of her soiled clothes too.

"Come on, baby girl, calm down so Daddy can change you."

Just saying Daddy is bizarre. I never pictured myself with kids—ever. Now I'm gifted with one and I can't believe I was ever stupid enough to never want this. This feeling of belonging, of unconditional love... it's a blessing. But the bond I share with Sunday already is something I've never felt before. It's something that can't be described, only felt and shared.

Undoing all of her little buttons, I pull her legs out of her onesie. She screams louder, her pink, skinny legs kicking up a fuss.

I scrub a hand down my face, feeling exhausted already, before pulling her arms out of the sleeves. Next is her vest, and the minute I get the buttons undone, I pause, feeling hopeless at what to do.

There is no way her head is going to fit through that tiny little hole. "Fuck!" She screams louder.

Oh, God. I can't do this. She's in distress and I can't even change her.

I pull one of her arms out, wincing at how tight the fit is and praying I don't break it. The other is easier, so I move onto her head. I softly grab the neck, pulling it until the fabric creaks before lifting it gently over her delicate head.

Her whole body is red, along with her face as she screams down my flat. I look around for the nappies, panicking when I can't see the package I watched Mum point out.

"Oh, God!"

I pull her into my arms, and she relaxes somewhat, her cries turning into sniffles. "Come on, let's go find these nappies." I walk out of my room, checking the front room and living area, but don't see them. Ready to call my mum, I step back into my room, my eyes going to the changing unit. There they sit, on the side, piled among all the other baby stuff. I sag with relief, grabbing one, as well as a pack of water wipes.

Mum had changed her nappy at the hospital, showing me everything I needed to do. I watched on, panicked as she quickly changed Sunday, her movements not as gentle as mine. My girl didn't like it, not one bit.

It was the first time I wanted to shout at my mum. She read my expression, though, and explained that babies never like their bum done. It's the feel of the cold air hitting their sensitive skin that make it uncomfortable for them. The quicker you do it, the quicker it is over for them.

I lay Sunday down on the towel I asked my sister to put on here, so Sunday didn't have to lie on the cold mat. Just as I unclasp the Velcro, she farts so loud it echoes through the quiet room. I look down at Sunday with surprise, wondering how something so loud came out of someone so tiny. I hold the nappy against her tummy, waiting.

"Oh, God, no."

I wait a few minutes, watching my girl suck her fist. It happens again, the distinct sound of her filling her nappy.

"You couldn't have done this before all the women in my family left?" I ask her, tilting my head to my shoulder and taking a deep breath.

A few minutes later and she's screaming again. I lift the nappy away from her tummy and the smell hits me.

I gag, moving my head into my shoulder. My eyes burn and I gag again. It's horrendous. How can someone so beautiful produce something so vile and foul-smelling?

"God, Sunday, that's one messy poop," I tell her as I lift it back again.

Once again, I gag, but this time sick rises up my throat. I turn and bend over the bin just in time to empty my stomach.

A towel catches my eye when I go to stand up straight. I wipe my mouth with it before wrapping it around my mouth and nose and facing my daughter head-on.

I've got this.

I can do it.

I try to be as quick as I can, but five minutes in and I realise I just don't have the same skill my mum does. She made it look so effortless, so easy. It's not. This shit is hard as fuck.

Hoping like hell I've put her nappy on correctly, I grab a new set of clothes from her new drawers. I pick out a pink Minnie Mouse set and head back over to the changing unit. I put her back down, going through the process of placing the vest over her head.

Her arms going in are a different matter. The first one goes in, but the second... it's like I'm going to break her arm. There's no way mums put these on their kids without doing some damage. Her arm doesn't even bend that way.

"What were the manufacturers thinking?" I growl, stepping back a little to look it over. There has to be a way for it to fit. I watched Mum do it effortlessly. They wouldn't make them otherwise, right?

Taking a deep breath, I go back to it, pulling the material as far as I can without ripping it and pulling her arm through.

Her little legs and arms wave around frantically, so I relax, taking it as a good sign. I button her up before picking up the all-in-one. I undo all the buttons before pulling one of her arms through, smiling when I see it has gloves attached.

So, they were thinking right on something.

I lift her up, pull it around her body for her other arm to go through, when I notice it doesn't look right. There's an extra piece of material at the top that looks like it shouldn't be there.

I wonder if there are any instruction manuals for this...

I grab my phone, typing into Google on how to put an all-in-one on a baby, and frown.

"Shit, this is the wrong way."

I quickly pull her arm out, lifting the onesie up in front of me, then looking back down at my phone.

Ah, that explains it.

I pull her arm through the right one, then lift her and wrap it around her to pull the second one through, muttering, "They should make the vests this easy."

I pull it down her body, and pull her leg through the first one, then the second.

Google saves the day.

It takes me a while to finally get the poppers connected to the right ones, but I do, and when I'm done, I'm proud of myself.

I lift her up in front of me, beaming. "See, we got this."

Famous last words.

She projectile vomits all over my chest and herself.

Yeah, maybe I don't have this after all.

THREE

AIDEN

I CAN'T DO THIS. I'VE NOT EVEN HAD my daughter in my life twenty-four hours and already I'm failing her.

Tears run down my face. I'm tired, worn out and utterly exhausted. Take me out on an all-night bender, I'm good to go. But a night in with a baby girl... nope. I'm so royally fucked.

How do women do this, then get up and carry on like the world isn't imploding around them? They deserve fucking medals.

A knock on the door has me jumping up from the sofa, my eyes bleary with sleep. Sleep I didn't get.

I nearly hit myself in the face when I throw open the door. My mum stands there, her mouth open and eyes wide—no doubt at my appearance—before my dad steps in front of her. He chuckles and I narrow my eyes his way, wanting to lay him out.

I'm not in the mood. I feel like I haven't slept in days. When he steps to the side, my mum comes into view again, her face soft, but the worry lines are still around her eyes. She looks like an angel with the sun shining behind her and right now, an angel is what I need.

"Mum, thank God."

I move out of the way to let her in, leaving the door open when Madison, Hayden and my uncle Max pull up.

"What on earth has happened in here?" Mum calls.

I turn around and face her, unable to meet her gaze when I blurt out everything. "Sunday didn't sleep. Well, she did when she was in my arms, but the second I put her down, she would start crying."

"Is that why you have bottles, dirty nappies and cups of coffee littered around the place?" Dad muses, looking around.

I narrow my eyes on him. "Yes! If you're here just to make fun of me, then leave. I've not had a wink of sleep and I'm ready to pull my hair out." I give him one last warning look before turning to my mum. "How did you do this? Show me."

She chuckles, taking Sunday out of my arms. Even after she kept me up all night, I want to take her back, hold her close where she belongs. I rub my chest, hating the foreign feeling; emptiness.

She hands Sunday to Dad, giving him a stern look that says 'behave', before assessing the mess.

"Um, Aiden, why is there a pile of her clothes shoved into the corner?"

I run a hand down my face. "She kept throwing up. It was bad. And she had diarrhoea—it was everywhere, Mum. All up her back and down her legs. I wasn't prepared for it and ended up throwing up on her." I inhale, running my fingers through my hair. "Mostly, she was being sick."

She walks over, picking one off the top. "There's only a bit of dribble on here, Aiden."

I throw my hands up. "I didn't want her to be cold."

"Why didn't you put a bib on her?"

I look around, wondering what the hell she's on about. "What's a bib?"

She rolls her eyes, groaning, and walks into my room. She comes back out holding up a bandana. "This is a bib. It goes around her neck." I watch as she wraps it around my girl's neck, popping the buttons together at the back.

Well, shit. Who knew? I shrug sheepishly. "I thought they were for her hair."

She laughs. Max, Madison and Hayden walk in, whistling at the mess. "Seems you had a party without us," Hayden mutters, her eyes filled with mirth.

I narrow my own. "I'm not in the mood for any shit. I've not slept."

Both girls put their hands up in surrender.

"So, you don't want to hear what happened to Maddox last night, then?" Max says.

My head snaps to him. "What about him?" I ask, intrigued. Maddox is one of the eldest of us cousins, but you'd never believe it. The guy is a kid through and through. How he manages to run a successful business is anyone's guess, but he does, and customers wait months to hire Maddox and his team.

Madison giggles. "He called me this morning to ask me to pick him up from the police station. I didn't want to get up, so I called Mum and Dad. They're going to pick him up."

"He got arrested?"

"We don't know the full story. We're waiting for him to get here to find out. Mum said she wanted to come over and see if you needed anything."

I sit next to my dad on the sofa, watching as Mum starts picking up bottles and taking them into the kitchen. The girls follow suit. I'm too tired to argue, to tell them I'll do it in a minute. I rest my head on the back of the sofa, closing my eyes.

"Rough night, huh?"

I don't bother opening my eyes to answer Max's question as he flops down next to me, leaving me sandwiched between him and Dad. "She wouldn't stop crying. Every time I got her to sleep, I'd put her down, and it would all begin again." I pause, opening my eyes and turning to my uncle. "Have you seen the outfits they make to put on babies? I swear they should be labelled a hazard. I felt like I was going to break her."

"Babies are flexible. It takes a lot to break a bone, son. You did good. She looks peaceful," Dad whispers. My lips twitch when he runs his finger down her cheek, looking lovingly down at her. "It's been so long since we had a baby in the family."

I grunt. "Well, let's hope we don't follow you guys and start a tradition."

"What do you mean?" he asks, pulling his eyes away from Sunday.

"Well, according to Grams, Aunt Denny got pregnant first, then Harlow and you followed suit, trying to fill your own stadiums."

Dad grunts but Max gasps, sitting forward. "Nope. Hayden isn't having sex. Over my dead body. And as cute as Sunday is, I'm not ready to be a grandfather. I've just got Liam and Hayden to move out. I can finally fu—I mean, have alone time with my wife. I don't want to be called at all hours to watch over my grandchild. Not yet."

"So, you let your only daughter move out, where you can't watch her or see who she has coming or going?" Dad asks, his lips twitching. "You never were bright."

I have to admit, he has a point.

"I'm in the room," Hayden yells from the kitchen doorway.

Max stares at Hayden, eyes wide and slightly panicked, finger pointing at her. "I mean it, Hayden: you have sex or get a boyfriend, I'll kill him. I don't want you to have children yet."

"Will you relax already? One, I don't have a boyfriend at the moment," she states, and I feel Max sag against the sofa, relief pouring through him. "And two, I've been on the pill since I was fifteen; ask Mum."

With that, she walks back into the kitchen, leaving Max gaping like a fish.

Me and Dad watch him, waiting for the inevitable explosion that is going to happen in, three… two… one…

"I'm going to kill her! We discussed this. *We discussed this!*" he growls, standing up and grabbing his phone out of his back pocket, completely oblivious to the rest of us watching him. "We agreed: giving her the pill would just give her the green light to have sex."

"When did you agree to this?" Dad asks, looking genuinely interested.

Max looks away briefly from his phone, muttering, "The day she was born," before walking out.

The second he's no longer in view, we both burst out laughing. Hearing us, he pops his head back in, pointing at me. "Laugh all you want, Aiden, but you've got all this to come."

I choke on my laughter, straightening in my seat before turning to my dad, horrified. "She can't date. Not ever. I mean it. I'll kill any fu—fudger, who goes near her."

Dad bursts out laughing, pulling his granddaughter closer. "Don't worry, with how big our family is and how much bigger it's getting, no lad will have a chance to get through all of us."

I relax instantly, but still, the image of my girl growing up and dating turns my stomach.

Maybe I could keep her at home, home-school her?

Car doors slam in the distance, and Dad looks at me, his eyes lighting up. "I can't wait to hear what the little shit did this time. I'm surprised Malik hasn't kicked his arse yet."

"If it weren't for the fact he's Maddy's twin, I'd think he was Max's son and that Landon was Malik's. Both Landon and Malik have that whole moody and broody shit going on. I've even tried to perfect their stare, but I just look constipated," I admit.

Dad nods, understanding. "He's always been like it. Don't forget, we didn't have the same upbringing you guys did."

My heart hurts at the reminder. We don't know what happened; we just know it was bad and they never wanted to talk about it. "We know. We're lucky to have you as our parents."

"I don't know why I bother," Harlow yells, walking in. She starts to head to the kitchen but pauses halfway there when she sees Sunday with Dad.

"What did he do?" Dad asks.

She groans, rolling her eyes. "Let the fool explain. I thought I'd heard it all, but clearly not."

I laugh, a little more awake after hearing that. We've all been taken in for petty stuff, but the only one who has a criminal record is Landon. The rest of us either didn't get caught or were let off. I'd like to think it was because of our good looks and charm, but it had more to do with explaining to a judge what we did than anything. It's like they don't want to report the stuff we did.

Maddox walks in next, with a fuming Malik behind him. He looks like shit—worse than me—with red-rimmed eyes, one of them black, and as I look closer, a few scratches down his face.

"What did you do?" I ask, smiling wide.

He groans, sitting down on the floor just inside the doorway, clearly too tired to walk any further. Mum comes in, handing me a cup of coffee before taking the other over to Maddox.

"You don't deserve this, but I want you awake when you tell us. I'm intrigued to hear what you did this time."

Maddox looks to his dad, who stands in the doorway, his arms crossed over his chest. "Do I have to?"

Max pushes past Malik and sits down next to me again, grinning. "You know the rules. You get caught, you have to tell us what you did."

"It was stupid really," he says.

"Go on," Hayden urges, bouncing on her feet.

He scrubs his face, looking rough and haggard. "Okay, so I had this amazing idea. I promise, it was when I thought of it."

"What was it?" Maddy asks, grinning.

"I was watching *The Bachelor* with Lily and Charlotte a few weeks ago…"

When he doesn't say anything more, instead looking to his bent knees, Hayden giggles. "Isn't that the pompous show about a guy who thinks he's all that and gets women with no dignity to fight over him?"

Maddox glares at her. "*Anyway*, I thought that the dude was on to something. All those chicks, he had the pick of the litter, ya know?"

"What did you do?" I laugh, clutching my side.

"I set up an account on Tinder and arranged dates with a bunch of women, asking them to meet me at The Gin Inn last night. I thought I'd re-enact *The Bachelor*. It really did seem like a good idea at the time."

What a div!

"What happened?" I ask.

He shrugs, looking anywhere but at the people in the room.

"Tell them," Harlow snaps, hugging Malik.

His cheeks turn pink when he answers. "I kind of hired the pub out for the night. Once I thought all the girls were there, I took the stage."

"They have a stage at The Gin Inn?" I ask. It was our local hangout and I'd never seen one before.

He waves me off. "I hired that too."

"Of course you did," Malik mutters.

"And?" Mum asks, sitting on the arm of the sofa, next to Dad.

"I told them they had ten minutes to convince me which one would be perfect for me, that sexual advances were welcome," he looks away from his mum when she starts forward, "and that the winner would have the pleasure of being my girlfriend—until I got bored." Malik coughs and Maddox sighs, leaning back in the chair. "And that I'd take her to Italy for two weeks."

"And how did they react?" I ask, trying my hardest not to laugh.

He forces a smile. "A few were interested; I could see it in their body language and eyes."

"And?" I ask, grinning from ear to ear, no longer tired.

He sighs, looking defeated. "They started pushing towards me. At first, I thought I'd died and gone to heaven, and was about to have a—"

"Baby girl in the room," I growl before he can finish the sentence.

"Oh right, yeah. So, I thought *that* was about to happen, but when they reached me, they started attacking me. I barely made it out alive."

"So, why did you get arrested?"

"For disturbing the peace and causing a riot."

"What has Jimmy said?" Madison asks, talking about the bar owner who we've known for years.

"I promised to do his back room for free," Maddox answers.

"Dude, I can't believe you thought that would work."

"I just wanted to give them a chance."

"On that note, I'm going to go and finish the washing," Mum says, shaking her head in disappointment at Maddox.

"Aren't you missing work?" I ask him, resting my head back on the sofa.

"Yeah. I called Todd to run things while I'm gone. I'm gonna head back and get some sleep, then head over to The Gin Inn and apologise once again to Jimmy for last night."

Glad some of us can get some sleep.

I close my eyes for a moment, listening to Malik give him shit.

GROGGILY, I RUB the sleep from my eyes and look around my clean apartment. There isn't a cushion out of place, unless you count the one someone has stuffed under my head.

Sitting up, I stretch my back, groaning at the click. It feels good. I also notice there's no one here.

Everything from the past twenty-four hours comes shooting back at me, and I jump up from the sofa, panicking.

Where the fuck is Sunday?

I glance down in the Moses basket, not finding her there. It's dark out, which means I slept the whole day away.

I'm just about to grab my mobile from my back pocket when Mum walks out of the kitchen, drying her hands with a kitchen towel.

"Mum, where's Sunday?" I ask, unable to hide the panic in my voice.

She gives me a warm smile. "Sleeping soundly in her cot. I put her down not long ago, after bathing, changing and feeding her.

My shoulders relax. "Thank you so much. I must have needed the sleep."

"You're welcome," she tells me, moving further into the room. "I need to get going before your dad has a hissy fit. But before I go, I wanted to tell you how proud I am of you. I may not have expected grandchildren from you at such a young age, but I love that little girl with my whole heart. And I know you're going make an amazing father."

I feel a *but* coming on.

"But?"

She grins, shaking her head at me. "But… you need to relax. Stop panicking over the tiniest things, and if she cries, let her for a little while before picking her up." Seeing the 'I'm not doing that' expression on my face, she laughs. "Trust me, it will be hard to sit by and listen, but once she realises you won't pick her up every time she whimpers, she'll settle down easier. She's your child and I won't tell you how to raise her, but that is my advice to you."

I scrub the back of my neck. "I don't know if I can handle her crying, Mum. My heart hurts every time I hear it."

"Trust me, I know. I went through it with you lot. But it does get easier, I promise."

"Thank you for staying, Mum, and for cleaning up my mess. You didn't need to do that."

"I'll help any way I can, Aiden," she tells me, grabbing her coat. "I've washed all of her clothes and put them away. Just make sure you use the powder I bought for her clothes and not the one you use. I've made you some dinner, too; it's in the oven. Try to get some sleep before she wakes up."

"I will. I can't believe I slept all day and I'm still shattered."

"That's babies for you." She picks her bag up before turning to me. "Oh, and your brothers and cousins said to meet them at Harvey's for breakfast around ten. They want to go get some things for Sunday with you."

"Um, I don't have a pushchair."

"Your dad already went out and bought one," she informs me, pointing towards the door. I glance over and find a new pushchair that looks an awful lot like the Moses basket.

My throat tightens with emotion. "Tell him I said thank you."

"I will."

"Um, Mum?" I call out when she reaches the door.

"Yeah?"

"Is Sunday allowed out? She's only a few days old."

She laughs. "Of course she is. Fresh air will do her good. It's going to be warm tomorrow so don't wrap her up too much. She'll get overheated."

"I won't."

"Call me if you need me."

I walk over to her and pull her into my arms. "Thank you, Mum. I love you. You're the best."

"I love you too, Aiden."

FOUR

AIDEN

MY HEAD SNAPS UP WHEN I hear banging, before Sunday's high-pitched scream startles me out of bed.

I tried to listen to my mum's advice, but I could only last thirty seconds before I picked her up. No baby as precious as Sunday should be left to scream. She deserves to know she is loved and wanted. I never want her to think I've abandoned her.

I growl when drills and more banging picks up, rocking Sunday in my arms. Enough is enough. I've tried to get on with the neighbour, really tried. But she just woke up a newborn baby, who I only managed to get to sleep… an hour ago. Before that, she was awake six hours, only sleeping for short amounts of time.

Whoever came up with the saying, 'slept like a baby', clearly never had fucking kids.

I storm out of my room, holding Sunday, who's calmed down now she's in my arms, and head outside. Builders are carrying bags of cement through the gap between the properties, towards her back garden.

I glare at the one who makes eye contact with me. "Morning," he calls out.

"No, it's fu—fudging not. You guys ever heard of sleep? It's six in the morning."

"Whatever, mate," he scoffs, before walking off.

"I'll shove his 'whatever mate' up his fu—fudging arse," I mutter under my breath, before looking down at my girl, who's sucking her fist. I smile, still amazed she's real. She takes my breath away each and every time. "Baby girl, you're gonna have to tune Daddy out for a moment. I'm gonna have words with the mean old lady."

Walking up to the door, I waste no time in banging my fist against it. Then, seeing the sign above the doorbell that says, 'ring me', I hold my finger down on that, too, until they answer. See how she fucking likes the noise this early in the morning.

The click of a lock has me stepping back, removing my finger from the doorbell, and dropping my arm to the side. The second the door opens, I take another step back, holding my breath.

I didn't know what I expected her to look like, but an angel wasn't it. Her hair is platinum-blonde, almost white as snow—and fucking natural. I can tell because she has no dark roots and has fair, pale skin. It falls to her shoulders, cut in choppy layers. It's sexy as hell. She reminds me of a blonde Snow White, with her pale complexion and ruby-red lips.

Her eyes… Fuck, her eyes are ocean blue, so deep they sparkle. They stand out like a beacon. I've never seen eyes like that in my life.

She's petite, with a small, slender waist, her white tank top showcasing firm, perky breasts. I can't help but let my eyes linger a little too long.

Fuck, she isn't wearing a bra.

My gaze rakes down her slender body, down to her legs, to the tiny shorts she's wearing.

I snap out of it when she clicks her fingers in my face, and I look up to find her glaring at me. I shrug, trying to play it cool, when really, my body is screaming at me to hit on her.

She is so fucking hot.

"Can I help you?"

Even her voice sounds angelic, almost musical.

"Yeah," I croak out, my voice gruff. I clear my throat, standing straighter. "I need you to tell the builders to come at a later time. I have a newborn baby who is trying to get to sleep, and you've woken her up. She needs her sleep. I don't mind the noise in the day—I can take her somewhere else if it unsettles her that badly—but during the morning, could you keep it down?"

I want to slap myself for rambling. I'm more self-controlled around women than this. I sound like a fool.

"Can you repeat that for me, please? I didn't get it all."

I glare at her. I can't help it; I'm tired. "Were you not listening?"

I notice her staring at my lips and fight back a grin. If I wasn't holding my daughter, I'd have her shorts around her ankles and be balls deep inside her.

"I'm sorry. You're talking too fast."

This chick is crazy. Fed up and needing to get ready to meet the others soon, I turn to leave. "Tell the builders not to come in before eight. There's no need to wake the neighbours up this early."

"Wait! What did you say?" she calls out, but I ignore her, shaking my head.

All blondes are dumb. I should have known something as sweet-looking as her would have a fault somewhere.

I guess you can't always have the full package.

BY THE TIME I finished packing what I would need for a few hours, I left the apartment with half of Sunday's belongings. I never knew a kid would need so much. I feel like I packed everything but the kitchen sink.

The Cheerio's I left open on the side; the ones I didn't get chance to eat because Sunday started crying.

Even the shower was a quick dunk, wash and out job. I was afraid to leave her too long on her own.

It was a nightmare. And trying to fit everything in the changing bag Mum had bought to match the pushchair was a joke. She needed a fucking suitcase, not a purse.

Three bags later, twenty minutes late, I was finally at Henry's. I could see most of my family already inside, knowing the rest had to work.

"Hey, guys, I'm sorry I'm late," I tell them, trying to juggle the door, three bags and a pushchair.

Landon steps up, taking the bags off me, while Charlotte holds the door. Mark and Lily get up to help me with the pushchair, and between the three of us, we manage to get her in safely. I push a chair out of the way, making room for her pushchair. I don't want her too far away.

I nod my greeting to the rest, watching as Liam stuffs his face with bagels. Ashton is watching me with an amused expression.

"What?" I snap when he doesn't stop staring.

"Nothing. Being a dad suits you."

I glare at him before taking Sunday out of the pushchair, turning to my sister. "Lily, could you get a bottle out of her bag, please? I didn't have chance to feed her before we left. She was asleep and I didn't want to disturb her."

She looks down at the bags Landon put down by me, frowning. "Um, are you taking washing to Mum's or something?"

Puzzled, I shake my head. "No, why?"

"What's with all the bags?" she asks softly.

"It's Sunday's stuff."

"All of it?" she asks.

I nod my head grimly. "Yeah. She needed a change of clothes, and a spare in case something else happened, then another just in case. I packed the entire pack of nappies because this girl can poo. Then I had to bring spare bottles, the sterilisers in case I need to sterilise new bottles, and then her milk powder. I have the ones in the tiny containers already measured out, but in case I run out, I brought the whole tub. She has three extra dummies, though she doesn't really like them—and I'm worried she'll choke on one. Then there's nappy bags, water wipes, cream in case she gets a rash, and three dozen bibs. They are a godsend," I tell her.

She giggles at me before looking down at the bags. "Which bag is the bottle in?"

Rocking Sunday in my arms, I say, "It's in the black one. Just mix the powder in the milk. I already measured it out."

"I know how to make a bottle," she tells me, giving me a soft smile. "You're doing amazing."

"Are you going to let us hold her today?"

I glance down the table at Charlotte, who is staring at my child in awe. "I will. Just let me feed her. I don't want her to be hungry. Then you can all have a turn."

She claps her hands excitedly, and I smile. "Oh, before I forget, I baked you a cake to congratulate you."

The guys don't bother to hide their snickers and I glare at them before smiling at Charlotte. There is no way I'm going to be the one to let her know her cooking sucks. I'd be surprised if the cake is even edible. I don't even know how she manages to make something so terrible when I've given her recipe after recipe. But I can't talk. I can make an okay dessert, but my talent is in food. I love to cook.

"Thank you, Charlotte."

She beams at me, and I instantly feel bad that I'll be throwing the damn cake away before it can harm my daughter.

And I'm not joking. The last cake she made, Jacob didn't eat and instead left it on the side at home. He got into a fight with a friend of his from school and they ended up throwing the cake in a food fight. Both had an allergic reaction to it and ended up going to the hospital when they complained their skin burned.

Lily hands me the bottle, which is still room temperature. "Can you pass me a bib, too, please?"

"Here you go," she says, handing it over.

Gently, I lift Sunday's head and clip the buttons in place. "Shh, baby girl. Daddy's got your bottle," I coo down at her when she starts fussing. It stops as soon as the bottle touches her lips. She greedily guzzles it down, and I chuckle.

"Never thought I'd see the day," Landon, the quietest and meanest of our group, says—and I say meanest because no one on this earth would want to mess with him. He's been known to knock people out with just a punch. No fucker messes with him.

I notice another bruise under his eye and want to question him. The girls and parents don't know, but Landon fights illegally. They have the fights set up all around town in different abandoned warehouses or car parks. We told him months ago he needed to stop, that the level of violence the other fighters were demonstrating in order to win were getting out of hand. The only rule in the ring was that they couldn't use weapons, anything else was a go. But for some, it didn't matter, and many would slyly try to hit him with a set of brass knuckles, or a stick, or rock they picked up off the ground. The men running it didn't seem to care, and it was getting out of control.

A group bursting through the door has the entire table looking up. I groan the minute I see who walks in.

The Hayes brothers and their little sister, Paisley.

Well, most of the Hayes brothers anyway. The twins are still finishing school, alongside Jacob, my uncle Myles and aunt Kayla's son.

All of us, at one point, went to school with a Hayes. We've been somewhat friendly enemies for such a long time, none of us know what, exactly, started it, or how to behave around each other. My guess is that a girl was the reason the war began between us. We were always fighting, either over who had the biggest ego, a girl we fucked—or wanted to fuck first—or just because we could. It's been a rivalry that has gotten us into trouble more than once with the police and our parents.

The only one I can stand is Paisley. She was in the same year at school as I was, and she's nothing like her brothers. She's forever got her head in a book, and she's so shy she blushes whenever someone talks to her.

Harvey, the owner, groans from the counter. "Guys, you know the rules," he yells.

We all smirk at the Hayes brothers when they spot us, their eyes narrowing. Jaxon, the eldest, who runs a moving company, steps towards the counter.

"Come on, Harvey, we just want breakfast. We've been up since six and haven't eaten. And Paisley needs to eat," Jaxon says, making Paisley blush.

That was another thing; the girl was forever being fussed over when it came to what she ate. They were always throwing food or drinks in front of her. When we were at school, they would go apeshit if someone stole any of it.

"No trouble, otherwise you're paying for damages. I've barely finished paying for the last lot."

Jaxon pulls out a wad of cash from his back pocket, but I look away when Reid, one of the triplet's, grins over at us. The triplets are the same age as Hayden, Landon and Liam, but were a year above them at school. It caused fights to break out all the time, as both Reid and Landon had the same temper, although Reid wasn't as moody as Landon. No one could be. The fucker only smiles when he's with Charlotte.

"Who the fuck gave you a baby?"

I cover Sunday's ears the best I can with one hand. "Watch your language in front of the baby," I hiss, and his eyes go wide.

"Reid," Paisley scolds quietly.

Wyatt, the second eldest, leans back against the empty table, nodding at me. "You're losing your touch if someone got one of your females pregnant. No one is touching our sister."

I glare at him. "She's mine—not that it's any of your business."

Isaac starts laughing, slapping his other triplet, Luke, on the shoulder. "He's shitting us."

"And the mum let you have her? Unsupervised?" Luke asks, staring down in horror at Sunday.

I want to wipe the look off his face, but I'm not getting in a fight in front of Sunday. She'll be traumatised for life.

"Probably fucked off when she realised Aiden was the father," Alex says, laughing at his lame joke.

"Isaac, fuck off," Landon drawls, leaning lazily in his chair.

"Who the fuck do you think you're talking to?" Reid growls, stepping up for his other two triplets.

"Don't even think about it," I growl, sounding deadly. "There's a baby girl right here. I'm not gonna have you *pussies* fighting in front of her."

Isaac laughs. "Never thought I'd see the day. I wonder how Laura will feel when she finds out," he says, mentioning one of my fuck buddies. Not that I care about her. She just fills a need. "Might give her a go. Dunno yet. I'll see how needy she is. Having been with you, she's probably horny as fuck. I'm told you couldn't satisfy her. Does the kid's mum know you stick it anywhere?"

I stand up, passing Sunday to Lily, then the bottle, before moving forward. Jaxon steps in front of me, putting his hand on my chest, just as the sound of chairs being scraped back echo in the room. I know the others have my back.

"I said, watch your mouth around my daughter, otherwise I'll make it so the doctors wire it shut," I growl. "And in future, don't mention her mum. She died giving birth. As for Laura, go ahead. You were always going after my seconds."

"Not what she said a few months ago when she was kissing me and begging to suck my cock."

Anger begins boiling within me at the language he's using around my daughter. She might not understand it, but I do. I don't want her around that shit.

A grin stretches across my face, a baring of gritted teeth. "How'd I taste?" I taunt.

He loses the cocky grin, stepping forward. I laugh, ready for him. I might not want to fight in front of my daughter, but it doesn't mean I'm gonna get my arse kicked in front of her either. No way am I having her think I can't protect her.

"That's enough, you two," Jaxon snaps, pushing Isaac back. He glares at me before turning to his brothers. "Guys, you can get your food to go. I'm gonna make sure Paisley eats."

"Can't she do that herself? She's not a little girl anymore," Landon drawls, raking his eyes up and down her body.

The movement doesn't go unnoticed by anyone, including Paisley, who looks always, her face bright red. I want to slap him around the head myself.

There's one thing taunting these losers, but there's another to mess with Paisley. The brothers are as protective of her as we are with the females in our family, if not more. Since she's their only sister, she has it twice as bad.

"Keeps your eyes off my sister," Wyatt snaps, blocking Paisley from view.

"Guys, go. Now," Jaxon orders, his expression cold. They look torn for a few moments, before heading back to the counter to grab their sandwiches.

I don't move until every one of them has left the shop. If it wasn't for Sunday, I'd already be punching the living shit out of Isaac, because there was no way Jaxon Hayes would stop me.

I lift my arms out to take Sunday from Lily, but she pulls her closer to her chest. "You've had her for two nights with no sharing. I want to hold my niece."

"She's really yours?" Jaxon asks.

"She's beautiful," Paisley whispers.

I smile at Paisley. "She's the prettiest girl I've ever laid eyes on. She's perfect."

"Paisley, your order's ready," Harvey yells.

"Congratulations," Jaxon says. "And I'm sorry about her mum."

"Thanks."

"Don't think being nice gets you out of Family of The Year," Mark tells him. "We're gonna kick your arse."

Family of The Year is a fundraiser to help families in need. Every year we compete in the trials to win the competition. There's the wheel race, which is lifting and throwing a wheel for a hundred metres; a cooking contest, which allows two minutes to eat as many spicy wings as you can; and other fun stuff. And every year, the Carter's and the Hayes' end up the last two families competing. It ends with tug of war.

Jaxon scoffs. "Like you stand a chance. We won last year."

"Because some fucker told the judges Charlotte was doing the cake contest," I growl, eyeing him suspiciously. None of us could prove it, but we think one of the Hayes brothers paid the judges to change the name on the form for the cake contest from Faith to Charlotte. And you can't change names at the last minute.

"There's nothing wrong with my cakes," Charlotte says, looking adorably confused.

Jaxon eyes her like she's got a screw loose. "There's nothing right with them, either."

"Watch it, Jaxon," Landon growls, always protective of Charlotte.

They stare at each other for a beat before Jaxon sighs, looking away. "I'm too fucking busy to deal with this today. Later."

The girls immediately relax when he leaves to sit with Paisley on another table. She chose to sit at the one furthest away from us.

Clever girl.

Taking my seat, I watch as Lily tries to bring up Sunday's wind. Between her pursed lips is a ring of white; milk bubbles still around the edge. I smile, finding her cute face adorable.

"Here, let me. If it's not brought up properly, she'll get bellyache," I tell Lily, taking Sunday from her. Learning the trick I watched on YouTube, I tilt her back a little, then forwards, then back again before rubbing her back. She burps, making me proud.

"You really are incredible with her, Aiden," she says.

"I'm gonna go order everyone's food. Does everyone want the same?" Charlotte asks, standing up. We all nod.

"You aren't paying for everyone's food again. I'll come help you," Landon says.

"I made a list of things I might need last night," I tell Lily. "Do you think they have some drawers in the shop you're taking us to?"

"Of course. They have everything a baby will need. And Dad gave me some money to get her some things."

I grin. "He's smitten with her. He's already spoiling her."

Lily returns my smile. "He is. He was gonna go out himself, but Mum told him to let you handle it. Then he threw loads of money at me."

"I'll thank him later."

"What are you gonna do about work?" Mark asks, listening to our conversation.

"I don't know. Mason said I could have a few weeks to sort myself out, but after that, I'm gonna have to organise something for Sunday. Mum and Maggie both offered to babysit while I work, but I can't picture leaving her. She's still so small."

"You need to work to support the both of you," Lily reminds me softly.

"I know."

"And you don't want social services thinking you can't provide for her. Ask Mum and Maggie what days they can do. I'm sure Mason will work with you so you aren't working long hours."

"All right. Either way, I've got two weeks off—with pay. Hopefully, it will feel easier to leave for work by then."

No one looks convinced as they watch me cuddling my sleeping daughter. It still doesn't feel real.

FIVE

BAILEY

I'VE NOT BEEN ABLE TO STOP THINKING about the guy living in the apartment above the garage next door. I've nicknamed him 'Hot Neighbour' because I've never seen anyone so good-looking before. He's the type of guy who belongs on the front cover of magazines or in underwear ads. Everything about him is sexy, even the way he moves. He has swagger most guys think they have, but in reality they just look like morons.

I've been waiting to get a glimpse of him ever since he came over again this morning. I almost jump when I hear cars pull in, their lights shining briefly into my living area.

I move the netting away from the window just slightly, peeking out at my neighbours to see two cars stop just outside of the garage.

At first, I thought the guy living above Maggie's garage was her grandson or something. When I went over to ask her if she would give him my note, to make sure he was okay, she explained he's helping her out around the house. My grandparents never mentioned Maggie was even back in the UK.

When we chatted through Skype, my grandma explained that someone had vandalised Maggie's house while she was living abroad with her daughter and family. The guy she offered to let live there offered to do the work for cheap rent, so she could afford to replace the furniture she lost.

I don't remember much of Maggie. When we visited, we were only kids. By the time I came to live with my grandparents, she was gone. We were lucky our house wasn't vandalised, too, because we were gone a year, the house empty for the duration.

My breath catches when my neighbour steps out of the passenger side, going towards the back like he's in a rush.

My first impression of him wasn't a good one. I thought he was a little crazy, if I'm honest. He was kneeling in a bed of stinging nettles and it didn't even faze him. I had seen him storming over towards the house and had hesitated about answering the door. When I finally got the courage, he was on the phone to someone and looked so lost. I wanted to be the one to guide him to where he needed to be. I don't even know what had compelled me to have those kinds of thoughts; I just knew I wanted to help him.

I was going to turn around and head back inside, to give him privacy, but then he dropped to his knees in those nettles and I couldn't walk away. Something pulled me to him. It was frustrating when he wouldn't turn to look at me so I could read his lips. I still don't know if he said anything to me that day. It didn't help I was flustered over seeing him with no shirt on. He was beautiful.

Our second meeting didn't go too well either. He was talking too fast for me to read his lips, and because of his deep voice, it just sounded like someone was speaking too closely into a microphone. And that was after I managed to pull my gaze away from the tiny bundle in his arms.

My eyes draw together when he pulls said baby out of the car, still in her car seat. Her legs are kicking up a fuss and her arms are flailing around, so I imagine she's screaming. He looks down at her lovingly, his lips moving sensuously before leaving the others to empty their boots. I'm curious to know if the baby is his. He never had her the first time I met him, and he seems so young—too young to be a dad. He has to be about a year or two younger than my just turned nineteen self.

I look at the women's faces, wondering which of them is the mother. Both women are drop-dead gorgeous. One has dirty blonde hair that reaches her shoulders, and a slim frame. Even from here I can see she has expressive eyes. They look big and round and stand out as one of her best features.

The other has curves, but she works them and looks sexy as hell when she walks. Her hair is a reddish-brown colour, and suits her creamy skin tone. I watch as she smiles at the scary guy next to her, and dimples form, making her look sweet.

Maybe she's with him and not the hot dad.

The guy, my new neighbour, is all kinds of hot, and I sigh when I find I can no longer ogle him.

I drop the curtain, heading back to the room I've made into my office, and sit down at my desk.

When my grandparents said they were remodelling the house and would be leaving it to me until they decided to come back—if ever—I had been surprised. They even went to the trouble of ordering my office supplies, sparing no expense when I told them I wanted to come home. They wanted me to feel at home, so they set up my office with everything I would need and more. For a web and logo designer, I picked up a lot of work. My latest one was for a new carpet factory opening and they wanted me to design opening day boards, their web page, and posters. It was keeping me busy.

My disability doesn't stop me from living life, but it also doesn't make some aspects of it any easier. I'm glad it doesn't affect my work because it's the only thing that keeps me sane, and I can do it from anywhere.

Every time it affects something in my life, I'm reminded of how I ended up the way I am. I can hear sound, but it's muffled, like I'm under water. I can't make out what someone is saying to me without looking at them and reading their lips. Otherwise I can't trust what is being said.

I was given hearing aids, but all they did was make loud white noise in my ear, to the point I suffered with migraines. It was like they couldn't pick up the right frequency. After the third fail, I stopped trying further treatments. The last one improved my hearing drastically, and I could hear words more clearly, but it still made me get really bad migraines to the point I'd be in excruciating pain. They also made my ears sore. I was already angry enough that I was deaf, I didn't need to keep getting my hopes up for them to be let down. It was too heart-breaking. And after my parents and little brother died, I didn't care much about anything. It was my fault they were dead.

I've perfected lip reading over the years. However, I have to be looking at the person talking head on, which is why I couldn't tell what the guy next door was saying. This morning, I couldn't keep up with him.

I look out the window that faces my neighbour's home and give out another breathy sigh when a light flicks on.

I never wanted to come back here. However, my grandparents kept moving from place to place and it was tiring travelling all over the world. I wanted a bed that was my own, and some privacy. I didn't get any of that while we were travelling. There were times we'd have to share a room if a hotel was fully-booked.

Coming back here after everything that happened has been so hard. I haven't felt safe, not since I've been in this town, so much so that I haven't even left the house during the day or night since I've been back. Now I'm back and I'm worried the group of girls who made my life hell will find out. I'm constantly fearing one of them will turn up or try another stunt to hurt me.

Instead of risking another run-in with them, I've stayed in, had shopping delivered to my door, and gone for walks early in the morning when I know I'll never run into them. Those girls probably haven't seen eight in the morning since they left school.

I've prayed they've grown out of their bullying stage, but I know those girls. They will never grow up. They will be living out their school years for years to come.

The screen on my computer flashes, alerting me of an incoming call on

Skype, snapping me out of it before I go down the long, dark road of my past. I laugh, like I do every time I see the photo they have as their profile picture. Both grandparents are flashing cheesy grins, their eyes filled with happiness.

Answering the call, I smile at the screen, greeting them, "Hey, guys, where are you now?"

Grandma smiles, shoving my grandpa out of the way so she can lean closer to the camera. I've tried explaining the further they sit back, the more I can see of them, but they don't listen.

"We're in Vegas, and guess what?" she yells, not waiting for me to answer. "We got married!" She lifts her hand up and shows me the same rings she's worn since she first married my grandpa.

"You're already married," I remind her, laughing.

Grandpa rolls his eyes, moving Grandma out of the way so he can see the screen. "We got married *again* last night. She thinks because we were married in the UK, we aren't legally married here."

"I didn't want to live in sin," she snaps at him before turning to the laptop, her expression softening. "If you know what I mean."

Gross.

You have to love them though. There isn't much they could do that would shock me anymore, not since they took me to a nude beach and stripped down to their birthday suits.

"Did you do it the proper way: go gamble at some tables, get drunk, then go get Elvis to marry you?"

Grandma pushes Grandpa away again, leaning even closer to the screen. "We had these lemon-drop thingies. They tasted so good. Made me feel twenty-two again."

"That's a yes, then," I laugh, swinging my chair side to side.

"It was a good night. We wish you could have stayed with us; we've missed you," she says, smiling softly. "Don't worry about the wedding though, we have it on video. The lovely lady at the front desk said she'll show us how to email it to you."

"Looking forward to watching it." I smile, genuinely excited to see it. I can only imagine how it went.

"Never gonna see us marry again, kid. We don't have much time on this earth. We've got to do things while we're still young."

"You're old," I remind him, fighting not to laugh when he narrows his eyes at the screen.

"Bite your tongue," Grandma scolds. "We rocked this bed——"

Grandpa covers her mouth. "The kid doesn't need to hear what we did last night, woman." He pushes his face closer to the camera, pushing Gran to the side so she's out of view. I giggle. "How's it going there? Everything going okay with the renovations?"

"Good," I say, not wanting to tell them I had another run-in with my neighbour. They'll only worry, and since I didn't hear a word he said to me, I can't tell if he was angry with me or not. His facial expressions could always be like that. That's what I choose to believe, anyway. It hurts a little to think he was angry with me. "Actually, is there any way you can tell the builders to come around eight from now on and not six? They keep waking me up, and I've been working late some nights to get this project finished."

I have to have the doorbell attached to me when I go upstairs, otherwise I can't tell if someone's at the door. Downstairs, my grandparents had lights installed in the corner of the rooms that flash when it's rung. The device I carry vibrates. I would leave it outside my room when I go to bed, but something always stops me. What if someone rings it to make sure no one is home before they break in? I've read in magazines that it's happened before. So instead of leaving it, I've let them ring it until I'm up and answering the door. It's driven me mad, especially when some nights I work until the early hours of the morning.

"What time have they been showing up?" Grandpa asks, all business and serious now.

"Before six."

He eyes my grandma before looking back at me and shaking his head. "I'll have a word with the manager. Did you not tell them yourself?" I bite my lip, wondering if I should tell them or not. "I know that look. What is it?"

Releasing my lip, I inhale before telling them. "I don't like them. One guy pinched my arse, another keeps asking me out, and a few of them keep asking me to use the restroom, even though they have a Portaloo at the side of the house. They give me the creeps, so I tend to lock the doors and pretend I'm not here."

The builders were meant to be working on the new garden for my grandpa. He wanted a brick gazebo, a BBQ set up, and a pond put in at the back. They've also been working on the conservatory, but luckily, the back of the house can be closed off from the kitchen, which is what I've done.

I was glad it wasn't them who put the scaffolding up, but a different company. Knowing the men who were working here now, they would perv inside my room.

I've been dreading the time they have to come in and start work on the inside of the house.

Grandpa's face turns red. "I'm firing them. You should have said something sooner. I'm gonna talk to Maggie. She said the guy living with her has a family member who runs a construction business. They even do remodels. Do me a solid, kid, run next door and ask your neighbour for the number. Tell them we will pay ten percent over costs and labour for their service."

"But—"

"I'll ring them low-lifes now and fire them. The only reason they'll be there tomorrow is to get their stuff," he growls, taking his mobile out.

"Now, you take care, Bailey. We've got a dance club to get to. But we'll ring you tomorrow, same time," Gran rushes out.

"But—"

The call ends and I sit back, wondering how I was the one who got roped into asking for the number.

If I don't do it, Grandpa will just come back and do it himself, and I want them to have a good time. They've looked after me since my parents and little brother died three years ago and have done everything they could to make my life better.

Thankfully, the builders left early today, probably thinking I wouldn't notice, so I won't have to worry about them being outside to hound me.

I grab the keys to let myself back in and head out, nerves hitting me when I see the cars are still in the driveway.

I swallow, wondering if I should come back later. He's got company; it will be rude of me to turn up uninvited.

I look back towards my grandparents' house, ready to run back inside, but the thought of having those builders come back if I can't get these ones to work for me has me moving to the stairs leading to the apartment above the garage.

I place my palm on the door before knocking with my other hand, making sure it isn't too loud, since he has a baby that could be sleeping.

For the first few months after losing my hearing, I would shout instead of talk, and slam things down rather than placing them normally. It was a huge adjustment to work without my hearing.

The door opens slowly, revealing my hot neighbour and the baby girl in his arms. I want to smile down at her adorable face, but I'm too nervous and scared of what he might say.

I realise I've been watching her too long because when I look up, he's frowning, his lips moving too quickly for me to keep up.

I want to run back home and whine to my grandpa for making me do this. It can't possibly get any worse.

SIX

AIDEN

A KNOCK ON THE DOOR HAS ME GLANCING at Lily and Mark, raising my eyebrow. "Bet you that's Mum."

Lily laughs from where she's emptying the shopping bags on the bed. "She's busy helping Dad today with the new house they bought."

"Are you gonna help with this?" Mark pants, looking down at the parts for the chest of drawers we bought.

"No, you and Landon have got this," I tell him absently, not wanting to put Sunday down. I don't like her being cooped up in the pushchair. Even close by, it still feels too far away. I didn't realise becoming a parent would be this emotionally challenging.

"I'm going to wash these," Charlotte tells us, carrying a huge pile of new clothes out of my room. Apparently, you have to wash baby clothes before putting them on the baby. It made me panic because I can't remember Mum washing anything before we started putting clothes on Sunday. Even the clothes Uncle Mason brought to the hospital were put on her straight out of the packaging.

I step out of my room, walking over to the front door. Opening it, I'm startled to find the chick from next door. She looks sexy as hell in her denim skirt and white tank top. I almost pout when I find she's wearing a bra. I wouldn't complain if she decided to not wear one ever again when I'm around.

When she doesn't say anything, I frown. "Can I help you?"

She continues to stare at Sunday, and I become worried. Maybe she's a baby snatcher. I pull Sunday away a little.

"Look, if you're here to take my baby or ignore me again, you can leave," I tell her when she starts to look up, her eyes on my mouth again. My cock stirs when she licks her lips. "Is there something you want, babe, or are you gonna stare all night?"

"I—I, um… sorry," she says, looking ready to flee. She takes a step back, her face pale, and I watch in horror as the heel of her foot slips off the stop step. Holding Sunday with one arm, I reach out and grab her with my other, a tingle shooting through me where we touch.

"Watch it," I warn, pulling her away from the stairs. It makes me frown, my own face growing pale when something occurs to me.

Sunday will be at an age soon enough when she'll be crawling around and might do the same thing. Holy crap! I need to baby-proof that ASAP. And after listening to one of the staff at Mother Care talk about baby-proofing homes, I know I need to take this shit seriously. Who knew a toilet could be dangerous for a baby? And that wasn't even the worst of it.

"Is there something you wanted?" I rush out, ready to hit the internet to see what I can use to make the stairs safer.

"I'm sorry, but can you speak slower?"

Trust me to be hot for the crazy chick. "What. Do. You. Want."

Her shoulders relax and she smiles, taking my breath away. She's fucking gorgeous normally, but when she smiles, she's fucking breath-taking. "My, um, my grandpa…. He told me to come and get a number."

"You want my number?"

"What? No!"

I grin when she turns bright red, her gaze focussing over my shoulder. Lily steps up behind me, peeping around me to the door, so I step aside, letting her stand next to me.

"Um, hi," the chick from next door says, waving.

"Hi, I'm Lily."

"I'm Bailey, it's nice to meet you."

"Yeah, yeah," I say, interrupting. I ignore it when Lily slaps my stomach and face my neighbour. "Whose number do you want, if not mine?"

It's not like I have time to date, but maybe once I'm settled with Sunday, I can get a babysitter and give her what she wants.

"I think you said which number do I want, but I can't be sure. I think you mumbled the last bit."

Of course, *I mumbled it*. Didn't she hear me?

"Are you deaf?" Lily asks, and I stare wide-eyed at my innocent sister. She's never been bitchy or rude to anyone in her life.

"Lily!"

"I am." Bailey smiles, and I look between them, confused.

"I thought you were insulting her for a moment. I didn't know whether to congratulate you or shout for at you for being mean."

"Aiden, she was watching our lips. It was easy to see."

"Yeah, I knew that," I tell her, wanting to slap myself. It explains why she didn't answer the first time I went round, and why she couldn't answer me this morning.

"Come in. Did you want a drink?"

Sheesh, invite the neighbourhood in, Lily, why don't you. While you're at it, ask if they need some food.

Speaking of food, I'm starving.

"Only for a minute. I really need to get back."

I watch Bailey enter, my eyes never leaving hers. There's something about her that makes her different. I just don't know what. It's not even that I want to fuck her, because there's a lot of girls I want to fuck. It's her.

"Aiden mentioned a number?" Lily says, starting conversation when she sees Bailey become nervous.

Charlotte steps into the room, quietly watching us, and I know it won't be long until Mark and Landon follow. One look from Landon and I'll probably never lay eyes on the beautiful neighbour again. He's enough to scare a serial killer away. Fucker doesn't know how to be relaxed.

"Yes. My grandparents were speaking to Maggie and she mentioned that…," she pauses before pronouncing my name, as if hoping to get it correct, "Aiden, had family who worked in construction. He wants to fire the people he has working for him."

I step into her view so she has no choice but to look at me. "Why are you firing them?"

She wrings her hands together. "I don't like them. They wake me up too early. Too early for anyone to be up and—and I, um… I just don't like them."

I can see there is more to the story, but she's too nervous to tell it. I want to pressure her, but it's none of my business. And I have a baby to think about now; I can't get involved with her.

"I said that to you this morning. They keep waking me up with all the banging."

She winces. "I'm sorry for them waking you up. And I couldn't understand you this morning. You were talking too fast and kept looking away."

Shit. Now I feel like a bigger prick. By the time I finished breakfast with the family, I was convinced she was a spoilt bitch.

"Sorry. I'd not long gotten Sunday to sleep before they woke us up."

"I'm so sorry. Is she yours?"

I beam down at Sunday before looking back up. "She is. Beautiful, isn't she."

"Very," she answers quietly before looking at Lily. "Are you her mum?"

Lily gives her a sad smile. "I'm her aunt. Sunday's mum died giving birth."

Bailey's eyes water when they glance at me. "I'm so sorry for your loss."

I shrug. "Thank you. It was a one-night stand though. We weren't a couple. I didn't really know her," I rush to explain. And for some reason, I feel like I had to. I don't want her to think I'm heartbroken over my girl's mum. Yes, I hurt for Sunday—she'll never have her mum—but for me… I'll be fine.

"Um, okay," she says, her hands still twisting and clenching. "So, can I have the number? I'd really like the work done before my grandparents decide to come home—if they ever do. They're enjoying their time away travelling."

"Here, hold Sunday for a moment and I'll ring him," I tell her, and for the first time since I picked Sunday up from the hospital, I hand her over to another person without that empty feeling in my chest. It's bizarre. I shake off the feeling quickly.

I hear Lily's sharp intake of breath and ignore her surprised face as I watch Bailey cuddle Sunday close, smiling gently down at her.

"You are beautiful," she coos, letting Sunday grip her finger.

Lily clears her throat. "You were going to call Maddox?"

I look away from the beautiful sight in front of me, my heart hurting for Sunday. She should be held by her mum.

"Yeah," I tell her, grabbing my phone from my back pocket before clicking on Maddox's contact. He answers straight away.

"You miss me already?"

I sigh, pinching the bridge of my nose as I move into the kitchen to get some privacy. "No, the chick next door is firing the builders working on her grandparents' house. She was told to come get your number. Do you have any time to fit her in? I know you've been busy but she seems like she wants rid of them fast."

"Who was working on her house?" he asks, and I hear papers ruffling in the background. This is the side of Maddox only his workers get to see. Any other time he's laid back and a goof. You would never believe he runs a successful business. "I'll see who we have free."

"Hold on," I tell him, poking my head out of the kitchen. "Hey, Lily, ask her who works on the house now." I wait for Lily to ask before listening to Bailey's answer. She glances towards me with a cute frown on her face. Instead of answering her silent question, I move back into the kitchen. "Smiths General Contractors."

"Fuck!"

"What?"

"No wonder she wants them gone. They're one of my biggest competitors in town, but since they hired Ford and his team, they're losing customers. They've had sexual harassment suits build up against them, but because his family are rich and have contacts in high places, they've gotten away with it. Doesn't your neighbour live on her own?"

Fuck is about right. I scrub a hand down my face. "Yeah, she does. So, can you do it?"

"I don't really have the men, but if she doesn't mind, I can pop by tomorrow and go over what needs to be done, see if I can pull some men away from jobs that are nearly complete. Mark, Landon and Liam are three of my best men, so I'll ask if they mind swapping around a bit."

I don't know why I feel relief when he agrees to help her, but I do. I look back into the living room where she's slowly rocking Sunday side to side and narrow my eyes.

She must be a witch. There's no way around it. She's put me under some sort of spell and made me a fucking pussy.

Either that, or Sunday has made me go soft. Then again, the chick trying it on with me today in Mother Care didn't even make me tingle in the balls, so it has to be Bailey.

I'm just gonna have to stay away until whatever spell she has me under fades away.

"You there, dickhead?"

"Yeah," I croak out. "Sorry, I was just watching Sunday."

He laughs down the phone. "I still can't believe you're a dad. And I'm still pissed you won't let me put a picture on Facebook. Chicks will be all over me if I post that on there."

I roll my eyes. "You're not using my daughter to get chicks. Now fuck off. And I'll let her know you'll be around tomorrow. Do you know what time? She's deaf, so she probably needs to know when to look out for you. Don't be fucking late."

"I don't know sign language. Want me to bring Liam; he knows it? He learned it when he wanted to bang that deaf chick a few years ago."

My family can be arseholes.

"No, she can lipread just fine. Just speak clearly and don't look away."

"All right. Tell her I'll be by around midday."

"Speak to you later," I tell him, then hang up. When I reach the living area, Bailey looks up, her body tensing. "He said he'll be by tomorrow around midday to go over everything. That good for you?"

Her body relaxes and she smiles brightly at me. "That's perfect. Thank you so much. I don't know what I would have done if we couldn't hire him. Is he your friend?"

"No, he's my cousin. We're family. And he's really good at his job."

"Thank you again," she tells me. "I'd best be going; I've got loads of work to catch up on."

She turns to leave, and I watch as she heads for the open door. I want to reach out, tell her to stay and grab a drink or something, so we can get to know one another.

Then my eyes widen when I remember she's still holding Sunday. I rush over at the same time she turns around, her face flushed with embarrassment.

"I'm so sorry. I didn't mean it when I thought about taking her home with me. It was a joke because she's cute and all."

I chuckle at her rambling, taking Sunday from her arms. "It's fine. She kind of does it to everyone."

"I bet," she says, before laughing musically. I smile at the sound. "Right, now I'm definitely going. Have a good night."

"You too."

"And it was nice meeting you both," she tells Charlotte and Lily.

"We'll pop by in the week to talk about that thing with you," Charlotte says, and my eyes widen when Bailey nods. Then she's gone.

I turn to the girls, eyeing them both suspiciously. "Why are you going to her house?"

They both look at each other, biting their lips. Neither can lie to save their life. They're too kind and soft-hearted. I'm nearly knocked off my feet when they both shrug at me, keeping their lips sealed.

"Come on. You two hate lying."

"Not telling you anything is not lying to you," Charlotte states matter of fact.

I'd laugh at her cleverness, but I'm dying to know. You know, the curious cat and all that. "Lily?"

"Don't ask me, please. I don't want to lie to you. And I'm only going because I like her. She's really nice."

I eye Charlotte, wondering what she's keeping from me and what she could possibly want with Bailey. We'll find out eventually, and when I tell Landon, he'll soon get it out of her. If the fucker doesn't already know. Those two have been best friends all their lives.

When they share another conspiratorial look, I nearly push for answers, knowing they'll give in eventually. But I have a better idea. When they show up, I'll make sure I'm there to invite myself to the little party. That way I can check out Bailey and get to know her story.

And if there's one thing I'm certain of, it's Bailey having a story. You can see it in her body language, in the way she speaks, and in those eyes.

She also wasn't born deaf—she speaks fluently with no problems—which also questions why she doesn't have a hearing aid or something. I'd like to know what happened to her.

Why? No fucking clue. No girl has ever had me this worked up. The only women I care about are the women in my family.

Until her.

She seems different, and I'm gonna make it my mission to find out why.

So much for staying away from her.

SEVEN

BAILEY

THE CONTINUOUS VIBRATIONS OF the doorbell wake me up from a deep sleep. A cold sweat breaks out over my skin and I begin to shake, slowly getting out of bed as it continues. Someone has their finger on the bell and aren't removing it.

My worst fears have come to life: the four girls who made my teenage years a living hell are here.

Flashes of my childhood run through my mind and I start to feel frustrated with myself. I promised myself, after the last time, I wouldn't let them rule my life. I want to take a stand, to not let them see how scared I really am inside.

Not wanting to be half naked when I confront them, I grab my hoodie off a chair and pull it over my head. I also don't want to be taken off guard again, either, so I rush to my bottom draw and dig out the last hearing aid I was given. It hurts too much to wear normally, but there is no way I'm letting one of them sneak up on me. If that means putting this torture device to my ear, then so be it. I push the earmold into my eardrum, before attaching the tiny clip to my lobe, wishing one of the ones that sat behind my ear was the ones that I got on with. I switch it on, wincing at the sound that echoes through my head.

I close my eyes, fighting off the wave of tears that threaten to spill at hearing sounds around me. I can hear banging on the door this time, and I jump, quickly heading for the stairs.

It has to be them. Who else would be ringing my bell like there's a fire? My grandparents are well known around here, so everyone who is important know they are travelling. If news has gotten around that I'm back and alone, those four will jump at the chance to come and tell me where my place is.

You see, my mum and dad owned a hardware shop and we lived nicely in a middle-class area. My grandparents are rich, having shares in all sorts of businesses, and live on a private road. When it came to going to school, my grandparents won in sending me to a private school so I could take the art classes I was passionate about. It's all I've ever wanted to do: to draw and design.

I had been so excited to attend my new high school, more so when I saw their art department. It was heaven. I left that day thinking it was hell. I'd never felt so secluded or alone in my life. Those girls sucked the life out of me. Because my grandparents paid a lot of money for me to attend and we begged my parents to let me, I couldn't turn around and say I didn't want to go anymore.

Instead, I lived through years of bullying. No matter what my parents tried to do to stop them, nothing worked. It only made things worse. Then I got pulled out half way through my last year and attended our local school. It was easier there, but because I hadn't had any friends at the private school, I was anti-social. I didn't know how to interact with other people, so I kept to myself. It was how those same four girls managed to get me alone every single time. Even at different schools, they still managed to find me. There were times I would take the long route home, but as always, they managed to corner me. It was beyond terrifying.

I shake the bad memories from my mind, my throat tightening.

My hands begin to shake as I move into the hallway and head to the front door. I peek through the peephole, my eyebrows bunching up when I see Ford, the site manager who has been working on the house. I wipe my clammy hands down my thighs.

Crap, Granddad already spoke to him. Last night I had hoped he wouldn't have been able to get in touch with him. I should have expected this.

With a gulp, I turn the lock and pull open the door. I'm met with an angry snarl and a finger pointing in my face.

"Am I hearing this right? You've got us fired?" he roars, eyeing me with disgust. My fingers go to my hearing aid, already wanting to rip it off. The sound is loud, echoing in my ears and making me wince in pain.

"My grandpa wanted someone else," I lie.

He grabs my arm, pulling me out of the door. "Ring him up now, you silly fucking bitch. We've worked hard on this house. Look at all these men. They've got families to support."

And drugs and beer to buy, I want to add. I may be deaf but I'm not blind. I've seen them smoking weed and drinking in the garden.

I pull my arm out of his grasp, glaring at him. I'm fed up of bullies trying to dictate to me. "No. It's his decision."

He scoffs, stepping closer to get in my face. "Then make him change his mind, you silly cow. Or you can pay for the money we'll lose from us being kicked off this job."

I rear back. The audacity of him! "I don't think so." I won't be giving them a penny of my money.

"Like you don't have the money. Rich bitches like you always have a big bank account. I suggest you go get it, because I'm not going to leave until you do," he yells, just as a car pulls up next door and a beautiful woman steps out. I watch as she stares over at us in concern before quickly moving towards the stairs.

"I'm not giving you money."

"Yeah, you fucking are. You've cost us a fucking job because you think you're all high and mighty."

"Yo, slag," I hear shouted, and turn my head in the direction of the muffled sound. I cringe when I see the rough-looking guy who is always eyeing me like I'm fresh meat. "Who the fuck do you think you're reporting us to, our boss? Uptight bitches like you need to loosen up." I cringe when he drops the tools he's carrying to hold his junk, shaking it. "You can sit on this."

Ford's muffled laughter fills my ears. "Maybe we should teach her how to lighten up."

I take a step back when the sound in my ears becomes too much. I can see the men laughing, and it's all too much at once. Tears fill my eyes because I want to rip the thing out, but I know I can't with these men. They'd take advantage of my vulnerability; bullies always do.

"I suggest you all leave before I call the police and have someone else come and get the rest of your equipment."

"Hear that?" is shouted, but when I look around for the source, I can't find it. I begin to panic, hating this feeling. This is why I don't go out without my grandparents. I hate confrontations, especially ones I can't fully understand or hear.

"Call the fucking police? Bitch, you won't get near a phone if you keep chatting shit. Thinking you're something fucking special," Ford scoffs, stepping forward again. "You can give us the money we're gonna lose, or else… And trust me, you don't want to get on my bad side."

"You don't want to get on mine either, dickhead," I hear next. I glance to the side and see Aiden prowling towards us, his growling voice as deep as I imagined. My jaw hangs open at the sight of him shirtless, his ripped chest defined and muscled. "Step the fuck away from her."

Yikes, he must work out.

Closing my jaw, I wipe at my mouth in case I've drooled a little. Thankfully, I haven't.

Aiden's expression softens when his gaze reaches mine. I give him a small smile and he winks, before masking his expression into a cold glare, aiming it at Ford. I shiver.

"Kid, you don't want to mess with me right now," Ford snaps.

Aiden laughs humourlessly. "No, it's you who doesn't want to mess with me. For weeks you've woken me up early—too fucking early. Then I've watched as you guys leave around noon, or I see you drinking on the job. So it's you who shouldn't mess with me."

"This is none of your fucking business, wanker. Go run back home to your mum and let the big boys deal with this."

Aiden steps between me and Ford, and a warm feeling swarms my body at the protective gesture.

"I beg to differ. Bailey is my friend and my neighbour; I won't have you bullying her. If you did your fucking job in the first place, you wouldn't have gotten fired."

"You don't know what you're talking about," Ford snaps, his face turning red.

The muscles in Aiden's back tense, and I look around for help, knowing I won't be of any use if this turns into a fight. The woman who got out of the car earlier is standing in Aiden's doorway, rocking Sunday, a phone to her ear and talking rapidly.

"Yeah, I fucking do. I'm a Carter. I know all about you and the sexual harassment complaints you've had from clients. How many more times do you think you can be fired before you're laid off for good? Does it make you feel good creeping girls and women out? Does it make you feel like you've got a big dick when you scare them after they complain about you? You're nothing but a dickhead who can't get laid 'cause he's got a small dick."

I scream when Ford roars, his fist flying towards Aiden. Aiden doesn't turn but instead reaches back to push me out of the way, before planting his feet apart. I trip over a stone and end up falling to the floor. My hearing aid falls out, giving me a moment of relief before I remember what is happening around me.

I turn in time to see Aiden duck the punch Ford was aiming at his face, before twisting and landing his own punch in Ford's gut, forcing him to the floor. Aiden straddles him, punching him once more before movement by the gates snags my attention.

I feel like I'm watching a bad horror movie when two cars pull up, stopping right outside our gate. Three men and four younger guys step out, looking intimidating and scary as hell.

I have to do something. Aiden can't possibly take all of these men on.

When I turn back to Aiden, a scream bubbles from my throat as I see another guy has joined the fray and is beating on him too. I get up from the ground to help him, hating myself for not sending him home to his daughter when I had the chance. Just as I reach them, the guy who's joined in rears his fist back to punch Aiden, and his elbow catches me in the eye. I cry out, feeling disorientated for a moment as I'm knocked back a few steps.

"Stop! I'm calling the police," I scream out, pulling my phone out of my pocket, tears falling down my cheeks as Aiden punches Ford relentlessly while the other jumps on his back.

From the corner of my eye I notice one of the guys from the car step towards me, his expression unreadable. I flinch, taking a step back and clutching the phone to my chest. The others from the cars try to break everyone apart, but it ends up getting into a fist fight once again.

I stare in fascination when one of the guys from the car catches my attention. I try not to laugh when he throws his arms around in a karate gesture before punching the guy who ganged up on Aiden in the mouth. His lips move, and I swear he says, "Fucker, I'm gonna have you shitting out your teeth." His face turns away before I can read if he says anything further, but I'm positive that's what he said.

Movement close to me has me remembering the big, intimidating guy. He's watching the fight, his mouth shouting the word, "Max!"

I quickly dial the police, but before I can connect the call, he snatches the phone out of my hand.

I look up at him, my eyes wide. "Hey!"

"Sweetheart, I'll deal with this."

"I won't have you beating up my nice neighbour," I snap, wondering how quickly I can get to the next nearest neighbour's house. I look over to the woman who has Sunday, knowing she has a phone. But she's no longer on it and she doesn't seem as concerned as she did before. If anything, she seems relaxed.

A tap on my shoulder has me looking back to the guy next to me.

"I'm Maverick, Aiden's dad. Just go wait over by my wife, Teagan, and I'll sort this out, okay?"

He's Aiden's dad? He looks too hot and too young to be a dad. Okay, he's not young—he has to be in his forties at the most—but he looks good.

"Okay," I whisper, before rushing across the grass, over to her. The guys have stopped picking up their equipment and glare at me as I rush past them. I can't help but watch the words spilling from their lips.

"Bitch."

"Whore."

I look away, wiping the tears staining my cheeks. When I reach the top, the woman Maverick called Teagan is talking to me rapidly, her hand reaching out to rub my arm.

I can see where Aiden got his looks. He has stunning parents. This woman doesn't look a day over thirty.

"I'm sorry. I lost my hearing aid—not that it's much good," I ramble, my headache turning into a migraine. I wince, clutching my head when the pain becomes unbearable. "I'm sorry about your son. We need to call the police."

Teagan shakes me gently and I look up, feeling dizzy from the pain. This is why I hate wearing the hearing aids I was given: they become too much and I end up like this. My grandparents offered to pay for a better quality one, but after my parents' and brother's death, I didn't feel like I deserved to hear, not when I'm the reason they're dead.

The black eye I can feel swelling doesn't help my migraine. The throbbing right under my eye makes it hard to keep it open. I can see this being a bad one.

"I'm deaf," I tell her, grimacing when Sunday stirs and I realise I said it too loud. "Sorry."

"It's okay. Why don't you come and lie down? You look like you're about to pass out."

I don't even know this woman—or Aiden—enough to lie down in their house, but if I don't, I'll embarrass myself and pass out in front of everyone. And I'm ashamed enough as it is.

"What about Aiden?" I whisper—well, I hope I did.

"His dad, uncles and cousins will sort it."

I nod, letting her lead me inside. I thought she'd lead me over to the sofa, but instead she takes me through to another room. I look around, a small smile tugging on my lips when I see a beautiful cot with pink bedding and other baby things. One side of the room looks all man, while the other side looks like a unicorn threw up pink. It's beautiful.

My eyes scrunch together when Teagan pushes me down on the bed. I look up at her, silently questioning her since it hurts too much to speak.

"Close your eyes for a bit. When I get headaches, that's what I do, and I wake up feeling refreshed. Would you like some paracetamol?" I nod, feeling my throat tighten at this family's kindness. "Lie down; I'll only be a minute."

I look down at the rumpled sheets, feeling my cheeks heat. Aiden sleeps here. Hell, the bed still feels warm.

I lay down, inhaling the scent of musk and man. I sigh, closing my eyes to take it all in, memorising the smell.

EIGHT

AIDEN

I THOUGHT MY MORNING WAS GOING great until Mum started banging on my door frantically. I had just finished feeding Sunday and was ready to get her changed when she arrived.

I still can't believe that dickhead was harassing Bailey. When I walked out, all of them were gravitating towards her. A feeling I only felt when I thought one of my family were being threatened overwhelmed me, and I was moving before I even knew what I was going to do. She had looked petrified, so fucking small curled up on herself that I wanted to punch him there and then. The only reason I didn't was because of Sunday and Bailey. One: I couldn't get arrested now I had a baby, and two: I think if I had started the fight, Bailey would never have been comfortable around me ever again.

I spit blood out of my mouth, onto the floor, and lick the cut on my bottom lip. One of his friends had sucker-punched me when I wasn't looking.

I bend down, my hands on my knees, when the last of their trucks leave, looking over at my uncle Max lying on the grass.

"Uncle Max, what the fuck were you doing? Having a dance off?"

Mason bends over, roaring with laughter. "I've been waiting for someone to bring it up. It was awkward for a moment there."

"Fuck off, those were my ninja moves," he snaps, before grinning. "I've not had that much fun since I ran Hayden's last boyfriend off."

"Not as much as we did when we took her last one to the secluded spot and threatened him," Landon adds, not even looking out of breath. Fucker doesn't even have a mark on him as he casually leans against Mum's car.

"You put me off what I was doing, Dad. I kept worrying you were having an epileptic fit, or a heart attack," Liam comments, grinning.

"Fuck you. I'm still young I'll have you know," Max snaps, glaring at his son.

"You're lucky we got here as quickly as we did. Your mum was frantic," Dad warns me.

"I didn't start the fight," I tell him. And I'm telling the truth. I may have goaded the fucker into hitting me, but I can, hand on heart, honestly say I never threw the first punch.

Dad rolls his eyes, sighing. "You're a dad now, son."

"I know," I snap, wishing he would believe me.

"Maverick, he's telling you the truth," Mum says, and I stand up straight, glancing at her. "He was trying to help Bailey when that guy attacked him."

Dad still looks doubtful. I inhale, turning around to face Mum. "Where's Bailey?" I ask. "Is she okay?"

"She's asleep in your bed."

"What?" I ask a little too loudly, confused as to why.

Mum walks down the steps, pinching my chin and tilting my head side to side. "You need to go get this cleaned up. You all do."

"I don't," Landon pipes up.

I glare at the fucker. "Was you even fighting?"

He narrows his eyes back at me. "I had five of them on me."

Liam sits up from the grass he was laying down on. "He's right. I was next to him fighting one and was wondering how the fuck he did it."

"I took them all on," Uncle Max says, getting up. "Now I've got to get back to school before P.E. starts."

"You came from school?" I ask. I'd presumed it was teachers training day or something.

"No. I had the morning off and was going over some things with Mav and Maddox about some work on the house."

"Oh."

"Dad, you don't have a mark, either," Mark says, sounding envious. The left side of the poor lad's face is completely swollen, as if someone trod on it.

Dad grins, looking smug. "I only stared at the two guys who were gonna come at me and they ran off to get their tools before leaving."

Mum giggles and I roll my eyes. "Can we get back to the real issue?" I ask, then look at Mum. "Why is Bailey in my bed—asleep, I might add?"

"She mentioned something about a hearing aid and she looked in pain, the poor thing. I went to get her some paracetamol for the black eye but she was asleep by the time I got back."

"Hearing aid?" I ask, before my eyes widen. "A hearing aid? She's deaf!"

Dad steps towards us, handing me a crushed device. "Think this is what she was talking about."

"Crap! I wonder why she doesn't wear it, then," I muse to myself.

"Well, Great-grandma Mary's first one used to irritate her ear and give her migraines. If I was to guess, that's what's happened here. She looked pale and in so much pain."

"And who the fuck punched her? Did you see?" I growl, wanting to go look for them fools and finish what they started.

"I'm not sure," Mum tells me gently.

"She tried to get in between you and the guy who jumped you. As he pulled back, his elbow landed in her face," Dad answers.

"And you didn't do anything?" I growl.

He gives me a dry look. "Of course I fucking did. He's the one they carried to the truck."

I relax, looking up the stairs at my apartment. "What do I do?"

"Let her get some rest. She looked like she needs it," Mum tells me.

"And it's not like she's gonna hear you or Sunday," Liam adds. I turn my glare to him. "Wow! Calm down. How long have you known this chick? Sheesh."

"Officially, yesterday," I admit, rubbing the back of my neck. Mum and Dad share a look, before she heads back upstairs, smiling. "What?"

Dad grins. "Nothing."

"You're pussy-whipped," Max adds, laughing.

Glaring at him, I snap, "No, I'm not." They all start laughing and I growl, clenching my fists. "Shup up, dickheads!"

"Look at you getting all mad," Liam laughs.

"I wouldn't antagonise him," Dad warns, before clapping me on the shoulder. "Don't worry, we've all been through it."

"I'm not going through anything," I assert.

"Yeah, you are, but it's worth it," Uncle Mason calls out.

"I'm really not."

"Yeah, you fucking are. Just don't fuck up," Max adds, holding his hand out to Mason, a silent request to help him up. Mason keeps walking, and I chuckle as Max narrows his eyes. "Right, Maddox, you can take me to school before they fire me. I'm gonna have to tell them I was mugged."

I chuckle, wondering how many times he's had to explain bruises to the school.

"I'll get a lift back with Teagan and meet up with you later," Dad tells the others.

"Thanks for coming, guys."

"It's what families do," Mason tells me, squeezing my shoulder.

"I'll be back in a few hours. Text me if you need longer," Maddox tells me, winking.

I roll my eyes at him before saluting them goodbye and heading up the stairs. Mum is placing Sunday down in her Moses basket when I step inside.

"I'm gonna have to head in. Maddison and I have a big order to fill out. We've got four weddings this weekend."

"Thanks for coming, Mum."

"Always. I wanted to come check on you. I'm gonna come by tomorrow evening. If you want to go out for a drink with your siblings and cousins, I'll watch Sunday for you."

"Nah, I'm good. I'm not ready to leave her just yet."

She smiles softly at me. "Okay, honey. Get cleaned up. You don't want to get blood all over Sunday."

"I will. I promise," I tell her, reaching over to kiss her cheek, chuckling when she gets a bit of blood on her face.

She glares at me before wiping it off.

"Bye, son. Speak to you later. Look after those girls."

I look down at Sunday, who is sleeping soundly in her basket, then at the door to my bedroom, knowing Bailey's in there. "I will."

I see them out before heading into the bedroom to get a change of clothes, since I was only wearing my jogging bottoms when Mum came over. I walk in and pause in the doorway. Bailey is lying on her side, cuddling my pillow, partly under her head, to her chest.

Her innocence shows on her sleeping, peaceful face, her chest rising and falling with each soft breath she takes.

Quietly, I step closer to her. Her dark eyelashes fan across her high cheekbones, and her lips have formed a cute pout that brings a smile to my own. I don't know what compels me to do it, but I end up walking over to the edge of the bed and lightly brushing her hair from out of her face. She sighs, snuggling further into my pillow.

Girls have always been simple to me. There are ones that flirt and are looking for a good time, there's the shy ones who crush on you and picture your future babies, and there's the ones who pretend they're only after a good time, when really all they want to do is tame you. Then there are the rare creatures who deserve more, the ones who will always be worth more than the person they meet. The women in my family are those rare creatures. No man on this earth will ever be good enough for them. Not to us guys, anyway.

But Bailey... Bailey is one chick who is a mystery to me. She doesn't flirt or look at me like I'm a slab of meat. Although, I bet she's had some right dirty thoughts about me. How could she not; I'm fucking sex on legs. She's not shy, and she's had no problem talking to me, even though she does seem like the girl who keeps to herself. And she doesn't strike me as the type of woman to manipulate a man to get what she wants. Call it intuition or what have you, but I just know she's different.

And a complete fucking puzzle I can't work out.

A Carter always gets what they want. And finding everything out about Bailey is what I want right now. Whether she knows it or not, she'll tell me everything.

MOVEMENT FROM THE bedroom door catches my attention from the corner of my eye. I look up, smiling at Bailey's just woke up look. She nervously straightens her hair and hoodie, looking around the room in confusion.

"How long have I been asleep?" she asks, her eyes drifting back to me.

I look up from changing Sunday's nappy to answer. "Only an hour. How are you feeling? Did you take the tablets Mum left out for you?"

"I did, thank you," she says, still looking dazed, before her eyes widen in horror. "Oh, my gosh, you're hurt. I'm so sorry. This is all my fault. I should have phoned the police when I looked out of the peephole."

"Sit down before you fall down," I tell her when she starts to sway. She reluctantly does, surprising me when she sits down on the opposite side of Sunday, stroking her cheek.

"I really am sorry," she whispers, glancing up at me. "What happened after I came inside?"

"Stop apologising," I tell her as I lift Sunday in my arms, bringing the bottle to her lips. She's been crying for the past twenty minutes, and she never finished her bottle this morning, refusing to drink it. Now she gulps it down. Once I know she's happy, I look back up at Bailey. "What happened wasn't your fault. I should have warned you last night after I spoke with my cousin. They've been known to harass the women they're working for."

"I can't believe it got so out of hand. Did the police come?"

I grin. "Nope. We handled it. They won't be coming back here again, I promise. We've threatened to call the police if they do, and they know my sister is engaged to one."

"Lily? I didn't see a ring."

"No, my other sister, Faith. We're a big family."

"I could see. I thought those men were there to attack you when they came out of the car," she tells me, before giggling. "It was like a mob movie. All they needed were black cars with tinted windows and guns at their hips."

I laugh. I can't wait to tell Dad she said that. He'll get a kick out of it. "No. Mum called them before I even came out to you." I take the bottle from Sunday's mouth and begin to bring her wind up before continuing. "How are you feeling?"

Her fingers go to her eye, and she winces. "I've had worse," she jokes, but something in her tone tells me she's serious.

"Maddox wants to come around soon to go over the plans for the house. He'll need to do an evaluation and all that. If you agree to it, he can start work as soon as you're ready."

"That's great news. The house is so old, and the bad weather we had last year tore a lot of the roof down, causing leaks. I've also got copies of the plans for the garden. I drew them up myself, and we already bought the materials. My grandpa was gonna do the work himself, but after a few attempts of trying to build a barbeque, he gave up and said he'd hire someone."

"Where are your grandparents?"

She smiles, adoration shining in her eyes. "Still travelling. They're in Vegas right now. I have no idea where they are going next."

"You didn't go with them?" I ask as I lie Sunday back down in my arms, bringing the bottle to her lips.

"I did for a while. I came back a few months ago. It was becoming too much to travel with them. I hated living out of a suitcase and sleeping in different beds. I just wanted some peace. For their age, they have more energy than me."

I grin. "Is that right?" I flirt, eyeing her up and down. The words just slipped out. It's a habit. She blushes, though doesn't say anything to my remark, so I clear my throat and change the subject. "How come you don't wear a hearing aid all of the time if they help you hear?"

Pain flashes across her features and I tense. She shrugs, looking away for a moment. "I only tried a few. I guess I was upset about becoming deaf in the first place and didn't want to rely on something. They give me migraines and make my ear sore. After my parents and brother died, I didn't want to look for more options."

Fuck!

"I'm sorry about your parents and brother. How long ago did they die?"

"Thank you," she answers, her voice thick. "And they died a few years back, in a house fire."

"How did you lose your hearing?" I ask, wanting to know everything about her, for reasons I don't understand.

Seeing the anguish and pain on her face, I immediately feel guilty. "I don't… I don't want to talk about it."

"Sorry," I whisper, ducking my head. Needing to lighten the mood, I change the subject. "Do you go to school?"

She shakes her head. "I did online courses. I'm a web and logo designer, but I do other designs too. I just started designing book and game covers."

Wow. Didn't expect that response.

"That sounds awesome."

A knock on the door has me jumping. Bailey, seeing my reaction, looks around the room. "What?"

"Someone's at the door. Can you take her for a minute?"

She takes Sunday from my arms, and the smile she shares with her steals my breath. I shake it off, hating the effect she has on me. I fuck around; I don't do monogamy. I'd never be worthy of someone like her. And it's not like I'm after a committed relationship, so I don't know why I'm getting so worked up over a chick I don't even know.

Opening the door, Maddox's bright smile greets me. I grin back when I see the bruise that has formed on his cheek.

"Nice whopper you got you there."

He chuckles. "You should see the other guy."

"Come in."

He steps inside, and I check behind him to make sure he didn't bring the family. He didn't and I'm grateful. For some reason, I don't think Bailey would appreciate having a house full of people she doesn't know.

"Fuck me," he hisses out, whistling through his teeth. "You kept it quiet that your neighbour is smoking hot."

I elbow him in the stomach, glaring. Bailey looks back and forth between us, an adorable crease in her forehead.

"Did you say something to me?" she asks shyly, tucking her hair behind her ear.

Maddox grins, and I know what's coming before he even starts, so I step in front of him, knowing she can't hear him. Call me sadistic, but I'm glad she can't. He has a way of charming the pants off women, and I want him to stay away from Bailey. The possessiveness isn't something I'm used to.

"Baby, I'll say whatever you want me to say if you agree to go out with me."

"She can't hear you," I growl.

"Huh? I'm standing right here."

"She's deaf, remember?"

He smiles bigger. "Move the fuck aside then and let her see me."

"Don't bother. I'll go fucking mad if you try it on with her."

"You fucking her?"

I want to punch him in the mouth; the urge is strong. "No, fuckhead, I'm not. She's my neighbour and I like her. I don't want her hating me because you fucking used her."

"Um, you do know it's rude to hide so I can't see you, now you know I'm deaf and all," Bailey says, and Maddox starts chuckling. I move aside and sit down next to her.

"Walk me through what you're wanting, then, darlin'."

I sit back and listen to the plans on the house. I can't keep my eyes off her;

the way her delicate mouth forms her words, the way she will often bite her bottom lip or tuck a stand of hair behind her ear. Every time she moves, I find myself fascinated.

NINE

BAILEY

I WRING MY HANDS TOGETHER, pacing by the front door as I wait for Charlotte and Lily to turn up. Both girls are special, both sweet and innocent and filled with warmth. I've only met them once, but there's something about them that screams at you to treat them with care. You can't help it. The way they move, look at you, and speak… they're all filled with an undeniable kindness.

When they treated me like I had been their best friend all our lives, I was blown away. I grew up with no one. The few people I did have drifted away, unable to handle the bullying I endured. The new ones I tried to make ignored me once they were warned to stay away from me. Hanging out with me was a ticket to becoming bullied, so people tended to stay away.

Charlotte had surprised me at Aiden's when she asked me for a favour and if they could come around. A part of me feared it was fate playing another cruel joke, but the thought passed quickly.

Now, I'm nervous as hell. I don't know how to act around other women, let alone what to say to them.

I had made myself sick with worry last night, praying this didn't go bad. I've craved a friendship for so long. It's sad, really. These two were offering it to me, and I knew, in the deepest part of my heart, they had no ulterior motive. They were both too gentle and soft-spoken to be anything other than who they were.

I can trust them.

The doorbell device vibrating against my leg and the lights flashing in the corner shouldn't surprise me, but still, I startle.

They're here.

I wipe my sweaty palms down my thighs and unlock the door, smiling at the two beautiful women in front of me.

"Hey, come in," I greet them. The two of them look different appearance wise. They're both incredibly beautiful too. It's like God had decided at making something perfect and used it up on these two. I'd never met anyone like them. Everything about them screams pure.

"I made you these," Charlotte says, handing me a plate of muffins. They look yummy.

"Thank you."

"Your house is beautiful," Lily tells me as we step into the living room. I can see what she means; everything about this house is big, even the high ceilings. Every bit of the building has been carved with detail. Nothing about the house screams plain.

My grandparents are the reason this house doesn't seem like a museum and instead feels like a home. It isn't cold, like most houses of this magnitude, but is instead filled with warmth and harmony. Pictures of family members before me and those I know and grew up with fill every space free for a picture frame. Snow globes my gran collected on her travels sit in a glass cabinet, and another is filled with items I created growing up or little presents I bought them with my pocket money. This is a true home, and where I felt loved after my family died.

"Thank you," I whisper, smiling. "Would you guys like a drink?"

They share a look before nodding. I smile at how sweet they both are. "Do you have tea?"

"I'm British; of course I have tea," I tease. They follow me into the kitchen and I start on making their drinks. "Take a seat and tell me what this favour is that you needed."

Since the kettle is boiling, I face them, waiting for Charlotte to answer. A pink tinge appears on her cheeks, which has me curious.

"Well, none of my family know—only Landon and Lily—but I write romance novels. Instead of publishing, I've only ever posted chapters on my website. At first, I thought it would just be a hobby, but people keep asking me to self-publish. I've decided, since the second book is complete, to do it, but I need covers and other logos. I also need my website revamping; it's been a while."

"Ah, that's why your eyes lit up when I told you what I did for a living." I smile, and then something occurs to me. "You seem close to your family... Why don't you want them to know? They seem like they'd be really supportive."

I've only met a handful, but they seem kind and willing to do anything to help others.

Maddox was really helpful with the plans for the house and went over the drawings I'd worked hard over when I brought him here, Aiden tagging along like a chaperone. I also showed them the work—or rather lack of work—done by the other builders.

Charlotte grimaces. "Our family are really supportive, but I want this to be mine for a while longer. I don't want them reading what I write."

I grin, intrigued. "Do you write dirty novels?"

She shrugs, her cheeks turning redder. "Not really, but they do have some naughty stuff in them."

"Tell her why you don't want them to know," Lily says, grinning wildly.

I didn't think it would be possible, but Charlotte turns even redder. "I'm a virgin," she blurts out, surprising me. Her expression is horrified, and I can see her throat bob as she swallows.

"Um, okay…" I say, unsure where she's going with this. She covers her face with her hands and I look to Lily questioningly, pointing to my ear.

Lily smiles softly, a rose blush tainting her cheeks and neck. "She's a virgin who writes sex scenes. She needed some inspiration as to what happens, so watched porn. In her latest book her main character works in a strip club. Charlotte had never been, so for research reasons, she visits a strip club weekly while she writes. The men in our family would go mad if they found out. And not only that, she'd be mortified if they teased her about it."

Lily's shoulders shake, and I smile. "My gran tried taking me to a strip club when we went to Amsterdam, so I can completely relate. As soon as I figured out where we were going, I decided to stay in. The street was filled with women and boobs."

"It's not funny," Charlotte says, her face heated. "Landon comes with me. I tried to go by myself, but I lasted ten minutes before I walked out. I decided the first time a woman shook her tatas at me that I'd just write it from my imagination, but I couldn't write anything afterwards. When I planned to go back, I had blown Landon off, not wanting him to know. He knew something was wrong so he followed me. Let's just say, he wasn't happy. But I couldn't write the book I wanted by staying at home, so he agreed to go with me, so I wasn't alone. He always looks pained when we're there though, like he would rather be somewhere else. I always thought men liked places like that. I hate that he had to suffer, but I was kind of grateful I wasn't alone. It was awkward enough."

I giggle, pulling the plate of muffins over to me and grabbing one. "I think he'd rather be there alone, without his…" I look to Lily for answers as to who Landon is to Charlotte.

"Cousin and best friend," she answers.

"Without his cousin cramping his style."

Lily gives me a look when I peel the paper from the bottom of the muffin, her wide eyes warning me of something with a subtle shake of her head.

When I glance back at Charlotte, she's talking. It takes me a while to catch up. "I don't think I can go with him ever again."

"What did I miss?" I ask, watching Charlotte for her reaction as I take a bite out of the muffin. Or try to. The outer edge is soft, but the middle is rock solid.

I think I just chipped a tooth.

Oh, my God, she hates me and is trying to kill me.

I turn around before she can answer, grabbing a tissue from the side and spitting the muffin out, gagging at the foul aftertaste in my mouth.

I feel someone beside me and see Lily there, placing her hand on my arm and smiling apologetically. "She's a terrible cook, but none of us have the heart to tell her."

I look over my shoulder to see Charlotte isn't there, before facing Lily. "Where is she?"

Her entire face lights up with amusement. "She's ringing Landon to cancel this week's outing to the strip club." She laughs, throwing her head back, before glancing back at me. "Are you okay?" When her eyes travel down to the muffin I spat out, I groan.

"They are terrible," I tell her, then wince. "Sorry."

"It's fine. We all feel for you, truly. We just don't want to hurt her feelings. She loves cooking and giving to people."

"So, she wasn't trying to kill me? She didn't give them to me because she hates me?"

The fear of her hating me is real. I don't know why I care so much, but I do. I want friends in my life—good ones.

Her eyebrows scrunch together, like she's thinking something over. "Charlotte doesn't have a hateful bone in her body. She gives these to all of us."

"I didn't mean it in a bad way," I assure her.

"I know you didn't," she tells me, looking down at the plate, then back up at me. "I thought these might be a little better. After we got arrested and they tested her muffins, she's been trying to perfect them."

"She got arrested? Charlotte and you?"

She nods furiously, her facial expression so expressive I laugh inside. "It was the worst night of my life. I thought we were going to prison for a very long time."

"What did you do?" I gasp out, utterly shocked. Both girls look like they couldn't hurt a fly.

Lily looks over my shoulder, her attention gone before she has chance to answer. And I really want to know the answer.

Someone's here.

Charlotte steps back into the kitchen, beaming at us, but her shoulders are tense, and she looks kind of nervous. Aiden follows behind, pushing Sunday in her pushchair.

"Look who I found outside."

"I can't believe you were having lunch and never invited me," he says, winking at me. I duck my head a little, feeling the need to fan myself all of a sudden. He's so freaking sexy it's hard not to stare at him. "Oh, are those muffins?"

Before I can warn him, he picks one up and takes a huge bite. He grimaces, his eyes wide as he slowly brings the muffin away from his mouth, teeth marks now marring the baked good.

Oh, dear.

"Actually, I'm not that hungry," he says, glancing briefly at Charlotte.

I giggle, looking away as he steps over to my fridge and pulls out a carton of orange juice. I wait for him to ask where the glasses are, but he doesn't, instead drinking what is left in the carton in a few large gulps.

"Well, when you are, you can take some home with you. I'm sure Bailey won't mind," Charlotte says.

I beam teasingly at Aiden. "Take as many as you'd like."

I can see him struggle to swallow as he nods. "Yeah, thanks."

Charlotte's cheeks have turned a tinge of pink once again as she looks at Lily, then me. "I forgot I have to do something at home. Maybe we can come another day?" Her expression totally gives her lie away, and I can see it all over Aiden's face that he knows it as well.

"You've not even had a cup of tea," he says, raising an eyebrow at the empty cups on the side.

She flushes, wringing her hands together. "I forgot. I always forget things," she says.

"And you don't have time to stay for a cuppa?'"

Charlotte glances at Lily, her eyes round. Lily steps forward. "You're here now; *you* have a cup of tea."

He doesn't say anything but continues to watch Charlotte with a blank expression, before pulling out his phone.

Charlotte see what he's doing and begins to look panicked. Before she confesses everything, I step forward, gaining their attention.

"That's fine. Wait here a second while I write my details down. We can, um… reschedule it later."

Her relief is palpable. "That would be great."

Quickly, I rush down the hall to my office, grab a pen and paper, and write down my phone number and email address. Hopefully she has a rough idea of what she wants so I can design some mock ups.

They're chatting as I walk back into the kitchen, Lily bent over the pram to see Sunday. I still can't believe her mum died. And his comment about her being a one-night stand was so blunt and forward. A part of me is asking myself why he would tell me that, hoping it's because he likes me. I feel for that little girl not having the chance grow up with a mother. Mine had been my best friend.

Pasting on a smile, I hand Charlotte the slip of paper. "Looking forward to seeing you again."

"Right, we'd better get going. Thank you for inviting us today," Charlotte tells me.

Lily smiles softly. "Yes, it was lovely seeing you again."

"It was lovely meeting you two, too," I tell them honestly. "Let me walk you out."

After saying goodbye once again, I close the front door with a sigh. If only briefly, I got to experience what it's like to have girlfriends. The tension I felt all morning was for nothing.

I relax back against the door and close my eyes. *I have friends.* Friends who could become people I'm close to.

A scream lodges in my throat when I open my eyes to find Aiden leaning against the wall. How the hell did I forget he was in my house?

"What's taking you so long?" He raises his eyebrow.

I narrow my eyes at him. "I forgot you were here. You scared me half to death."

He gives me a wounded look. "*You forgot I was here?*" He points to his chest, pouting at me.

I roll my eyes. "Yes," I admit, stepping around him and heading into the kitchen. Sunday is sleeping soundly in her pushchair when I stop next to her.

She's such a beautiful baby—and lucky to have so many people around her who love her. I notice four bags, filled to the brim, attached to different parts of the pushchair.

I turn around. "Are you going on holiday?"

"What?" he asks.

"The bags…"

"Oh, that's Sunday's stuff," he tells me, before heading over to the fridge and pulling out food to make a sandwich.

"Oh, is she staying out somewhere?"

He looks up from the round work bench, shaking his head. "No. I was gonna come and see if you wanted company today—in case they came back."

"You were?" I ask. I'm surprised by his kind gesture; we hardly know each other.

He grins, winking. "Yeah. That and I ran out of food this morning and I'm starving. When I saw the girls pull up I got her stuff together."

"Is she moving in here?"

His shoulders shake. "No, she's not."

"Then why all the stuff? You could have just popped back home when you needed it."

He shrugs. "I've only left the house with her once before, and, honestly, I still left stuff I might need at home. I never knew a baby needed so much stuff."

"They do," I murmur, running my finger down her soft cheek. "How old is she?"

"Four days old today."

"You're doing really good for only being a dad for four days."

"I've got the nappy thing down. Any time she poos, I wear one of the mouth masks Maddox brought over. After the first few incidents of being sick, I knew I had to do something. The only other thing I find difficult is changing her vests. The things are a hazard."

I laugh, remembering the time I first babysat my mum's friend's baby. I had to change her vest, and pulling it over her head, then putting her arms through was a challenge.

He finishes making the sandwiches and slides one over to me. "Do you eat in here or is there a fancy room in this house with a dining table?"

Shaking my head, I grab half the sandwich and take a bite out of it. He starts to laugh, sitting down on one of the stools and grabbing his own.

"This kitchen is the shit. It looks like it belongs in a restaurant."

I glance around the fully-furnished kitchen. "Yeah, my gran loves to cook. She would always be baking something in here."

He winces as he glances at the plate of muffins. "I still can't believe you didn't warn me about the muffins."

Briefly, I look down at the one he left, smiling at the teeth marks. "I think I chipped a tooth," I tell him, then run my tongue over my teeth.

I watch, mesmerised, as his shoulders start to shake, wishing for once that I could hear the sound of his laughter, wondering if it's as contagious as it looks.

"She can't cook worth a shit, but she tries hard every damn time. She gave us food poisoning once and made herself so ill from the guilt. She was literally throwing up and crying all the damn time. After that, none of us could bear to tell her anything bad about her cooking. She's one of the kindest, most selfless people I know. She feels differently than all of us, though. She lets everyone's feelings, and her own, overwhelm her. She cares about everything and anything. Even the people she's never met but sees on the news, she'll cry over them. She got depressed once when someone posted a video of people hunting sharks on the internet."

"Sharks?"

He laughs again. "Yeah. One of the deadliest animals in the world and she got heartbroken over it for weeks."

"She does seem like a special person."

His expression softens. "She is—her and Lily both. We're really protective of them." I don't like the look he gives me, but I know looking away would be rude. "What is it she wants you for?"

I suck my bottom lip into my mouth. I don't like lying to him, but I can't betray one of the only friends I've made since I was in nursery.

"Please don't ask me to lie to you. I know you know she was lying in there. If she wants you to know, she will tell you."

A bewildered expression spreads across his face, and I notice him shift, looking nervous. "Um, okay. Yeah. I'm sorry I asked you," he says, not looking away from me. His deep, penetrating gaze sends shivers down my spine.

"It's okay," I whisper, unable to look away from him.

He licks his bottom lip and my eyes immediately are drawn to them, wondering what they would feel like pressed against mine.

"Just tell me one thing: will she get into trouble with what she's up to, or get taken advantage of?"

Shaking the lustful thoughts from my mind, I answer him. "No—God no. It's nothing like that, I promise. If it was, both she and Lily would have told you, and if they hadn't, I would have."

He nods, pleased with my answer. "Good. We've had a lot of people take advantage of or use those two. We try to protect them as much as we can."

"You really are an enigma, Aiden," I blurt out, completely amazed by him.

He grins, winking at me. "It comes naturally."

I laugh at his comment. "Would you like some tea?"

"I'd love some coffee if you have it. Sunday doesn't understand sleep yet, or that she's supposed to sleep during the night and not all day."

I laugh, looking over at Sunday, who is still sleeping soundly. "I'll make it strong."

Before I move, he taps my hand for me to look at him. "What do you do for fun in the day?"

My cheeks heat. He's going to think I'm lame, because the truth is, I'm boring. I enjoy my own company and finding small things to amuse me. Even sitting and reading entertain me. But most days I catch up on work or promote my business to get some new work.

"Um, I kind of work most of the day."

He looks at me incredulously. "Well, I'm not having that today. I'm here, so you can't work. I'm taking you out."

I bite my bottom lip, wondering how I'm going to get out of this. I don't want to risk running into the girls who ruined my life.

"You okay?" he asks when I don't answer.

"Um, I don't really want to go out," I tell him, looking away briefly, feeling my throat close.

An emotion passes across his face before he nods. "That's okay. I can spend the day here. I'm sure there's something we can do. I'm too tired to go out anyway."

"You're spending the day here?" I ask, eyes wide.

He gives me a smile I find charming. "Oh, Bailey, when I leave tonight you're gonna miss me."

I duck my head to hide my smile, because there is no doubt in my mind that I'll miss him when he goes home.

I just hope I can make it through the day without mauling him.

TEN

BAILEY

TODAY HAS BEEN ONE OF THE BEST days of my life. I've not enjoyed a day full of laughter and fun in a very long time. I never hoped or believed I'd get to feel like this again, ever.

Getting to know Aiden and helping him with Sunday has been an out of body experience. I've felt like I've been walking on cloud nine all day.

I learned so much about him; that he loves to cook, which he showed me at dinner time, and will be starting cooking school in the fall. His entire face lit up when he spoke about it, and he was so animated about it all, his hands gesturing to this and that. I could have watched him speak for hours and never tired.

It made me long to hear his voice all the more.

He spoke about his family, and from the sounds of it, he has a big one. I couldn't remember all their names, as there were so many, but I could see the love and devotion he has for every single one of them. I like that he's a family man.

I spoke about my parents and little brother, but it hurt too much thinking of them and tried to stay clear of any topics that would bring them up. I miss them every day, and with each day that passes, it doesn't hurt any less. I want to phone my mum and tell her about Aiden. If she was alive, she would give me advice and gush over his good looks.

It makes me sad to know she'll never meet my husband or future children. It pains me so deeply.

Aiden has just finished telling me about the time he got suspended from school for gluing all of his teacher's stuff to her desk. He tilts his head to the side, smiling at me.

"What was school like for you? I've talked your ear off most of the day, but you hardly talk about yourself. Tell me something—anything."

I can see in his eyes he's surprised by his question. Aiden doesn't seem like the type of lad who wants to get to know a girl on a deeper level. Knowing he wants to get to know me has my heart racing.

Today has been eye-opening for me, and for the first time I feel like opening up, no matter how hard it is for me to talk about. There are some things I'll never be able to tell him, the humiliation too much to bear.

"It was horrible," I tell him.

He sits up, his eyebrows drawing together. I look down at Sunday, glad she'll never have to go through what I did. I could never see a member of his family letting it happen—or himself. As much as I loved my parents, they were blind to most of the bullying I went through. But it was only because I didn't let them see. I faked my happiness so well in front of them.

His fingers wrap around my lower arm and chills run all over my skin from his rough, warm touch.

I glance up, our eyes meeting.

"Why was it horrible?"

I can feel the tears burning in the back of my eyes, but I don't let them fall, too afraid he'll run away if I started crying.

Instead, I look down at Sunday, pulling myself together. "My grandparents got me into a private school that had a great arts program. I was so excited. But the first day, I was cornered by a group of girls—four of them. They ran the school. Apparently, I had caught the eye of one of the school's most popular boys. I had never even laid eyes on him, but they didn't care. After that, they called me names in the corridors, behind me in class, or during break." I pause, looking to Aiden for his reaction. His jaw is clenched but he nods at me to continue. I swallow, taking a deep breath.

"The bullying got worse after that. They'd hide my gym clothes, destroy my locker, or trip me over in the dinner hall," I tell him, leaning my head back and sighing before looking at him again, feeling the tears build in the back of my eyes. "I was spat on, pushed and shoved, and the school did nothing. All four girls came from wealthy families who donated to the school. My grandparents didn't have any history with the school. They may have paid my way in there, but unlike those girls, whose parents had previously attended the school, they didn't have ties. I was a nobody there.

"My mum and dad tried everything to get it to stop when they finally found out. But I could see the stress and worry it was putting my mum through, so I told her it stopped. The bullying continued to get worse, and soon I was always covered in bruises from the beatings."

His fingers lace with mine, grasping my hand in a tight grip, and I look up in surprise. "Did you not report them to the police?"

I swallow past my nerves and nod. "We did at first. The other times I lied to my parents about how bad it really was and how I got some of my injuries. But it cost me my family's life," I choke out.

He looks so confused, before shaking it off. "What do you mean?"

Knowing he needs to know so that what happened this afternoon doesn't happen again, I tell him. Now he will understand why I don't go out and declining his offers won't be so awkward. "The last day of school they beat me so bad I lost my hearing. I was in hospital for three weeks because of the swelling on my brain."

His hand tightens around mine, making me wince. I look up, seeing the pools of anger in his eyes. "Did they get arrested?"

I laugh dryly. "No. We couldn't prove it was them—since their parents gave them all alibis. Before they beat me, I'd overheard them talking about fireworks as I was rounding a corner. Knowing who was there, I turned back. I tried to keep quiet but ended up knocking a bin over. They heard me. I think they beat me because they thought I heard the whole story."

Aiden gulps, before asking: "What happened after?"

"I tried to adjust. I went to doctors' appointments for months, trying to find the best way to hear again. I could hear better back then, but still needed the extra help. One day, I had just picked up a prescription for my brother, who was sick with the flu, and didn't hear them. They pulled me into an alley and started in on me again. I managed to get bits of what they were saying. They didn't like that I had gone to the police. It was that beating that made my hearing go."

"And the police didn't do anything?"

I pull my hand out of his to wipe my tears. "No. They came to the hospital to get my statement, but then told me there wasn't any CCTV footage, and again, those girls had alibis as to where they were. I knew it was a lie, but the police didn't.

"My parents went home that night, promising to see me in the morning. They never made it."

"What?" he asks, the veins in his neck bulging.

I wipe at my cheeks again. I haven't talked about this to anyone but the therapist I had at the time and my grandparents. Speaking of it now is hard.

"That night, after they left, those girls must have thought they'd be staying with me, because they lit fireworks in our letterbox and a fire at both the front door and backdoor. My parents and brother were found dead under the bed in my brother's room. He was seven."

"Fucking hell!" The look on his face is a mixture of anger and disbelief. "Please fucking tell me those bitches are sitting in a prison eating sloppy rice."

I shake my head sadly. "No. They took everything from me and got away with it. I've not seen them since that day they attacked me in the alley, but then, I've never gone out and certainly never alone. I don't want to give them another chance to hurt me. Everything I do riles them up and I only have my grandparents left in this world—all my other family were never really close. I can't risk something happening to them. And going to the police for help has never helped me in the past. How can I protect them if I keep putting myself in those girls' crosshairs? Being a recluse is easier."

"That's fucking bullshit. My sister's fiancé is a copper, a damn good one—but don't tell him I said that; he'll think I like him. I'll get him to do something."

"There's no point. It's done now. Nothing can bring my parents back."

He gives me an incredulous look. "No, but they can fucking rot for what they did. Fucking bitches." He shakes his head, looking utterly disgusted, and I shrink into myself. "This is why we protect the girls in our family. For lads, when we have issues, we fight it out then it's done. Girls… they're evil. They gang up on you and tear you down. You did fuck all to deserve what they did to you."

"Maybe so, but it doesn't change it."

"I'm so sorry this happened to you," he says, deep emotion written all over his face.

I wipe at the last of my tears and shrug. "I miss them every day, but nothing is going to bring them back to me."

"You're so fucking strong, Bailey. You really are. I'm in awe of you right now. I don't think I'd be sane if I went through even a touch of what you have."

I blush at the praise. "Thank you," I tell him. "And thank you for listening. I've only ever spoken to my grandparents and the therapist I was assigned about it. I know it's a heavy subject, and not something you thought I'd talk about when you asked me what school was like for me."

He shuffles closer, taking my hand back. "No, it wasn't. I was hoping for naked pillow flights," he teases, winking at me. I laugh despite everything we just spoke about. He runs a finger through my hair, tucking it behind my ear, and I shiver. The way he's looking at me has butterflies fluttering in my stomach and sweat forming. "I'm so fucking wonderstruck by you. You're amazing and I'm glad you told me. I know it must have been hard for you, but I wanted to know everything about you."

"Thank you," I manage to choke out.

His dark hazel eyes study me carefully, like he's looking at me for the first time, before his gaze travels down to my lips. I fight the urge to run my tongue over my dry lips, feeling nervous and on edge.

He sits forward, his finger tucking another loose strand of hair behind my ear, his gaze never leaving his study of my lips.

"I shouldn't be doing this," he tells me, and for some reason I imagine his voice low and seductive, matching his eyes; dilated and filled with lust. His runs his thumb over the pad of my bottom lip, and the urge to flick my tongue over the edge causes me to stop breathing.

"Doing what?" I whisper back shakily, hoping my voice doesn't sound as squeaky as I imagine it to be.

His lowers his head, and before I can take a calming breath, his lips are hovering over mine. I close my eyes, overwhelmed over the fact I'm about to be kissed by someone like Aiden.

When the feel of his lips doesn't come, I open my eyes in case I imagined it. I didn't. His eyes are shut tightly, a pained expression on his face. Before I can ask what I did wrong, the vibrations from Sunday's cry have me looking down at her.

I begin to rock her, too afraid to look up at him. Then Aiden's hands come into view, gently pulling Sunday from my grasp. There's an ache in the pit of my stomach at the feel of my empty arms. When I look up, Aiden is speaking rapidly, and I can't keep up.

I clear my throat. "Did I do something wrong?"

He stops, drawing back to look at me. "What? No. I—" He stops to close his eyes and run his fingers through his hair, something I've wanted to do all day, dying to see if it's as silky as it looks. His eyes flick open, and there's so much emotion shining in them. "Fuck! I'm not good for you. I've not had a relationship last longer than a week, and you're a relationship kind of girl. I don't want to hurt you."

I release the breath I was holding, wondering why his words have affected me. It's not that I'm denying that I'm attracted to him, because I am, even more so after spending the day with him. And I dare admit I think I'm beginning to have feelings for him.

"Okay."

His gaze looks away briefly before coming back to me. "I need to get going. Thank you for spending the day with us."

I stand with him. "No, thank you for keeping me company. It's been one of the best days I've had in a long time."

He seems to struggle with something before finally nodding. "I'll go grab her pushchair and stuff."

"All right." I help him gather up Sunday's things as he continues to rock her. I can see she's still crying. "Would you like me to help you next door?"

His tight expression relaxes. "Would you mind holding Sunday for me while I carry the pushchair upstairs?"

I rush forward, holding my arms out for her. "Of course."

We walk across the front garden and the security lights come on. My heart is in my throat when we reach the steps to his apartment, knowing this is where we say goodbye. He rushes up, keys and pushchair in hand, and deposits them inside.

I force a smile as he rushes back down the stairs, taking Sunday, who has calmed down, out of my arms.

"Goodnight, Aiden," I whisper, fiddling with the edges of my top.

A shiver runs down my spine at the heated look he gives me. "Goodnight, Bailey."

"See you around." I wave lamely, and before I can make a bigger fool of myself, I spin around and rush back to mine. I close my eyes once the door shuts behind me, groaning.

He was going to kiss me. *Me.* Lame Bailey James. If I hadn't felt his breath on my face or seen the lust in his eyes, I wouldn't have believed it.

But Aiden Carter was going to kiss me.

Shaking my head, I step inside my empty house. Being alone has never bothered me before—I enjoy my own company—but after a day filled with Aiden and Sunday, I feel lonely.

Walking into my office, my laptop sits open and I know what I have to do, so I walk over and fire it up.

All throughout the day today I wished I wasn't deaf. I longed to hear Sunday cry or the noises she made that would make her dad smile. And Aiden... it hurt every time his lips moved and I couldn't hear his voice, not knowing if it was deep, husky or low.

Tears spring to my eyes as I load Google, typing in the search bar for a doctor who specialises in my condition.

For the first time since my family died, I want to live. And if someone can help me achieve that, give me back my hearing, I will do whatever it takes. I'm longer the scared girl who lost her family and her hearing. I'm no longer angry at the world, at everyone who forgot three lives were taken in that fire, or that those girls still walk around like they didn't commit heinous crimes.

I may not be healed, but I don't think anyone really heals from something like I've been through. But I've been dealing. I got my degree in art and design, just like my parents wanted for me. I started my own business to make them proud.

But if I really want to make my parents proud of me, then I need to start living. I have to stop letting those girls rule my life, and where and what I do in it.

With that in my mind, I send a request for an appointment with a doctor nearby. My grandparents are going to lose their minds when they find out. They've been trying to get me to see someone for a while, but I always refused. My family were dead; I didn't feel like I deserved my hearing back.

Feeling better in myself than I have in a very long time, a smile lifts my lips. I feel lighter, freer.

In the mood to do some work, I open my emails, finding one from Charlotte at the top. I click it open and see a list of links for things she's looking for in her covers.

Ready for a long night, I sit back in my chair, looking out my window to next door. The curtains move, making me tense, because even though I can't see him, I know he's there. I can feel it.

A small smile plays on my lips as I open the first link, trying to get my mind off the hot god who lives next door, who looks incredibly sexy whilst holding a baby.

Working will distract me from thinking about him.

But even as the thought runs through my mind, I know it's a lie.

Because if there's one thing Aiden Carter isn't, it's forgettable.

ELEVEN

AIDEN

For the entire week I've avoided Bailey. She makes me feel things I shouldn't, and whether that's from having Sunday in my life, I don't know. I just know for the first time in my life, there is someone outside my family I'd do anything to make sure didn't get hurt.

Staying away is harder than I imagined it would be. I've never had a problem when it comes to girls before. Ever. This is all new to me.

I glance out at the back garden when I see her step outside, wearing only a pair of denim shorts and a thin-strapped tank top that barely covers her magnificent breasts. She smiles brightly at the guys, gently resting a tray of drinks on the table.

"They can get their own damn drinks," I mutter.

My hands clench when I see Mark, Liam, and even Landon checking her out as she leans over to grab one of them a drink. She passes it to Mark, laughing at something he says to her.

I wish I could see his lips from here, make out what that fucker is saying to her.

"Sunday, me and you are going next door. Daddy needs feeding," I tell her. She kicks her tiny feet, so I take that as a good sign. "Yes, you want to go see the sexy lady next door, too, don't you? Yes, you do."

She kicks harder, making me smile. The front door opens, and I look up to find Mum walking in with some bags. I groan. There goes my excuse to go around Bailey's. I was hoping she'd take one look at my puppy dog eyes and feed me.

And okay, spend time with me.

"Hey, Mum," I greet.

"Hey, baby. I'm just gonna put the shopping away," she calls out from the kitchen.

I look down at Sunday in her Moses basket and roll my eyes. "Should we tell her she's just ruined our plans?" I ask, using a baby voice. Her lips twitch into a smile and my heart completely stops. "Did you just smile?"

I look around for my phone when she does it again. "Mum!" I yell, quickly moving to my bedroom to get my phone. I trip over the nappy box with an "oomph".

Fuck!

I crawl over to my bedside table, taking my phone off charge, and in the process, ripping the charger from the wall. I don't even care as I rush back to my girl.

Mum comes rushing out of the kitchen, her face pale and full of concern. "What's happened? Is she okay?" she asks, looking down at the phone in my hands.

"Mum, she freaking smiled. She smiled at me," I tell her, before looking down at my daughter. "Didn't you? Yes, you did."

When she doesn't smile, but instead, her bottom lips trembles, I pick her up, glancing to my mum. "She smiled, I swear to God."

Mum starts laughing, walking over to run her finger down Sunday's cheek. "Son, she wasn't smiling. She's got wind."

"No, she hasn't." I pretty much yell, startling Sunday. I rock her in my arms. "She smiled," I declare, looking down at her.

"She has wind. She's not old enough to smile. I promise you, she didn't smile."

I exhale, my shoulders deflating. "Mum, I swear, she smiled at me."

She pats me on the arm. "You'll know when she really smiles. You guys all smiled when you had wind."

I shrug. "I don't care. It was the most beautiful smile in the world." I look up when Mum doesn't say anything to find her staring at me with such love in her eyes. "What?"

"You."

"What about me?" I ask, looking behind me. You know, just in case. The way she's looking at me is making me nervous.

"You're all grown up. You're eighteen, going on to college, starting a new job, in a new house, and have become a dad in a few short months." She inhales, straightening her back. "I'm going to be honest; out of all my kids I worried about you the most. I'm proud of all my kids, don't get me wrong, but I didn't think you'd find your way. But seeing how much you've grown, then seeing you with Sunday…" she pauses, getting choked up as she wipes away a tear. I take a step towards her and wrap my free arm around her. One thing I hate is my mum crying. I'd put anything down that upset her, but as it's me this time, I can't. "Seeing you with Sunday, I've never been prouder. You've taken responsibility where some men wouldn't. You've stepped up while some men step out. I love you."

I squeeze her shoulder. "I love you too, Mum. And thank you. I—I'm not going to lie: I didn't want to go to college; I just finished school. I wanted to have fun. But everyone in our family was moving forward while I was still in the same place. And I love cooking. I just didn't want the guys to laugh at me."

"They'd never laugh at you."

My lips twitch at her heated words. "Mum, Uncle Max called me a bitch and pointed to the kitchen."

"Your uncle Max doesn't count," she tells me quickly. "Your dad said he was dropped a lot as a kid."

I laugh, hugging Sunday and Mum closer. "Okay. And as for Sunday, you guys raised me right. Family is everything to each of us." I take a breath to really think about my next words. "At first, I really would have given her to you. I was scared out of my mind. But it took one look at her to know I'd never leave her, that she comes first, despite my fears of becoming a dad. And it's because of you and Dad that I knew I could do it."

She runs her finger over Sunday's cheek once again. "What do you mean?"

I meet her gaze, my lips twitching into a smirk. "Because if you two could handle me and Mark and still make it to forty, then I can raise one little girl."

She lightly pushes my shoulder, laughing at me. "You terror. Did you want me to have her for a few hours? You could pop over and see your cousins. I saw the van in next door's drive."

Yep, not ready for that yet. "Nah. We were actually going to pop over and see them. But we can keep you company instead."

She steps out of my embrace. "Nonsense. You go on over. I need to get back anyway. Your dad wants me to bring him lunch."

Her reddened cheeks give her away and I grimace, gagging. "Come on, Sunday. Let's get ready to go before Nanny tells you why she's really going over."

Mum laughs again, grabbing her handbag from where she dropped it by the front door. "Like your dad says, I'm not dead."

My face scrunches up. "Eww! Just go. And keep yours and Dad's activities private next time."

She opens the door and looks back over her shoulder. "It's you who jumped to conclusions."

I shake my head at her. "Mum, your face is as red as a tomato and you didn't make eye contact when you were speaking to me."

She shrugs. "I'll be by in the week. Love you."

I chuckle. "Love you too." Once she's gone, I look down at my girl and exhale. "Come on, then, let's go next door before one of those jackasses hits on my other girl." My eyes widen in horror. "I mean—Bailey. I meant Bailey."

Maybe going over there isn't such a good idea.

I glance out the window that faces her back garden and the view to her office. The same window I've watched her through many nights this past week. Even when I wake up to feed Sunday I'll sometimes find her sitting at her desk, a look of concentration over her face.

A deep growl fires up my chest when I see Mark's hand on her arm, taking the large plate of sandwiches from her. She throws her head back, laughing.

"That fucking does it. They should be *my* sandwiches."

———————————

I CAN HEAR their voices in the garden as I make my way around. The sound of Bailey's laughter does something to my chest, and jealousy hits me that they're the ones that are making her laugh and not me.

Landon notices me first, giving me a chin lift before going back to work. Maddox, Mark and Liam notice me next and share a look.

That's when I realise I'm glaring at them. I straighten my expression in time for Bailey to turn around. She must have seen the guys were distracted.

I watch as her chest exhales, her entire body relaxing when she sees me and a blinding smile blossoming across her face.

"Hey."

I smirk when I notice she's breathless. "Hey. We came over to see you. Sunday wanted to see her second favourite person."

"Bro, that's cheating using the cute baby," Maddox whines.

I give him a shrug when Bailey steps over and looks into the pushchair before looking up at me. "Who's her first?"

I puff out my chest. "Me, of course. She smiled at me earlier."

Her smile brightens. "She did?"

"No, she didn't. She's too young," Maddox says.

I glare at my cousin. "What would you know?"

"I helped Lily with one of her coursework projects once. It said babies smile between six and eight weeks old. She's probably got wind."

"Fuck off!" I growl, before tapping Bailey on the hand. "Is it okay if we go inside? I don't want Sunday near all the building work, or to be out in the sun too long."

Her forehead pinches together. "Oh, my God, yes. I'm sorry. I just need to make these another load of sandwiches. They've already eaten the first lot I made them."

"They can make their own damn sandwiches," I tell her, harsher than I planned. I school my expression. "Maddox just said he's full now and for you to have a break."

I don't even feel bad for lying, or for using her impairment against her.

"He did?" she asks innocently, glancing over at Maddox. He looks upset but gives her a smile.

"Yeah, we're full. Plus, we've got to grab some more slabs soon. We can grab something then, if we get hungry."

"If you're sure? I don't mind."

I tap her hand again, loving I have reasons to touch her and don't need excuses. "He's sure."

"All right, then. Come on in."

I follow her up, lifting the pram up the three steps into the conservatory.

"Wow," I mumble, looking around the sweet get up. It has three white fabric sofas, all with various coloured cushions to brighten it up. There are two chairs with red cushions on and two tables. A TV is mounted onto the wall of the house, and the windows are fitted with blinds so she can watch it without the sun glaring across the screen.

It's huge, the biggest conservatory I've seen. I'll have to tell Maggie to get one because this is fucking awesome. I could live here. I even like the plants she has paced randomly around the room, and the mini bar in the corner.

"You okay?"

I realise I've stopped to admire the room and turn to Bailey with a smile. "This place is sweet. Has it always been a part of the house?"

"This is my favourite part of the house. It's only been here for six years or so. My gran loves being in here when it rains. We'd often come out and read when it did. It's the best time to be in here."

"I bet," I murmur, finding her more and more interesting.

We step inside the kitchen and she faces me. "Did you come around for something? Is everything okay?"

I smirk at the blush rising up her neck to her cheeks. "Yeah. Want to order food and eat with me? I can't order to next door." After hearing how that sounds, I quickly add, "And we saw you out the window and thought we'd come see you."

Her nose wiggles adorably, her forehead creasing. "Why can't you order to next door? Is it 'cause they take it to Maggie's?"

It's my turn to be embarrassed. "No, we're banned."

"Banned? From all take out foods or just a certain one? Or has Maggie banned you?"

I scrub the back of my neck. "Um, all take out restaurants. It's a long story."

She grins, sitting down on the stool. "Now you have to tell me. How? Why?"

"It was a misunderstanding," I tell her, quickly defending myself.

"Okay," she says slowly.

I roll my shoulders. "The first time was because we had food missing from our order. One of us blamed the delivery guy for leaving it at the restaurant and one of us accused him of eating it. It ended up in a fight."

My hopes she'll be happy with that vague answer is shredded when her grin spreads wider. "Who blamed him for leaving it?"

"Maddox," I easily admit.

She nods like she could have guessed it.

This isn't even the worst incident we've dealt with when it comes to food either.

Once, we went to an all you can eat Chinese restaurant, and between us and the Hayes brothers, we ate them out of everything. And within an hour of us being there, we had trashed the place by getting into a fight. I'd rather Bailey not see that side of me, not when I know what she went through.

"Who accused him of eating it?"

I shrug. "I don't remember."

She eyes me closely, before she arches an eyebrow and laughs. She slaps her knee before pointing her accusing finger at me. I can feel my cheeks heat, and groan. "It was you."

I hold my hands up. "Look, it was a legitimate argument. He had crumbs on his shirt."

"What did he say they were from?"

"Crisps." I shrug, ignoring her laughter. "After that, they wouldn't take orders from our address. We're band from most places anyway, what's one more?" I grin when a thought occurs to me. "But don't worry, I have you to order for me now. Just don't tell the others. It can be our little secret."

Her cheeks turn pink. "Okay." She takes in a deep breath, tucking her hair behind her ear. "What would you like me to order for us?"

"Whatever you fancy. Do you have the online food app?" I ask, knowing she can't ring.

She nods. "I do. I love cooking but I love to pig out some days too."

My kind of girl.

Sunday starts crying, so I reach over while Bailey leaves the room. I pick her up, rocking her. She had her bottle before Mum came so she can't be hungry.

I sniff her bum—under protest, but it saves me from stripping her then spending an hour trying to line up all the buttons. She doesn't smell and my shoulders sag. I hold her up in front of me, smiling at her cute face. "Aw, did someone just want Daddy's attention?"

Her expression should have warned me, but before I can move, vomit is landing all over my mouth, dripping down my chin. The second load lands on my shirt, and I gag, moving over to the sink. With Sunday still in my arms, I empty my stomach. The smell of stale milk has me gagging once more, and I end up vomiting again.

Like father like daughter.

Warm hands reach for Sunday, and for once, I don't argue, letting Bailey take her from my arms. I lean over the sink, running the cold tap and furiously try to get it all off me. When I taste it in my mouth, I gag again, but this time, nothing comes up.

Fuck!

When I've composed myself enough to stand away from the sink, my top is soaked. I look at Bailey apologetically. "I'm sorry about that. There's a lot of things I can handle, but someone being sick isn't one of them. The minute I gag, I end up being sick."

"It's okay, but you might want to go and get changed," she tells me softly. "And, um… do you have nappies and stuff with you?"

"Why?" I ask, before looking down at my jeans. I haven't pissed myself, have I? Nope. All clean.

"Sunday was more than sick," she says, wincing a little.

I nod, stepping forward to take her, but the smell hits me and I gag, rushing back over to the sink. Bailey giggles and I hear her moving about.

"You go change your shirt, whilst I change her. Do you have a changing mat?"

I rinse my mouth out before looking at her. "I can do it."

"You really should go and change your shirt."

I look down at my favourite AC/DC shirt and wince at the vomit stains on it. "Yeah."

"I'll change Sunday. I've changed nappies before."

Reluctantly, I agree. "Okay. There's a changing mat and blanket in the Minnie Mouse bag."

When she gives me a questioning look, I shrug. "I don't want her to be on a cold surface."

"You're so sweet."

I rear back. "I'm *not* sweet."

She laughs. "Yes, you are. You're a good dad."

I puff my chest out with pride, because I am a good dad. "Call me charming or something. Just not sweet. Or if you slip up, make sure it's not in front of them," I tell her, pointing towards the garden area. "I'll never hear the last of it."

"Okay," she tells me, grabbing the Minnie Mouse bag. "Now, go change your top."

"All right," I sigh, glancing at Sunday. "Um… she likes it when you do it quick. She hates having her bum done."

"All babies do," she says, not looking away from me. "Are you going to go change?"

I nod, still not moving. "Yeah."

"You need to leave to be able to do that, you know."

Coming unstuck, I head for the conservatory doors, stopping when I reach them. Bailey looks up from the pram she's placed Sunday in so she can get the stuff ready, raising her eyebrow.

"She needs the ointment that's in the side pocket too. Not too much, just a small pea-size."

"All right."

I take a step into the conservatory, before quickly popping back into the kitchen. Bailey looks up, her lips twitching. "Are you okay?"

I clear my throat. "Yeah. I was just coming back to say if you need me, just scream my name or come outside."

"You're going to be gone two minutes, not a lifetime."

I nod again, leaving, but as I reach the back door, I have to turn back, moving into the kitchen. Her sigh of annoyance is cute.

"Don't shout me and wait. Shout and bring her to me."

She rolls her eyes at me. "It's going to be Christmas at this rate. I'd have been finished by now and you'd be back with her in your arms if you'd just gone already."

I scrub a hand down my face and quickly rush out the kitchen, ignoring her tinkering laughter. The lads all glance at me when I step outside. They all smirk and I give them my middle finger. "Dude, put in a good word for me," Maddox yells. I come to a dead stop, turning to glare at my cousin.

"Stay the fuck away." I carry on, my steps slower, before turning back to them. "And make your own damn sandwiches."

He grins, leaning back against a pile of bricks. "Lily already made me some, but Bailey's taste so damn good."

I take a step towards him, readying to lay him out, when he licks his lips and winks at me.

"Fucker."

"Aiden, go get fucking changed. You look like someone pissed down you," Landon growls. "And going by the way you rushed out of there, you didn't want to leave Sunday."

Fuck—Sunday.

"Stay away from her, Maddox."

"Hard to do when I'm working here. Every. Damn. Day."

I keep moving towards my apartment, ignoring the others' laughter as I strip out of my top to save time. There's no way I'm going to let him try it on with her. No way at all.

Either I'm going to have to get over my fear of a relationship, or let Maddox ask her out.

Yeah, I'll rip his head off if he goes near her.

Life can be so screwed up. I just have to figure out what I want.

And for some reason, the second I picture what I want, Bailey's face is the first thing that pops up.

I'm so fucking screwed.

TWELVE

AIDEN

IT'S RAINING AS I STEP OUTSIDE AND rush around the back to let myself inside Bailey's house. When I notice no one is in the garden, I quickly backpedal to the side of the house and see that Maddox's work trucks are still there. Fucking arseholes.

My steps move quicker. I let myself in, wiping my feet and shaking the rain out of my hair.

The voices in the kitchen have me groaning. If they're eating food, I'm going to lay them out.

Bailey looks up when she sees me stepping inside, eyeing me apologetically. "It's not meant to rain long. I called the guys in so they didn't get soaked."

I don't bother telling her they usually call it a day when it rains, unless they're working inside. Instead, I force a tight smile and glare at my brother and cousins.

"She had some chilli in the fridge ready to heat up," Mark says defensively. I eye the food, my mouth watering.

Todd, Maddox's site manager, struts in from the hallway and I narrow my eyes dangerously.

"Where the fuck did you just come from?"

He smirks at me as he walks over to Bailey. I watch, feeling close to losing it when she smiles at his approach.

"Thank you for letting me use your loo," he tells her, giving her a side hug, rubbing her hip.

"It's okay. Glad you found it okay," she tells him softly, and I take glee in the fact she steps away, using Sunday as an excuse as she rocks her.

I smirk, giving him a smug look. "Fucker, touch her again and I'll break those fingers."

"Why? She 'ent yours," Todd fires back.

"Ooh, fighting talk," Maddox grins.

"Who's fighting?" Bailey asks, looking around the room before turning back to Maddox.

"There's a fight on tonight," he lies, winking. "We're thinking of going out to watch it."

Bailey pales, and I want to gut him for upsetting her. Any kind of violence upsets her.

"You should come with us. We're going to The Ginn Inn later," Todd says.

She glances at me, sucking in her bottom lip. "I would, but I have a ton of work to do."

Todd pouts as I reach Sunday, taking her from Bailey. She'll be the only thing to keep me from laying him out right now.

"Maybe you and I could go out to dinner?"

I grit my teeth and look away; too afraid she'll say yes. Maddox snickers behind his cup, and I kick him.

"What was that for?" he sputters out.

"Get him the fuck out of here before I kill him."

He rolls his eyes, and as he's about to answer, Bailey speaks up, a blushing mess. "Um, I—I'm really busy at the moment."

I have to turn around when his expression falls before she sees me laughing and thinks it's aimed at her.

"Todd, can you go into the office and make sure the tiles for the roof are ordered?" Maddox says, clearing the amusement out of his voice.

"Yeah," he mutters, before meeting my gaze. "If you 'ent gonna date her, then let someone else have a shot."

I shrug lazily. "Can't help it if women are crazy about me."

He rolls his eyes, giving the others chin lifts before escaping out of the kitchen door. I chuckle when he leaves, forgetting about my audience.

"Sucker!"

"Did you say something?"

I nod, lying without shame. "I said Sunday doesn't need a sucker."

The skin between her eyes creases adorably. "You don't give her a dummy?"

"Nope. I don't trust them."

Landon chuckles, shovelling food into his mouth like he hasn't been fed in a week. "This ought to be good."

"Fuck you," I snap at him.

Bailey doesn't seem fazed as she looks between us, reading our lips. I hate that she has to stare at their lips. I like it when she watches mine. Her eyes go all droopy and she gasps out tiny bits of air.

I lick my bottom lip, enjoying the way sparks flash in her eyes, her gaze drawn to them. I smirk.

"And what did the dummy do to offend you?" she asks, all breathless.

Yep, she's totally affected by me.

"Tried to suffocate my daughter," I tell her, grabbing a piece of garlic bread.

"Um, how? Did you give her one of those rock dummy's?" she asks teasingly, before moving over to fill me a plate. I wait for her to make it. What can I say, I'm an arsehole who loves his food.

Once I have her attention, I answer. "No. It's just too big for her mouth. It could suffocate her."

"They breathe through their nose," she tells me, laughter in her voice.

I roll my eyes. "I don't care. I tried and the thing looked like it would choke her."

"Mums breastfeed their babies. A dummy isn't much bigger than a boob." Her face turns bright red, like she said the naughtiest word ever.

Liam smirks. "Clearly you don't get out. You should have seen the tits I sucked on last night."

My lips twitch with laughter, glad Bailey wasn't looking in his direction. It would have only made her blush harder.

"Pretty sure nipples are the word you were looking for, darlin'," I drawl.

And there's that blush again. I'd love to know how far down it goes. My cock twitches at the thought. I shift behind the counter before I embarrass myself in front of the others.

"Even her bottles' teats are bigger than a dummy. You worry too much. People have been giving their children these things for generations."

"It can stop at mine," I tell her, shrugging.

She giggles, holding her hands out for Sunday. "Want me to hold her, or are you worried my breasts will suffocate her?" A second of silence passes before she groans, covering her face with her hands.

The lads look at her with wide eyes, while I look down at her impressive chest. Yep, I wouldn't mind being suffocated by them.

"Did you want me to answer?" I ask, smirking when she looks up at me.

"No." She shakes her head furiously. "Please pretend I did not just say that."

I laugh this time, liking this girl more and more.

"I need to go. I have to take Charlotte somewhere for the night and need to go get my things," Landon announces. I glance at my cousin, worried. He doesn't look away from my gaze, instead staring me down. We both know he isn't going to be with Charlotte all night.

No. He's going to be fighting again, something we've told him time and time again to stop doing unless it's in front of proper instructors, referees, and judges. Not in some abandoned warehouse.

"I'll let your mum and dad know. They were only telling Mum yesterday that they hadn't seen you for a while."

He narrows his eyes at me, getting angry. "I saw Mum and Dad the other day. Keep your nose out of my business."

"I will when you stop making stupid choices."

"You don't know what the fuck you're talking about."

"I know since losing Freya you've have some anger issues, but you need to move on, Landon."

He steps towards me, but before he can reach me, Sunday starts crying. He stops, looking down at Sunday with round eyes before meeting my gaze with a guilt-ridden expression.

"I'm sorry," he chokes out, before leaving.

"Landon," I call out after him.

"I'm gonna go check on him. Plus, I think he's forgot he's my ride," Liam says, before looking at Bailey. "Thank you for dinner. It was delicious."

Looking adorably confused, she just nods. "It's my pleasure."

I want to growl, because *I* own all her pleasure.

Where the fuck did that come from?

I shake it off, feeling like shit for bringing Freya up—in front of Bailey, too, who he doesn't really know.

Liam's phone beeps and he pulls it out, smirking. "That's Landon. He got to the end of the street before he remembered me. I feel loved," he teases, before looking at me. "Don't worry about it. We all agree with you, but he has to deal with this in his own way."

"I'll message him later to say sorry, man. I'm just worried about him. He seems to have more bruises lately."

A shadow crosses his face. "Yeah, well, we've all warned him."

"We're going to go too. I want to make sure all our jobs are on schedule," Maddox says as he and Mark get up.

"Something I said?" I jokingly add.

They laugh, slapping me on the back when they pass. Maddox, unable to help himself, pauses at the door. "Bailey?"

She's looking at me with a concerned expression.

"She can't read your lips from here."

She reads what I say, and her gaze turns towards the kitchen door. I turn as well, tucking Sunday higher up my chest, her bum fitting in the palm of my hand.

"Next time you cook dinner, light some candles. I'll bring dessert," he says, winking.

She giggles. "Bye, Maddox."

"Bye, darlin'."

I growl as he leaves, ignoring his taunting laughter. When they're gone, Bailey turns to me, biting her bottom lip.

"Are you okay? That was really intense."

I sigh, stepping over to Sunday's pushchair and gently placing her down. I smile as her body curls upwards, like she's seeking out my warmth. Seeing she's settled, I face Bailey with a grim smile.

"Landon likes to fight. I can't talk about why, but he has a lot of built-up anger and that's his outlet."

She pales, like I knew she would. "He just goes around fighting people?"

I shake my head. "No. There's an underground fighting ring that he fights for. He's one of their best contenders, and people are starting to take notice. The thing is, there's only one rule: no weapons. But it doesn't stop people from playing dirty. He's had people cover their brass knuckles with tape. I just hate seeing him like this."

She takes me by surprise when tears fill her eyes and she walks over to wrap her arms around my middle. I tense at the feeling inside of my chest. I feel like I can't breathe—all my nerves feel like they're on fire from her touch.

She pulls away before I have chance to hold her, to feel what it's like to hold an angel in my arms.

Her big doe eyes are nearly my undoing. My cock stirs at the sight of her, the moisture in her eyes and the tremble in her lips.

"He really is lucky to have you looking out for him, Aiden. I'm sorry he's going through something. He does look lost. You can see it in his eyes."

I sigh. "He's angry. He's mad at the world for what happened."

"You really are an incredible guy, Aiden Carter."

I grin. "Does this mean you'll make me dinner this week?"

She blushes, but a smile spreads across her face. "Yes. But only you."

I laugh, throwing my head back. "No going on a date with Todd?"

Her nose twitches. "Um, no." She groans, dropping her head onto my chest, and the tightness comes back. "I can't believe he asked me. I felt so torn. I didn't want to let him down in front of everyone," she mumbles against my chest.

I laugh, pushing her away gently so she can see me. "Well, then, guess I got lucky."

She bites her bottom lip and my cock twitches painfully against the zipper of my jeans.

"No. You're Aiden; my answer will always be yes," she whispers.

And in that moment, I feel like she just took half of my soul. The trust in her gaze; the surrender of her body… I know I could have her. I know if I tasted those cherry red lips she would kiss me back. I know, like I know my own name, that if I touched her, she would let me. She'd like it. And the minute I got a taste, I'd take everything she offered without giving anything in return.

Because I'm a selfish bastard.

Without hesitating, I'd take something I didn't deserve. I'd have no control, no say.

The only thing stopping me from leaning towards her, from tasting her, is my heart—my conscience. Bailey may be sexy as hell, but that isn't what makes me pause. No, it's her.

She doesn't deserve a quick fuck with a guy who doesn't know what he wants. She doesn't need her heart broken again.

Because I have a feeling that if I break her heart, I'd be breaking mine along with it.

The girl has me torn up in pieces.

And I don't even think she knows it.

THIRTEEN

BAILEY

I STEP OUT OF THE TAXI FEELING lighter than I have in years, and pass the money to the taxi driver. "Have a good day," I tell him brightly. "And keep the change."

He doesn't smile but he does give me a chin lift. "Cheers."

I don't let his attitude ruin my day, because I can hear. And I was told the best news today. News I couldn't wait to share with my grandparents. As soon as the doctor told me, my first thought had been wanting to tell Aiden. Over the last two weeks, he's spent a lot of time around my house. He always seems to turn up around the guys' break time. I'll go out to ask if they want something to eat and he'll distract me with Sunday. I felt bad for not making the guys food, but they didn't seem to mind.

I unlock the door and step inside, heading straight to my office to grab my phone. I left it in my rush to leave. I don't care that it's six in the morning where my grandparents are; I need to hear their voice.

I dial their number, bringing the phone to my ear with the new, cool device that will help me hear. There's no irritation, even though it's going to take a lot to get used to, and I don't hear any buzzing. I've also had it in for an hour and had not one headache.

I can feel my throat tighten with emotion at every sound I hear. It feels like I'm hearing it all for the first time.

"Hello?" my gran answers.

"Bella, honey, she can't hear you."

"Oh, sugar tits. Why is she ringing this early? If she's hurt, I'll kill a man."

"Bella, calm down before you have a stroke."

"Don't tell me to calm down. You calm down. My girl is calling me at… lord, we've only been asleep a few hours."

I start laughing. So, this is what they argue like when they turn away from me. "Gran, Granddad, calm down. I'm fine."

"See, she's fine," Granddad replies, before I hear his breath hitch. "Wait! You can hear us?"

I giggle, my eyes watering. "Yes! I've been going to the doctors over the past two weeks."

My gran starts crying, which brings tears to my own eyes. She's blubbering, and I can hear my granddad comforting her.

"I'm so happy for you, sweetie."

"Me too," Granddad adds.

"Did you go to the doctors we tried to get you to go to?"

"I did. I'm sorry I haven't gone until now. I just… I just couldn't. Not when—you know…." I trail off.

"We know, Bailey. What did the doctor say?"

I flop down in my desk chair, grinning from ear to ear. "Gran, you are never going to believe this but they think they can fix it."

"What!" she screeches, and I pull the phone away, laughing.

"Let her speak, darling."

"Let her speak?" Gran scoffs. "The girl just told us they can help her."

"And she wants to explain. Let her," he tells her, amusement in his tone.

I've missed this—listening to them. Their voices. I've longed to hear the deep rumble of my granddads voice, the sound of my gran scolding him.

"Go on, Bailey," she says after pulling herself together.

"They're going to try a method where they use umbilical cord hematopoietic stem cells

to fix the damage to the cochlea. They won't know the extent of the damage to the other parts of my ears until it's done. But they are hopeful I'll get seventy percent of my hearing back with this operation."

"Why have they never recommended this before?" Gran asks.

"I think they mentioned brain surgery to Mum and Dad at the beginning, but they were afraid they would lose me. They were still traumatised over my attack, which is why they went with the hearing aid suggestion. I knew there was a chance to have my hearing back—we've always known—but after losing them, I couldn't bear it. Why should I be fixed if they can't?"

"Oh, sweet girl," Gran says softly, and I imagine her head tilting to the side and her eyes going misty.

"When will they be doing this?"

"She will get back to me in a week. One of the best ears, nose and throat doctors will be performing the surgery," I tell them, then clear my throat. "The procedure, it's um... it's pricey, since it's done through a private clinic."

"Don't go worrying about that. We have that covered."

I relax back in the chair. I hated to ask. I received my parent's life insurance policies when they died, but I refused to take them, so my grandparents took charge of it until I become ready. I don't even want to think of the money; it's just another reminder.

"Thank you."

"Our pleasure. I'm so happy for you," Granddad tells me, his voice filled with emotion.

"Me too, darlin'. And I'm proud of you for going, but I have to ask, what made you change your mind."

I can feel my cheeks heat. "I—I..." I groan, not wanting to talk about this.

"Oh, it's a boy."

"No, it's not, Bella."

I giggle at the heat in Granddad's words. "He lives next door. We've been spending time together and—I don't know. I guess it made me realise how much I'm missing out on."

"Hearing a boy talk you into bed isn't something you're missing out on," Granddad hisses.

I choke on laughter. "Granddad!"

"Abel," Gran chuckles, and I can hear the slap of skin connecting.

"Ouch, woman!" he hisses. "But great-grandkids running around would be nice."

Oh, my gosh. My face burns with embarrassment. When my gran starts agreeing, talking about getting a playset built in the garden, I have to put a stop to it.

"Seriously, you two. Pack it in." I sigh; however I can't help the smile that is on my face. I'm so happy right now, and for the first time since I lost my family, I don't feel guilty for it either. "Plus, he already has a daughter."

"He has a daughter?" Gran asks, the happiness gone from her voice.

"And he's not with the mother?"

Okay, Granddad doesn't sound very pleased.

"She died during birth," I tell them. I don't want to lie to them, so I tell them the truth. They'll think he's grieving and will worry about me getting hurt. "He wasn't with her. He said it was a one-night-stand."

"Bailey," Granddad says, a warning in his tone.

"No, before you worry, you need to know he's not like you're thinking. Not to me anyway. And you should see him with his daughter, Sunday. He's an amazing dad. I swear, if he could take her to the toilet with him, he would. He loves her that much."

Granddad sighs. "We just don't want to see you get hurt, not after—"

I don't want to think about him. I can't. I still feel dirty whenever he crosses my mind. "I know," I whisper.

It's the one part of my past I'll never tell Aiden. I don't want him to look at me differently.

"All right. We'll drop it."

"Don't think you're getting out of Skyping us, either, missy. I want to see your beautiful face every night like clockwork."

I laugh at my grans attempt at lightening the mood. "I'll Skype, I promise. Now, I'll let you get back to sleep. I just couldn't wait to share the good news."

"Oh, we wouldn't have cared if you had woken us up earlier. We always love hearing from you."

"Love you."

"We love you too," Gran replies softly.

"I'll let you go. Speak to you later."

"All right, dear. Love you—and keep us updated."

"I will."

"Bye, darlin'"

"Bye, Granddad."

I end the call, looking down at my phone and smiling.

Now I just have one other person I desperately want to tell. Knowing he'll come outside if I go out back, I head towards the kitchen and make up some sandwiches.

Once I'm done, I head out. There are more men outside today, but with this company, I don't mind. Aiden has an amazing family, and although I think some of them flirt with me, I don't feel creeped out like I did with the others. Even the guys I know aren't related to them are nice and polite. I've felt more relaxed and even offered them the use of my kitchen if they need something to eat. With the last builders, I made sure to double check everything was locked up. I had dreaded the day they would head inside the house.

"Hey, guys," I call out, holding the plate of sandwiches up.

Mark grins at me and walks over, while Maddox groans from where he's cementing the barbeque together.

"I swear, she gets fucking hotter every time she walks out, and dickhead won't let us ask her out."

"I wouldn't let Aiden hear you say that," Landon, the scary one, replies. I blush, forgetting they think I can't hear them.

Mark's eyes widen when I tuck my hair behind my ear, revealing the ear piece. He chuckles, winking at me as he takes a sandwich, but does nothing to warn his family.

"Yeah, he'll kill you for checking her out," Mark says, and I blush further at his words. He can't really mean what he's saying, can he?

I turn back to Maddox when he gets up, wiping his hands on a towel nearby. "I can't help it. She's fucking hot. Have you seen her arse?"

Mark chuckles just as footsteps sound behind me. I don't turn, which is really hard not to do now my hearing is back.

"Fucker, I told you to stop checking her out, and why the fuck is she making you food? Again! Get your own damned food," Aiden growls. His voice is as sexy as I imagined it to be, sending a shiver up my spine.

"You need to learn to share," Maddox snaps, turning around so I can't read his lips. "And her cooking is better than mine."

"No. It's *my* fucking food. She's *mine*."

Mine.

My heart slams painfully against my chest. I desperately want to pounce on him, to tell him I am his and that he plagues my every thought, even my dreams. I can't escape him.

"Gonna ask her out?" Mark taunts, and my eyes widen.

Why would he ask that when he knows I can hear?

Not wanting to hear the answer in case he says something hurtful, I spin around and beam at Aiden. "I made plenty, and there's a lasagne I made this morning in the fridge for us. We just need to heat it up."

He smiles at me. "Hey, Bailey. I am hungry now you mention it." I giggle, ducking my head. "Ha, you fuckers get sandwiches while I get a good cooked meal."

I look back up, narrowing my eyes and reflexively snap, "That's not very nice."

His eyes widen in horror. He clears his throat, glancing at everyone before his eyes meet mine. "You can hear me?"

"Clearly."

A strangled cough comes from behind me, and I turn to see Maddox bent over, Mark slapping his back.

He looks up at me through watery eyes. "You heard everything I said?"

"What did you say?" Aiden asks him, sounding lethal and sexy.

"Nothing!" Maddox squeaks, looking pleadingly at me.

I beam, turning back to Aiden. "Do you want food or not?"

He doesn't take his eyes away from Maddox. "Yeah."

"Well, come on, then. I want to get a cuddle from Sunday before she falls asleep," I tell him. He's been trying his mum's idea of not holding her when she's asleep. So far, he seems to last five minutes before he picks her up again. I've been timing him. But who can blame the girl for wanting to be in her daddy's arms all the time.

And those biceps… I try not to let them affect me so much, but every time he flexes, I forget my own name.

I bet there isn't a woman out there who has looked at him and not forgotten who she was. He's drop-dead gorgeous.

"All right."

"I can't believe she heard me," Maddox whispers as we're stepping inside, sounding as if he's in pain.

"What did he say?" Aiden asks me as we walk into the kitchen.

I shrug. "Nothing much. Do you want garlic bread?"

He eyes me. "Yeah. After you've put it in, you can tell me how you can hear me."

"Don't need to; I can show you," I say, tucking my hair once again behind my ear.

"Is that new?" he asks softly, stepping closer to get a good look.

I nod. "Yeah, and they think they can get at least seventy percent of my hearing back with an operation."

"You're kidding?" he asks, grinning from ear to ear.

"It's incredible."

"What made you change your mind?"

My face has to be red because I feel like I'm on fire. "You."

"Me?"

"Yeah."

His expression changes to one I can't read. He moves closer, and I suck in my bottom lip nervously.

"You don't have to change for me," he whispers, stepping closer, his thumb untucking my lip. My knees lock together at his touch. And his words… somehow, they made me feel like I could touch the sky.

"I know. I just hadn't realised how much I was missing out on. It was time for me to move forward and forget the bad things from my past."

Desire fills the air as he takes another step closer, cupping my cheek. "You can hear me," he says in awe.

I nod and manage to breathe out, "I know."

"I really want to kiss you."

My entire body heats. "Then kiss me." I sway closer, looking up at him through my long lashes while my hands go to his hips, fisting his shirt to steady myself.

His expression fills with pain. "I'm not good for you, Bailey. Until I know what I really want, I won't touch you."

"Please, kiss me," I plead, touching my forehead to his as I grip him tighter.

"I can't," he chokes out, stepping back.

I nearly fall from the rejection, my heart filling with so much hurt. I can't meet his gaze, too afraid he'll see just how deeply he has hurt me, see how deep my feelings for him go.

Because the fact of the matter is, I'm falling for my neighbour. It isn't by choice, either. My feelings for him have been gradually building with each glance, each moment, and with every touch. He makes me feel alive again.

I could watch him like my favourite movie and never get bored. Everything he does mesmerises me, fascinates me. I like who I am when I'm with him.

"I'm sorry," I whisper, afraid I'm going to lose him. The last time I thought we'd share a kiss, I hadn't seen him for a week—other than the moments I saw him sneaking peeks at me through the window of his living room.

He spins to face me. "Don't be sorry. This is on me. I don't know what it is I'm feeling, Bailey." He rubs his chest like he's in pain, and I want to go to him—hold him—but I'm frozen to the spot. "I truly don't. I may have been a player before Sunday was born, but I've never promised anything to anyone. I've never been in a relationship longer than a week—if you can call what it was a relationship. With you; *you* matter. You mean something to me. And I can't stand the thought of hurting you."

I nod. "I understand."

He exhales. "No, you don't. But you will. I promise. Just let me work out what it is I'm feeling. I know that's not fair to ask of you. I just... Please?"

I can't deny him. I'd give him anything he asked for, that's how pathetic I am. And if I wasn't a hundred percent sure he was worth it, I would walk away. But he is. And I want him more than I've wanted anything in a long time. So instead of arguing, I nod and tell him, "Okay."

"Next week, we're going to my uncle's restaurant for a meal to celebrate me becoming a dad. Mum is having Sunday for me."

"You're letting her stay out?" I tease. "Get you."

He chuckles, rubbing the back of his neck. "I go back to work tomorrow so I've got no choice but to get used to it. Plus, my mum will love it."

"I bet she will." I force a smile, hiding just how hurt I am. "Are you excited for tomorrow? It will be your first time away from Sunday, won't it?"

He glances down at her, his smile sad. "I'm not looking forward to leaving her but I am excited to get back into a kitchen. I just wish she could come with me."

"She'll be fine. You have to work," I tell him, stepping around him to put the garlic bread in the oven.

"I know. I just wish I didn't have to leave her."

"How long is your shift?"

"My uncle Mason has me on for five hours tomorrow, which isn't too bad. He told me what it was like the first time he left after Hope was born. I just hope I make it. I don't want to lose this job."

"Your uncle won't fire you, will he?" I ask worriedly.

He laughs. "Probably not, but he can't let the others think they can get away with shit. It's why none of us work directly under him. It's different with Maddox; he doesn't give a fuck, and even has a lawyer draw up papers for his employees to sign before starting work. It states he doesn't need a reason to fire them."

"That's a good contract to have in construction work. You aren't promised hours. I can see what you mean though. Your uncle has to give you verbal warnings and then three written warnings before he can fire you. He doesn't need someone saying you didn't fire your nephew for such and such."

Aiden helps himself to some juice from the fridge. "That's it. He has agreed I can keep my phone on me. He lets all employees with kids have them, but if they're caught using them for non-emergencies, they're given a written warning."

"Sounds fair," I tell him, passing him to grab the tray of lasagne out the fridge.

"I'm just gonna miss her. I never pictured a life with kids, but now I have Sunday, I can't picture my life without her. I feel like I wasn't really living before. It was like one day I woke up and got slapped in the face with reality."

I laugh at his analogy. "She'll be fine with your mum; I mean, she did raise you."

The mock glare on his face has me laughing harder. "Are you trying to say I'm hard work?" he asks, stepping around the kitchen island. My laughter comes to an end, my stomach fluttering.

I start stepping the other way. "If it walks like a duck and quacks like a duck..." I say, shrugging, fighting my smile.

He chuckles, still moving around the island to get to me. "I'm thinking we have five minutes before Sunday cries."

My eyebrows draw together in puzzlement, glancing at Sunday. "Huh?"

My distraction has him moving faster, and I grin, feeling carefree.

"Oh, Bailey, if I was you, I'd run... and find a good hiding place."

When he lunges for me, I yelp—trying not to scream, for Sunday's sake—and jump back, out of his way. I laugh, running for the hallway.

I don't even try hard, since I'm having too much fun.

His arms wrap around my stomach and I grunt, squealing with laughter as he spins us around. He drops me to my feet and slams me up against the wall, gripping my wrists so my arms are above my head.

I pant, looking innocently up at him as he gazes down at me, smirking. "Oh, Bailey, Bailey, Bailey. What am I going to do with you now?"

You could kiss me. I don't say that though—too scared.

"I could think of a few things," I whisper. My lame-arse attempt at flirting works though, because I watch as his pupils dilate, his smouldering gaze darkening.

"Fuck it!" he growls out, leaning forward.

Sunday's cries echo down the hall. He drops his forehead to mine, panting just as heavily as I am.

"Go," I tell him, looking down.

He lifts off me and I drop my arms to my sides, watching his tensed shoulders and back as he walks into the kitchen.

I touch my lips, wishing I could feel his, imagining what they would taste like. I've only ever kissed one boy, but even then, I enjoyed it.

He was my biggest regret—I just didn't know it at the time.

Now, I pray like hell that Aiden doesn't become my new one.

I want him to be the best mistake I ever made. I want to feel the love he shares with his daughter. To feel what it is to make love to someone you truly love. To be wanted.

But most of all, I want to feel free to fall for him without inhibitions or doubt. I want to stop wanting him and have him.

But as my mum always said, 'I want, don't get'.

And that saying is perfect for this situation.

Because you don't get Aiden Carter. He had to want you too. And at the moment, he doesn't know what he wants.

FOURTEEN

AIDEN

THE BLACK LEATHER STICKS TO MY legs, and when I lift them, I feel like I'm peeling my skin from the seat. The heat today is suffocating and unbearable. Yesterday, it didn't stop raining, and it didn't look like it was going to stop. But this morning, the sun came up, and in no time, I had my windows open and fans on, trying to cool us down.

"Will you keep fucking still!" Dad grunts, flicking the indicator left to pull into the car park to Mason's restaurant.

"I can't help it. Do you think Mason will let me have one more day off so I can go check on Sunday?"

I had left her screaming and miserable. Mum had stripped her down to her nappy and had the fan on, but she was screaming bloody murder. I tried to comfort her myself before I left, but she just kept getting stuck to my skin. I couldn't even rub her back the way she likes because both of us were sweaty and clammy.

"No!"

I glance at my dad as he pulls to a stop. "What is your problem?" I growl.

He shuts the car off and turns his glare to me. "You. Stop whining and do your job. You have a child to support now."

"I know!" I snap. "I just didn't think it would be this way."

He sighs, unclipping his belt. "Trust me, it gets easier after the first day. When we had you, we couldn't wait to drop you off with your nan."

I look at him, affronted. "Are you saying Mark is your favourite?"

He grins, flashing his teeth. "Nope. The girls will always be my favourite."

I'm not even hurt. My sisters are pretty fucking special.

"What about Mum?" I ask warily as I open the door.

He gives me a dry look. "Do you really think your mum has a favourite? She loves you all equally, always has. That woman has so much love inside her, it humbles me. From the first moment I met her I knew she was special. Took my fucking breath away and then gave me life."

I roll my eyes but I can't help but picture Bailey. She's everything my dad just described. In one second, she can take my breath away, whilst in the next, breathe life into me.

"Does she know you have a favourite?" I ask once I've stepped out of the car and met him at the front.

His face scrunches up, looking at me like I said the stupidest thing in the world. "Do you really think I'd risk your mum making me sleep on the couch or not getting any?"

Gross.

"Yeah, didn't need to know that shit."

"Don't ask questions you don't want the answers to, then," he tells me as he opens the door.

I pull my phone out of my back pocket, checking to see if she's texted me. Sighing, I pull up our chat.

ME: Do you need me to come back?

Seconds, minutes pass before she messages me back.

MUM: No! I have everything under control. Enjoy work. Love you. x

She has what under control?

ME: What do you mean 'under control'? What's going on? Is she still crying?

"Yo, Dad, can you take me back? I think something is wrong."

He turns, frowning at me. "No, there's not. Your mum texted me to check in on Madison at the flower shop."

"When did she text that?" I ask, stepping into the staff room.

"Just now."

My brows furrow together.

MUM: No, she's fine. Currently smiling up at me.

ME: Send me a picture on Messenger.

Not a few minutes after does a picture of Sunday sucking her fist into her mouth pop up on my screen. I smile, rubbing my thumb over the screen.

I miss her so fucking much already.

The door to the staff room slams open and Mason rushes in looking stressed and worn out. "Don't put your kitchen uniform on. Take one of the bar staff shirts. All my employees miraculously called in sick," he scoffs. "Bit of fucking sun and they think it's Christmas and the only day of the year to drink."

I chuckle, grabbing one of the black shirts instead of the white kitchen uniform. "I'm not staying longer, just so ya know."

He glares at me before pointing to my dad. "You can help out as well. Hayden and Max are gonna come in too."

"You should ask Mum to come in and bring Sunday. She can help out while my baby sleeps. I can watch her at the bar."

Mason turns to grin at me. "You missing her already? How long you been gone?"

I sigh, finishing the last buttons. "Fifteen minutes—if that."

He laughs, sharing a look with my dad. "Well, you've got another five hours to go."

"Whatever," I mutter, and grab my phone from the shelf, firing another text off to Mum.

ME: You should pop down here, Mum. Bring Sunday. Mason's short-staffed.

"You're texting your mum to come down here, aren't you?" Dad asks as we step into the bar.

I undo a button when the heat hits me. The air con must not be working because Mason has the large windows open.

I dare to look at him as I answer. "Nope. Just texting Maddox to see if he's popping down for a beer."

"Brave."

This time I do look at him. "What do you mean?"

He shrugs, stepping behind the bar. "Just think you're brave in wanting your cousin down here. If he sees you like this, he'll rip you to pieces."

My phone vibrates, so instead of answering Dad, I open the message up.

MUM: I don't think the bar is the best place for Sunday right now. Isn't there a game on tonight?

Fuck.

ME: Yeah.

I hadn't thought of that. I really hope Mason doesn't expect me to stay longer, because he's got no chance. I'll be walking out of here the second my shift is over.

Since it's the weekend, food stops being served at six and tables are removed from the floor. A DJ will set up in the old booth and anyone seeking food will go to the restaurant downstairs. There, my uncle sells burgers, chips, hot dogs and pork baps. MC5 is always packed and the place to be if you want a good night out. My dad used to run the place but left Mason in charge of everything after a fire took place at Harlow and Malik's wedding before we were born.

They completely redone the place, starting a Monday through Sunday daytime restaurant, but on Fridays and Saturdays, the restaurant closes, tables are put away, and it's open as a club. The place is always thriving and has done better with the changes.

"Excuse me? Are you serving?" I look up and find a cute redhead fluttering her eyelashes at me.

I nod, stepping forward. "What can I get ya?"

"What are you offering?" she asks, biting her bottom lip.

My eyebrows draw together as I stare at her. "Um, drinks. If you want food, you'll have to take a seat and a waitress will be over to take your order."

Her cheeks turn red. "Y-yeah. I'll just have half a Strongbow please."

"Coming right up."

My mind is on my phone and whether I should text Mum to see if she's put cream on Sunday's bum.

I hand over the drink, taking her money and giving the girl her change before leaning back against the bar, grabbing my phone.

ME: Make sure you put some cream on her bum. The health visitor said she has nappy rash.

Dad chuckling has me glancing up, narrowing my eyes at him. "What?"

"Nothing. That your mum again?"

"So what if it is?"

"You have to leave her sometime, son. Trust me, she'll be fine. There is no greater person in the world than your mum to be looking after her," he tells me, before sighing. "I dread to think what you'll be like when she goes to school."

I pale. I didn't even think of that. She'll have to be around other people's kids, who could pick on her, call her names, or hell, come back with nits like the girls in our family have one time or another. And then she'll grow older, and me or my cousins won't be there to warn the boys away. I'll get arrested for hitting a minor. I know it.

I'll go to prison and not see my baby girl.

I'll be someone's bitch.

Hands slap down on my shoulders, shaking me. I look up, feeling woozy.

"What's the matter?"

"I'm going to prison," I whisper, feeling dejected.

"Huh? Since when?"

"A boy is going to hit on her, *touch* her, and I'll kill him. Or one will pick on her, or *touch* her, and I'll kill him. I'll get life."

Dad roars with laughter, punching my shoulder lightly. I rub it, frowning at him. "What was that for?"

"Just shut up and get to work. If we managed to stay out of prison, so will you."

Nope, someone else needs to have kids so she has someone to stick up for her. That's what needs to happen.

"I need to call Faith for a second."

"Why?" he asks, just as people stepping inside catch my attention.

"Magic," I whisper, watching as Faith, her fiancé, and my uncles, Max and Myles, walk in.

"What the hell are you muttering about now?"

I point towards the door. He glances over his shoulder before turning to greet them at the bar.

"Hey, baby girl. How you doing?" he asks, stepping around the bar to meet Faith. He hugs her before kissing the side of her head.

"Hi, Dad. We came in for a drink and to see how Aiden was doing on his first day back."

"I'm doing fine," I tell her defensively. Did they think I'd fuck up orders or something? I mean, I've only served one person, but still… I'm Aiden fucking Carter. I'm solid.

Beau pulls her into his arms, glaring at me. I glare right back. She's my sister; I've known her longer. I can speak to her however I like.

"I didn't mean anything by it," she says, glancing at everyone.

Max laughs. "Well, I came to make sure I won my bet."

"What bet?"

Dad hands them all a drink, already knowing what they'll order. I stand and watch, not bothering to serve the fuckers.

"I bet you'd last an hour before you went running back to Sunday."

I straighten, glancing at my dad then Uncle Myles. "That true?"

Myles nods. "Sorry, kid. I bet you'd last two."

"Thanks for the vote in confidence," I bite out, disgusted at my family. I glance at Dad. "What about you?" I think back to our conversation in the car park and him telling me to just get through the shift.

"The entire shift, because even if you went to leave, I'd stop you." He shrugs carelessly.

"Well, fuck you too."

My uncle Mason steps out of the kitchen, groaning when he sees his two brothers are here. "If you've come to keep him here, we stated we couldn't interfere with his decision to stay or go."

"You too?" I ask, gaining a few patrons' attention.

He looks at me like I'm stupid. I'm getting that a lot lately.

"Yeah. I don't think you'll last the hour."

I glare at him, then stare at Uncle Myles. "I can understand those knobs, but you? I thought you were different."

He shifts in his chair. "Sorry. I couldn't be the only one who didn't bet."

"Don't worry, Myles lasted thirty minutes before he went home," Max tells us, chuckling.

Myles turns to glare at Max. "You took a term off school because you couldn't leave your kids."

Max sits up, slamming his beer down on the bar. "I had three fucking kids who sucked the life out of me."

"Not my problem."

I laugh, and Max's attention turns to me. "Why are you so grumpy, anyway? Maddox said you're fucking your hot neighbour."

"Maddox is a moron," I snap.

"What, isn't she hot?" he asks, looking around at everyone in confusion. "She didn't look ugly."

I scoff. "I'm not doing my neighbour. And even if I was, it wouldn't be any of your business."

"Lily said she has her hearing back—with help of a hearing aid," Faith says to me, and I nod.

"Ah, so she's heard you whine like a bitch and kicked you to the kerb?"

I glare at my uncle Max. How my dad and uncles haven't killed him, I don't know. "Shut up," I tell him, before turning to Faith. "Yeah. They said there's an operation she can have to repair the damage."

"That's brilliant."

"It is."

My phone vibrates, and I step back from the others to see who's text me.

MUM: Will you please relax. I have experience, you know. I'm not clueless. Now, relax and enjoy some adult time at work.

ME: Never say 'adult time' ever again. Please. Just keep me informed.

ME: HOURLY.

ME: Actually, every fifteen minutes.

MUM: Do you want me to look after your daughter or be distracted by messaging you? I'll update you hourly, not a minute before or after.

ME: Okay.

Well, I got told. I feel my cheeks heat when I look up to find everyone staring at me.

"Mum tell you off?" Faith asks, hiding behind her drink when I narrow my gaze at her.

"No."

"She did; you have that look on your face," Max says.

Dad looks up from his phone. "She did. She just said to take your phone off you if you text her again."

I quickly put my phone in my back pocket, knowing he won't hesitate to take it from me.

"You're all arseholes," I growl when they begin to laugh.

"Back to the hot neighbour, to you and her—you know, not making any more babies, because I don't want my kids getting any bright ideas, especially Hayden," Max says without taking a breath.

God, please give me strength.

"I already told you no."

"What's wrong with her?" he asks. "From what Maddox said about her cooking, she'd make a good mum."

My hands clench into fists, ready to smash Maddox in the face. "Maddox needs to keep his nose out. And to stay away from Bailey and her food."

The chuckles from everyone grate on my nerves. "Ah, you like her."

"Oh, my God, will you shut up. I've got work to do," I snap, moving away from them.

"Don't worry, I got your back if you need pointers."

I spin around, meeting his eyes. "I think I'm good, thank you."

He loses his amused expression. "No need to get pissy."

I shake my head as I walk to the other side of the bar. A couple waiting meets my gaze, and I hold up my finger before turning back to check that Dad isn't looking. He isn't there, so I quickly pull my phone back out.

ME: What is she doing? Send me another picture. X

I just manage to hit send before the phone is snatched out of my hand. "Hey," I yell, spinning around and coming face to face with my dad.

He reads the message before shaking his head. "Nope. You can have this in an hour. You need to do work."

"But, Dad," I whine, going to reach for it.

"Nope. You were warned."

"What if there's an emergency?" I argue.

He grins. "Nice try. But your mum has everyone's number and I'll keep an eye on your phone. If she messages, I'll bring it to you. Now, get some fucking work done."

My shoulders slump. There's no use arguing because he'll never give in. And deep down, I know he'd tell me if something was wrong. Both dad and Mason would.

I just don't know how they managed to survive with us. Having kids isn't just feeding, bathing, and loving them. You worry about them twenty-four-seven. They literally suck all the energy out of you. And the love? God, I never knew love like I have for my daughter even existed. She's opened my eyes to a lot of stuff, but not as much as she's opened my heart.

I think it's why I can't stop thinking about Bailey. I've never looked at a girl through my heart or mind. No. I've always checked them out and saw them through my dick. It's all it's ever been for me.

With her, I feel. I feel so fucking much it scares me.

And it's that fear that's stopping me from pursuing her, from making her mine, and mine alone.

FIFTEEN

AIDEN

WORK GOT BUSY AFTER DAD TOOK my phone, helping me keep my mind off things. He kept me updated every thirty minutes, for which I was thankful.

Though that doesn't mean I wasn't tense for my entire shift. My muscles ache. I just want to go home—and hope Sunday sleeps long enough for me to run a bath and soak for a while.

Dad pulls into my drive and I open my eyes, frowning when I see Maddox and Landon's trucks in Bailey's driveway.

"What the fuck?" I growl, undoing my belt.

Dad pulls the car to a stop, chuckling. "It's a shame you don't like her like that, son. She seems to get on with the family."

"They shouldn't be bothering her," I tell him, stepping out of the car.

"Looks like she doesn't mind." Dad shrugs, grabbing Sunday's stuff from the boot. I take her out, her beautiful face relaxed with sleep.

"I'm gonna go over there. Thanks for the ride home, Dad," I say, quickly taking Sunday's bags from him.

"Thanks for the hundred quid I earned tonight."

I stop on the edge of her path and slowly pivot around to face him. "Are you serious?"

He grins, shrugging. "I'm a Carter. You can't blame me."

"I'm your son," I yell.

"And such a good boy you are," he tells me, before getting in his car.

"Fucker," I growl, watching him drive down the path. Sometimes I wonder why I put up with them.

Because you're as crazy as they are.

Taking a deep breath, I make my way up to Bailey's front door. I bang on it, pissed Maddox is here. Landon, I don't have to worry about; he has no charm or sex appeal. I'd be surprised if the fucker ever got laid.

The door clicks and opens. I paste on my best smile, wanting her to forget all about Maddox and his flirting.

Maddox's bare upper body greets me, sweat dripping down the hard lines of his chest. Slowly, afraid Sunday will sense the anger inside of me and wake up, I place her down on the floor, and then her bags.

"What. The. Fuck. Have. You. Done."

The second I see his smug smirk, I want to wipe it off.

He scratches his bare chest, leaning against the doorframe. "Whatever do you mean?"

"You know what the fuck I mean. I swear to god, if you weren't family, I'd lay you out right now."

Not that we haven't gotten in a fair few fights. There's a lot of testosterone in our family, so it's bound to happen.

"I was just about to take a shower, man. She's tired me out, you know. I'm all dirty and sweaty now."

Fuck him being family.

I take a step forward, my hands balled into fists, when the door swings open further.

"Hi, Aiden, do you want some dinner too?" Bailey asks cheerfully. "I've cooked everyone dinner to thank Maddox for fixing my shower for me. It was nice of him to come and do it in his spare time. Landon, Charlotte, and Lily are in the kitchen."

"I would love to," I tell her, beaming. I pick up Sunday and her bags and push past Maddox. I make sure the bags smack him in the chest, and I'm satisfied when I hear him grunt.

"Here, let me help you." Bailey takes two of the bags from my arm.

"Cheers, babe."

She ducks her head, cheeks turning pink. "It's all right."

"I'm just gonna go wash up," Maddox says.

Turning in his direction, I give him the middle finger. "Isn't it past your bedtime?"

"Nah. For Bailey, I'd stay up all night," he tells me, winking.

I growl, taking a step towards him, but Bailey's voice stops me. I don't think she even realises she's saved him twice tonight.

"Are you coming in or what? Let Maddox clean up before his food goes cold."

"Coming," I tell her, giving Maddox one last warning look. He just grins, uncaring.

I give a chin lift to Landon when I step inside the kitchen, and Charlotte a quick kiss on the head and a side hug, before placing Sunday on the floor.

When my eyes lock on Lily's, I walk over, concerned. I pull her into my arms, shivering from how cold she feels tonight. She looks tired, the dark circles under her eyes a tell. I worry about her a lot, hating that she won't let any of us live with her. The only person she lets stay more than once a week is Maddox. Why? I have no idea. Those two are polar opposites. But then again, Landon and Charlotte's friendship never made sense to me either. She's all smiles and Landon doesn't know how to crack one.

"You okay?"

"Yeah, just tired."

"You need to rest more," I tell her, before letting her go. She smiles, kissing my cheek.

"I'll be fine. You know me."

Her eyes are filled with pain and sorrow. The torment there has always been easy for us to see, but she has times in her life when it's hidden, or temporarily gone.

"I do, which is why I know you won't listen."

She pushes my shoulder, a cute pout forming on her lips when I don't budge. I chuckle, pulling out a chair to sit on.

"So, what's for dinner?" I ask, realising how hungry I am after today's shift.

"Just a cottage pie," Bailey says, grabbing a tray from the oven. The smell that fills the air has my stomach rumbling. Getting up, I walk over to help Bailey. She looks over her shoulder at me. "Sit down. I've got this. You've been at work all day."

I grab a pair of spare oven mitts and lean over, brushing my body against hers. She pauses, her body shivering, and I grin at the effect I have on her.

"I want to. You grab the gravy while I take this to the table."

"I've got the plates," Lily says gently.

"Do you want me to get everyone a drink?" Charlotte asks.

Sighing, Bailey steps out of my embrace, and I can't wipe the grin off my face when I notice the goose bumps raised on her skin.

"Yeah, there's some cans of pop in the fridge or soft drinks in the top cupboard," Bailey tells Charlotte. "And glasses are in the cupboard above where Lily just got the plates from."

"Okay," Charlotte answers.

I take the cottage pie over to the table by the window that looks into the conservatory and dip the serving spoon inside. I don't waste time piling up the plates Lily has set down, my stomach demanding I eat now. I make sure mine and Landon's are filled after putting enough on the girls and little on Maddox's.

Fucker doesn't deserve any.

Lily glances down at all the plates, raising her eyebrow at me. "You not hungry?"

I smirk. "Of course I am. That's Maddox's. He ate a big lunch."

"He said he was starving earlier," Lily whispers, so Bailey doesn't overhear.

"She's gone to all of this trouble to cook for us and he isn't even hungry. Why would he lie?"

"He was just being polite, Lil. Now, sit down before it gets cold."

Landon walks over, sees the plates, and I swear I see his lips twitch. He takes a seat between Lily and Charlotte, Lily to his left.

Maddox walks in and Bailey smiles at him. "Take a seat. Food's ready."

He rubs his stomach, which, thankfully, is now covered in a T-shirt. "Great. I'm starving."

"Fucker," I mumble under my breath.

"What did you say?" Charlotte asks.

"I said I'd best grab Sunday," I tell her, getting up to bring her to the table.

"Oh yeah, you don't want her to wake up and think you're gone," she says gently.

Shit! I hadn't even thought of that. I place her so the first person she sees when she wakes up is me. When Maddox goes to take a seat at the place set for Bailey, I kick him, warning him to move with one look.

He pouts, then looks down at his food with disgust. "Where's the rest?"

"Here it is," Bailey replies cheerfully, setting two pots of gravy down on the table.

"Why do I get a small amount?" Maddox whines as Landon shovels food into his trap.

I pour gravy all over mine as Bailey asks, "Were you not hungry?"

"Starving. I forgot to eat my snack earlier."

"You eat snacks?" Bailey asks, her lips twitching.

"Got to; I'd starve otherwise. I always have food to hand," he answers, before narrowing his eyes on my plate. "Hungry?" I grin, moaning over a bite. "Wanker."

"Here, have mine. There's too much and I'm not really hungry," Lily says, pushing her plate over and taking his.

I'd say something, but the tired look on her face shows she doesn't need any more stress right now. And me arguing with her best friend would do that.

Maddox looks down at her, his forehead creasing. "We'll help Bailey clean up and head home. Is it okay if I sleep at yours tonight? The new family that moved in next door are keeping me up at night with the noise, and I need sleep."

You can hear the lie in his words, but Lily, too tired to read into them, doesn't even blink. In fact, she looks relieved he'll be staying.

"Of course. You should have said they were keeping you up. I wouldn't have made you go home last night."

"It's fine. I didn't want to trouble you."

"Well, you're more than welcome," she tells him, taking a small bite of food.

I glance at Bailey, lifting a fork of food up. "This is amazing. Did you make this yourself?"

A light tinge of pink hits her cheeks. "I did. I was going to put the rest in the fridge and bring it over tomorrow for your lunch."

I narrow my eyes at everyone at the table, who look like they're enjoying my food.

"It's really good," Charlotte compliments.

"How was your first day back at work?" Landon asks, looking smug.

"Great. Why?"

"Just surprised you weren't home earlier, is all."

I roll my eyes. "Your dad told you, didn't he?"

He nods, not bothering to answer me. "Told him what?" Bailey asks as she pours more gravy on her plate.

"They all bet I'd leave work early to pick Sunday up," I tell her. "I was fine though. It wasn't as bad as I thought it would be."

Maddox covers his mouth when he starts choking on his laughter. "Dad said you were ready to go after ten minutes."

"Your dad wasn't even there," I tell Maddox snottily.

He shrugs. "He had Myles keep him informed."

"I think it's sweet you didn't like leaving Sunday. It just shows what a good dad you are. Some dads are quick to get out and leave the mum to deal with everything these days," Bailey adds.

"That's true. At the school its mostly mums that pick the kids up. There's only a few dads who show up," Lily says.

"I think I'll be fine next shift. I guess the first time is always the hardest."

She places a comforting hand over mine and our gazes meet, locked in a trance. Something passes between us, and I feel like I'm really looking at her for the first time. She gets more beautiful every time I see her.

"You'll be great. She's lucky to have you," she tells me, her voice low, almost seductive.

"Hey," Maddox says, interrupting our moment. I glare, really wanting to strangle him right now. "You should come to the pub with us next weekend. We're all meeting down there for a bit."

I feel her gaze burn into the side of my face, so I turn to look at her.

"Will you be there?" she asks, biting her bottom lip.

Knowing she doesn't feel comfortable being out, I nod. "I will. Mum is having Sunday for me that weekend, so I can catch up on sleep and work. We try to meet up all together once a week, but our lives have been busy lately."

"And you don't mind me coming?" she asks shyly.

"Nope. You can meet the other crazies in my family."

"Yeah, I wouldn't decide on a future with me until you meet the rest of my family," Maddox tells her teasingly, grinning.

"Good job she won't be with you then, isn't it," I snap.

"Are you sure?"

"I'm right here," Bailey interrupts. "And, Aiden, I'll come with you, but only for a little while."

"Good," I tell her sincerely, wondering if I can get some alone time with her.

Charlotte's phone dings with a text. I look up to see her face scrunch up with confusion.

"What's wrong?" Landon asks softly, glancing down at her.

"What does DP mean?" she asks. "A guy just asked if I wanted one."

I choke on my food.

"Who the fuck asked you that?" Landon demands, snatching her phone out of her hand. He reads the screen, his eyes widening, and a look of revulsion passes over his face. "What the hell, Charlotte?"

She still looks confused. "I don't know why you're so mad. Hayden told me about Maddox using it."

"Using what?" Maddox asks slowly, pushing his half-eaten plate away. I know how he feels because I push mine away too, no longer hungry.

"Dating App."

"One: didn't you learn anything from Faith's experience with dating sites? And two: why the hell would you do something he did?" Landon demands. "Nothing he does is a good idea."

"But he met loads of people on there. I can't stay a virgin forever, you know," she tells him.

His face reddens as he pushes his chair back and stands up. "Come on, I'm taking you home so you can delete this account."

"Okay," she says, her expression filled with sadness, before turning back to Maddox. "If you can recommend a safe app, can you send me the link, please? The men on this one keep asking if I want a DP or if I'm looking for a good time. Whenever I tell them yes, I'd like to go butterfly garden for our first date, they never answer me back."

"Come on," Landon growls, pulling her away from the table.

"See you later," she calls out, waving at us.

"Does DP mean what I think it means?" Bailey asks quietly after the front door slams.

"Dick pic?" Maddox says. "Yeah, it fucking does."

"He's gonna kill you," I tell him, grinning.

"I don't care. Maybe then he can knock the image of her sexting someone— even if she doesn't realise it's what she's doing—out of my mind."

"You mean someone was going to send her a picture of their... you know?" Lily asks, her face bright red.

"Yes," I growl, scrubbing a hand over my face.

"Oh, dear," she says, glancing at the door they left through. "He's going to be so mad."

"He'll sort it out," Maddox assures her. "You haven't—you know… signed up for one, have you?"

I look up, narrowing my eyes. "Please tell me you haven't."

"No!" she squeaks out. "After what happened with Faith…" She shakes her head as sadness fills her eyes. "If I knew Charlotte had signed up for one, I would have told her to delete it. I know they're not all dangerous, but you can never be too sure."

"Good girl," I say, relaxing back in my chair.

"I'll start cleaning this up," Bailey tells us, picking up Landon's empty plate and Charlotte's half-eaten one.

"We'll help," Maddox says, picking up his own.

"You two go," I tell him, glancing down at Lily, who yawns once again. "I'll stay and clean up."

"You sure?" he asks, and I nod. He helps Lily out of her chair, letting her lean against his body before turning to Bailey. "Thank you for dinner, and sorry it was cut short."

Her expression softens. "It's my pleasure. It's nice not having to cook for one for a change."

"Thank you," Lily says, sounding more tired by the minute. "I'll see you next week when we meet up."

"Looking forward to it," Bailey says.

We quickly finish clearing the table before Bailey walks over with a plate of brownies. I grin over the fact Maddox just missed out. I'll be texting him to gloat later.

"Those for me?"

She tilts her head. "Kind of," she says, passing me the plate.

"Kind of?" I rip off the cling film but she places her hand on top, stopping me.

"Charlotte brought them over and I don't have the heart to throw them away."

I nearly drop the plate like it burned me. "You could have started with that. I nearly ate one."

She laughs, and it's music to my ears. "Sorry. I just didn't want you to get offended."

"Trust me, as long as you don't say anything to Charlotte, you won't offend me. I'll even help you dispose of them."

"She made me eat one," she tells me, pouting. "They're terrible—tasted like cardboard."

"At least you weren't sick," I tell her, trying to cheer her up.

"Maybe I could give her one of my recipes."

I shake my head, dropping the contents of the plate into the bin. "Wouldn't bother. She'll still fuck it up somehow. We've tried."

"Can she cook?"

I place the plate in the washer before turning to face her. "Nothing edible. We can't even let her have animals in case one of them eats something she's cooked and dies."

"Have you tried teaching her?" she asks.

I'd told her about my plans to be a professional chef, but not even my skills could make Charlotte's cooking any better. "Wouldn't help. Her mum and dad can both cook so we don't know where she gets it from. It's like she's cursed."

Giggling, she passes me the plates she just swilled off so I can put them into the washer.

"Did you want to stay for a movie or are you ready for bed?" she asks.

Fuck being tired. If it means spending more time with Bailey, I'll push through it. I can have a soak in the bath tomorrow night.

"A movie sounds great."

She ducks her head, trying to hide her smile from me as she grabs a glass from the side. "Good."

Yeah, I could have gone days without sleep and still managed to find the energy to watch a movie with her.

SIXTEEN

BAILEY

TODAY, I DECIDED TO GIVE MY hearing aid a rest. I miss the solitude, the silence, which is I why I spent the morning without it in. I've got the doorbell device in my pocket, switched the lights to work if it rings, and my phone is set to vibrate. If anyone needs me, which I doubt they will, I'll have everything on me.

The past week has been a blur. The doctor said I'll have my appointment through in a couple of weeks and that everything looked promising. I'm excited and scared all at the same time.

Another highlight of my week was spending time with Aiden and Sunday. He fills my life with laughter and joy, but most of all, happiness. He makes me so incredibly happy that sometimes I wonder if he's real or not.

And the way he is with his daughter… they have a bond so strong it hurts to witness. It reminds me of my parents; of how much they loved me. Missing them has become a part of me. And my brother, Thomas; I see the seven old boy who was taken far too young. I sometimes dream about what we would be like now. Would he argue with me, tease me, like Aiden's siblings do to him? Would he still want to play video games with me, or would he have outgrown my presence and played with his own friends?

So many possibilities, so many scenarios, but I'll never know who my brother would have grown into, the man he would have become.

I wipe at the tear that drops down my cheek, blowing out the candle placed in a small cupcake.

"Happy birthday, baby brother."

Later, I'll place some flowers on their graves, and make sure to leave one of Thomas's favourite action hero figures too. He would have loved all the new action movies that have been released, and demanded for every game, toy and merchandise out there. And he deserved it. He was the best brother a girl could wish for.

A hand on my shoulder startles a scream out of me. I turn, ready to hit my intruder over the head. My gran's face brings a sob bubbling to my throat, and I throw myself in her arms.

Her chest vibrates against me, but I don't pull back to read her lips, instead I soak in her warmth. Granddad's arms wrap around us both, and I smile, so happy they're here.

I pull back, wiping at my tears with one hand whilst reaching for my hearing aid with the other. I put it in, and a door slamming open is the first thing I hear. I jump at the same time my grandparents do, my granddad grabbing a rolling pin from the side.

"Bailey?" Aiden shouts, running into the kitchen with Sunday in his arms, a look of panic on his face. "Thank fuck you're okay. I thought something had happened to you when I heard you scream. Shit, girl, I thought Sunday could scream."

I giggle through my tears. "Sorry, Aiden."

"You're the neighbour?" Granddad asks.

Aiden looks at him, just as my gran starts fanning herself. "Oh, my."

"Yeah, I live with Maggie next door. You must be Bailey's grandparents," he says, holding his hand out to shake Granddad's.

I ignore them, jostling my gran to get her attention. "Gran, what are you doing here?"

She cups my face, happiness filling her watery eyes. "We couldn't leave you today of all days."

"What's today?" Aiden asks, before he starts sniffing. "Please tell me Charlotte didn't make those."

I laugh as I look to all the cakes I baked. It's my brother's birthday, after all. After I baked the cake, I got carried away and started making loads of cupcakes. Now my kitchen side is filled with them.

"No, she didn't."

He walks over, his hand hovering over one, when the cake catches his attention. "Thomas is your brother, right?" he asks quietly.

"Yeah. He would have been ten today."

His expression changes from hunger for cupcakes to sadness. He steps over, shifting Sunday up so he can pull me against him and kiss the top of my head. "I'm sorry, Bailey. Why didn't you tell me it was his birthday last night? I would have been here for you."

I pull away a little to look up at him, surprised at his sincerity. I melt into him. "Because I didn't want to make a big deal. Today is hard as it is."

"Oh, my," Gran whispers.

"You should have told me anyway. I can be lazy and not make a big deal. And I can totally be on board to eat all these cupcakes."

I grin. "I was going to bring some out later."

"To Maddox and his team?" he asks, eyes narrowed.

"Yep." I slap his shoulder before turning to my grandparents. "You two could have called me—not that I'm not happy you're back, but you still have places to see, people to meet."

My gran's focus drifts from Aiden to me, but I can see it was a hardship for her as her eyes keep flicking back to him. She opens her mouth to answer, but no words come out.

I sigh.

"We wanted to be here for you. After your phone call about your appointment with the doctor, we had a long chat and decided to come home. It wasn't the same without you there, anyway, darlin'," Granddad explains when Gran can't.

"Apart from those three nights in Vegas," Gran whispers, still drawn to Aiden.

"But it was your dream," I say, my voice low. I can't bear the thought that they've cut their trip short for me.

"We want to be here with you. You're going to need us. Once the operation is done and you're all healed, we are going to move into the cottage. You're getting older now and don't need us oldies cramping your style," she says as her eyes drift back over to Aiden, checking him out.

"What about all the changes you're making to the house? Will you be selling it?" I hate that the first thought that crosses my mind is Aiden and that I'll no longer be the girl next door.

"Gosh, no," Gran says.

"We're signing the house over to you," Granddad tells me.

"But it's your home."

"And something tells me it won't be long until you make it yours," he says, his gaze flicking to Aiden.

I hear the backdoor open, and before my granddad puts that rolling pin to use, I explain. "That will be the builders. They're Aiden's family—well, some of them."

Aiden squeezes my shoulder. "Don't give them any cupcakes," he whispers.

"Yo, Bailey, do I smell cupcakes?" is Maddox's reply.

"It is," I yell, chuckling to myself as he lets himself into the kitchen. He looks like a wolf with the way he's sniffing the air.

"Hey, new people," he greets.

"Oh, my," Gran says, swaying on her feet. Landon, Liam and Mark follow in after him, and Gran gasps before falling. Maddox, already a few steps in front of her, quickly catches her before she hits the floor.

"Gran," I gasp.

Granddad sighs, helping Maddox lift her. "I knew this was going to happen.

She gets too excited. Maybe wear shirts next time you're around her," he tells Maddox, but his gaze flicks to Landon, who is also shirtless.

I lick my lips when I see the sweat dripping down his body, the hard lines of his abs glistening. Even his pecs are huge.

Now I can see why my gran fainted. I've never seen a body like that on anybody, and Aiden's body is pretty fucking sexy. Landon's was moulded by God himself.

"Wow!" I whisper.

"Put on a damn shirt, Landon," Aiden snaps.

I jump, quickly looking away and wiping my bottom lip. When I glance back up, he's grabbing a T-shirt from the back pocket of his jeans and pulling it over his head.

Granddad and Maddox walk back in, laughing and joking. Maddox walks right over to the cake but pauses when he sees the name on it.

He looks around, adorably confused. "Um, who's Thomas? Do I have more competition?"

"He's my brother," I tell him, my voice low.

"He passed away a few years ago. He'd be ten today," Granddad adds.

Maddox quickly drops the cupcake back on the side, looking at me apologetically. "I'm so fucking sorry."

"Eat them," I tell him. "I was going to bring them out anyway. Just don't eat the cake yet."

"Are you sure?"

I nod. "I am."

He doesn't waste another second before stuffing a whole cupcake in his mouth, moaning in appreciation. "So good," he mumbles through his mouthful.

Mark steps over to me and pulls me into his arms. I hug him back, smiling over his shoulder at my granddad. He winks before moving over to help himself to a cupcake.

"I'm sorry for your loss," Mark whispers.

My chest tightens. "Thank you."

He pulls away and I take a step back, happy when they all hover around the cakes in preparation to devour them.

Granddad comes over with a plateful and I roll my eyes. "How's Gran?" I ask him.

"She's just going to freshen up. She'll be down in a minute."

"She okay, then?"

He laughs. "Yeah. She did it in Vegas too. They had an underwear model shoot going on in the third hotel we stayed at. She walked out to use the pool and was swarmed with young men with no clothes on," he tells me, then sighs. "They called an ambulance."

I shouldn't laugh, but I do.

"Your gran okay?" Aiden asks as he tries to juggle a plate of cupcakes and Sunday.

"Here, let me have her while you eat those."

"Thanks," he says, passing her over to me. It's rare she's awake during the day, but I guess all the commotion woke her up.

"She's a beauty," Granddad says. "Make sure you get a bat ready to chase all the boys off when she's older."

Aiden quickly chews before answering. "I'm borrowing my uncle Max's baseball bat. He borrowed it from my uncle Mason, who borrowed it from my uncle Malik. It kind of got passed down. Only fair I get it next."

"Did your uncles ever use it?" Granddad asks before I can.

"Uncle Malik didn't use it when Maddison was old enough to date; one look had them running. Mason needed it for Hope and Ciara as Ashton, his only son, was the youngest and he couldn't really use him to scare them off." He pauses to take another bite before continuing. "My uncle Max just loved scaring anyone who tried to date Hayden. She's a triplet, the other two being her brothers."

"She had no hope of dating, then," I say, feeling sorry for her.

"Nope," he says, then laughs. "If they weren't scared of Landon, then seeing how crazy Max acted in front of them had them running off. Anyone else braver ended up in the boot of the car and dumped miles away from home."

Granddad laughs. "Looks like she has a good family looking out for her," he says, glancing down at Sunday.

"It still doesn't protect her from accidents. The amount of times we ended up in hospital for doing something stupid and getting hurt is a joke. I've been trying to think of a plan to wrap Sunday up, so she doesn't even get a cut knee."

I giggle, watching Sunday's bright eyes staring up at me. "Is your daddy silly? Yes, yes he is."

"Just get loads of plasters ready. When my daughter was a toddler, she was forever falling over and scraping her knee."

"Got that covered. I'm gonna make her play in shin pads," Aiden says.

I shake my head at them. Maddox groans as he licks icing off his fingers. "Did you cook lunch?"

I laugh when Aiden snaps, "She isn't your maid."

Maddox rolls his eyes, unaffected. "You're just jealous she cooks for us more than you."

I blush, looking away. "I didn't today. I've been busy making cupcakes. Give me five minutes though; I have some pork in the oven to do pork baps with stuffing and gravy."

"Again?" Mark asks, looking greedily at the oven.

"Yep," I tell him, laughing at his expression.

"I'll do it. You keep hold of Sunday. Don't let Mark hold her with his dirty hands."

Mark pouts at Aiden. "I washed them."

"Thank you," I tell him.

"I'll help. You can tell me all about how you met my granddaughter," Grandad says.

"Oh, she is just beautiful," Gran squeals as she walks into the kitchen. "I remember when you were a baby. You would only settle in your mother's arms."

"She's gotten used to her dad's. He's been trying to get her to grow out of it since his mum said it will make his life harder in the long run."

Gran nods, sitting down next to me in the conservatory, leaving the men to sort lunch.

"Oh, it will. Your mum had to strap you to her just to do the hoovering.

Didn't even matter if your dad held you; you would still scream the house down."

I laugh, remembering a few pictures I have of Mum doing just that. "I miss them."

"I know you do. I know," Gran says, wrapping her arm around me. I rest my head on her shoulder, never looking away from Sunday. "Now, tell me about Aiden. What's going on between you two?"

"Nothing," I tell her with a sigh.

She scoffs. "I don't believe that."

I lift my head, glancing up at her. "Believe it. I asked him to kiss me and he said no, that he wasn't good for me and didn't want to hurt me. From what his cousin and sister have said, he was a player before Sunday came along. He didn't do relationships. But, Gran, I can't picture him being like that. And I don't care. He's different with me; I know it. I feel it in my soul."

Gran runs her fingers through my hair. "The way that boy came charging into the kitchen, I believe you're right. He looked ready to take on the world one-handed if it meant you were safe."

"I just wish he wanted me the way I want him. I tried to keep my feelings neutral, but then we spent time together and I saw a new side to him. It made me fall for him more and more."

"You have a big heart, Bailey, never change that. He'll see reason. He's just been told he's a dad. He's still processing that and the huge change it's made to his life. If what you say about him is true, then he's not used to what he's feeling. I bet Sunday coming into his life was like a slap in the face. A love for a child has you seeing the world differently. What you saw as important before becomes irrelevant. So it's not that he's not capable; he's just taking time to figure things out."

"And what if he doesn't like me when that time comes?"

She shakes her head at me. "Silly girl. There is no way that boy will ever *not* want you."

"I hope so. I think I love him, Gran. I really do. He's nothing like—" I swallow, hating the thought of *him*. I clear my throat. "He's not like *him*. This time it's real. I'm not some naïve girl seeking affection."

"You were always more than that, my darlin'. Just give him time," she tells me softly, still running her fingers through my hair as I lay my head back down on her shoulder. "Just not too much. You have to make them work for it. I got your granddad by—"

"No! Stop!" I tell her, laughing light-heartedly. "I don't want to hear that story again. I've only just erased the images."

She chuckles. "All true loves have the best stories. I have a feeling Aiden's will be yours."

I smile, closing my eyes briefly. "I hope so, Gran."

"Love you, my girl."

"Love you too. I'm so glad you're here," I tell her.

"Me too. Witnessing my only granddaughter fall in love for the first time is something I never want to miss."

I don't reply, letting silence fill the lull in conversation.

I just hope my gran is right and that mine and Aiden's story will be epic; something we can tell Sunday one day and laugh about.

Because I can't picture my life without him in it. He fills the emptiness in my heart, the void in my life.

He's the air I breathe.

SEVENTEEN

AIDEN

H ANDING OVER SOME CASH TO THE taxi driver, I step out and open the door for Bailey. One look at her when I picked her up and I wanted to drag her back inside. She looks sexy as fuck tonight.

Wearing leather trousers that fit her like a second skin and a pink blouse that flashes the right amount of cleavage, her body looks hot.

Tonight though, she's wearing makeup, something I've never seen her wear. Her lashes are thick and long, and her eyes smoky and sultry. She has just the right amount of blush on to highlight her high cheekbones. She's fucking gorgeous.

Her hair has been curled and pulled to the side, showing one side of her slender neck.

"You look beautiful," I tell her, pulling her into my arms. I promised myself I would keep my hands off her, but then she came out looking like she did and all I wanted to do was touch her.

"Thank you," she replies breathlessly.

"Hey, you made it," Charlotte says, interrupting. I pull away, turning to my cousin with a sigh.

"Hey."

"Hey, Charlotte. Where's Lily tonight?" Bailey asks.

Fuck! I've still not explained Lily to Bailey. It's too complicated, and honestly, not my story to tell. Not that I know much of it. I think it's only my parents and Maddox who know more about her childhood than we do. We were just given the basics. We were never meant to know anything, but Lily slipped up one night and it came out that she wasn't really our biological sister, but instead, our aunt.

It doesn't matter to me though; she's my sister just as much as Faith is.

"She doesn't come out to bars," Charlotte answers, wariness in her voice as she looks to me for help.

Bailey glances at me, and I can feel the question in her stare. I scrub the back of my neck before facing her.

"Lily doesn't do well around alcohol—well, she can be around it, but not when it's people she doesn't know who are drinking."

"How come?"

"I'll meet you inside," Charlotte announces, leaving me to answer.

I give her a chin lift and take Bailey's hand in mine. "It's a long story, one only she can really share. She doesn't mind it when she's with us and we're drinking, but she won't come to a bar or club. She freaked out over Beau, my sister's fiancé, when he drunk a bottle of beer."

Her expression softens with sadness. "I understand. It must be hard for her when you all meet up."

Her thoughtfulness warms my heart. My sisters, my family, they mean everything to me. Bailey caring about them means a lot to me.

"Either my mum or dad keep her company or someone stays with her. My cousin Imogen is watching a movie with her tonight. They had organised it before we planned tonight. So, it worked out."

"That's nice for her, then."

I look to the bar, wondering if it's too late to leave. It is. Maddox is in the pub thrusting his hips and snogging the window. I groan. Bailey turns to investigate and starts giggling.

"Is he drunk already?"

"Nope," I tell her. "Trust me, he's worse when he's had a drink."

"I can believe it."

She goes to step inside but I grab her wrist and pull her back. She looks up at me with complete trust shining in her eyes.

"Whatever you do, don't agree to any of his bright ideas—or any of my family's. They seem to have a knack for getting into trouble or stuck in embarrassing situations."

She laughs like she thinks I'm joking, but I'm not. "I promise."

"You ready to meet my crazy family?" I ask her, wrapping my arm around her shoulders.

"I was five minutes ago."

I chuckle, leading her into the bar. It's not packed yet, but it will pick up around eleven. Maddox, Landon, Faith, Beau, Charlotte, Liam, Mark, Hope and Hayden sit in the section under the window. A few cousins couldn't make it, which is a shame; I wanted them to meet Bailey.

"Bailey, I want you to meet my sister, Faith. The ugly fuck next to her is her fiancé," I say. My sister stands up and pulls Bailey into a hug. Bailey looks at me from the corner of her eye, surprise shining in her eyes. I chuckle, shrugging.

"It's lovely to meet you. Lily and Charlotte have told us so much about you," Faith greets. A flash of disappointment crosses Bailey's face, and I don't understand where it's come from. "Aiden here just wants to keep you to himself, so he refuses to share information with us."

Bailey's face brightens.

Ah, so that's what made her sad; she thought I hadn't been talking about her. She should know by now she's all I talk and think about. My decision on what to do about the connection we share heavy on my mind.

"It's the food," Bailey answers with a shrug.

"If you say so," Faith says to her, before giving me a knowing look.

I gently nudge Bailey. "You know Landon, Charlotte, Mark, Liam and Maddox," I tell her. "Next to Landon is his and Liam's other triplet, Hayden. Next to her is Hope. The others couldn't make it tonight, but you'll meet them eventually."

"Hey, everyone."

They all smile, saying their own hellos before Maddox gets up. "Want a drink, Bailey?"

"Um—" she starts, but I interrupt.

"I can get her a drink, fuck-head."

He laughs, slapping me on the shoulder. "Come on, then. I lost a bet so Liam and Landon's drinks are on me."

"And mine," Hayden yells. "We come as a trio."

Maddox faces her, raising his eyebrow. "You weren't even there for the bet."

Hayden looks up from her nails, glaring at Maddox. "It doesn't matter. I'm still included. I'll have a vodka Red Bull."

Maddox groans. "Expensive-arse drink. And stop using the triplet card."

She laughs at his discomfort. "Why? You use your twin card whenever possible."

"Yeah, you made me pay for your cinema ticket when I promised Maddison I'd pay for her if she helped me clean out the attic," Hope complains.

"I wanted to watch Jurassic Park." He shrugs shamelessly. "And we come as a pair."

Charlotte pouts. "You took Lily with you."

"I paid for Lily, though," Maddox adds, grinning.

"And he didn't help clean the attic," Hope adds.

"Hey, I helped you clean that," I argue, glaring at Maddox. "And I didn't get anything."

Bailey pats my chest, giggling. I smile down at her, winking.

"I baked you a cake," Hope tells me.

I lick my lips, remembering that slice of chocolate cake. I gave the rest to a girl I was trying to impress.

Maybe saying I only got to eat one slice isn't the best topic to bring up in front of Bailey.

I pull Bailey away from the bickering and over to the bar. "What would you like to drink?"

Her eyes rake over the menu as she bites her bottom lip. It distracts me for a moment, before I remember she probably hasn't been out drinking before and doesn't know what to order.

"I'd go for something girly, so you aren't sick in the morning."

She meets my gaze. "I drank a Malibu drink when I went away with my grandparents. I just can't remember what it was called."

"Was it a cocktail?"

She nods, glancing over the menu again. "I think it was called sea breeze, but I'm not sure," she mumbles, concentrating on what she's reading.

"Wait, that's a Malibu sea breeze. Did it have cranberry juice, pineapple juice, and probably a little bit of lime?"

Her eyes light up with excitement. "They sell it here? That's exactly what was in it. I'm not sure about the lime, but the rest was in it. They even added fruit and stuff inside."

I chuckle, entertained by her innocence, and lift my hand to wave down the bartender.

I order our drinks, ignoring Maddox as he walks over. I'm grateful when he walks past, his eyes trained on something behind me. Turning to see, I shake my head in amusement as he sidles up to a blonde sitting with a friend.

Hayden, Liam, and Landon won't be getting their drinks anytime soon.

"Your family is big," Bailey comments. I quickly lay our money on the bar then grab our drinks before facing Bailey, handing over her drink. She takes it, smiling gratefully. "Thank you."

"My pleasure," I tell her, then look over to my where my family is sitting, shaking my head when Liam starts stacking glasses into a tower.

He's so going to pay for those later.

"And as for my family, we are big—and really close. We all live close to each other too. Aunt Harlow and Uncle Malik lived next door my nan and granddad—when my grandparents were alive, and Uncle Mason and Aunt Denny live at the end of their garden where they built their house. A few doors down from them live Uncle Myles and Aunt Kayla. All of them but Mason and Malik lived there at one point. But then my dad met my mum and some stuff happened so he got bought the house we grew up in, although, that is a few streets over from this street. My Uncle Max and Aunt Lake moved into a house across the street not long before the triplets were born.

"Jesus, do you own the whole street?"

I laugh, shrugging. "My dad is good at investing. He likes fixing houses up and selling them. He has a few he rents out, but only to those he knows. He hates fixing up after tenants wreck the place."

"And your mum owns a flower shop, right?"

I nod. "Yeah, my nan from my mum's side left it to her. She'd been running it for a while before my nan's death, since she couldn't keep up with the work. Madison works there too. She didn't enjoy school, even though she was good at it. She's just got my mum to agree to building a little lot outside the flower shop where they can grow vegetables. She's hoping she can start selling the fresh veggies at the market."

"Nothing beats fresh veggies. You should get her to speak to local bars who do a lunch menu. Most of them would probably buy from her."

"That could actually work." I grin. "I'll let her know."

"How has work been today?"

I groan. "Hard. We had a mad rush come in, and with the heat, it had been scorching in the kitchen."

"I bet," she says, smiling at me. "And Sunday?"

I raise my eyes at her. "Happy Nanny has her. I checked in and went to see her after I finished work."

She giggles. "Aw, I bet she's being spoiled."

I shrug. "She deserves it."

"She does," Bailey agrees.

"Want to go sit back down? It looks like Jimmy has reigned Liam in before he smashes a load of glasses."

She glances over her shoulder, a cute frown creasing her forehead. "Wait, is that why we're standing here talking?"

I watch as Liam pouts, standing on the table as he hands down pint glasses from the tower he made.

"Yep. He would have kept going until it either reached the ceiling or it fell like a game of Jenga."

She begins to laugh. "Has he done it before?"

I sigh. "He's trying to beat me."

She turns to look back at me. "You?"

I nod, feeling like an immature kid. "Yeah. I got to twenty-six pint glasses before they smashed. He and Maddox have been trying to beat me ever since."

Just as I finish speaking, Jimmy walks up to us with a tray of glasses. "I told you not to do that after the last lot got broken. It takes time for them to be delivered, and with the football going on, I need all the glasses I can get."

"I'll make him buy you another crate of them so you have extra," I tell him, my lips twitching.

He grunts. "I let you lot get away with too much in here."

Bailey starts laughing once he walks off. "That poor man. He looks ready to quit."

I rub the back of my neck. "Probably. But he'd miss us if we never came in. We keep him entertained."

"Bless him."

"Come on; let's go join the others."

I place my hand on her lower back and lead her over to the table. She sits down next to Charlotte, already joining in with their conversation.

"Hey, where's Maddox with our drinks?" Hayden calls out.

I grin at her. "You may as well go get the money off him. He's chatting up some blonde." I take a seat next to Bailey, Landon the other side of me.

Hayden scrunches her face up in disgust. "You'd think he would learn his lesson," she mutters. "Did you know he made the paper over that *Bachelor* scene?"

"He didn't," I gasp, coughing on my beer.

She laughs. "Yeah. Uncle Malik went mad 'cause it had Maddox's name and picture in it. Girls think he's a celebrity now. And the dumb act he plays has them eating it up."

Landon scoffs. "Celebrity. The guy acts like he can't tie his own shoe laces, but he's a fucking genius. I don't know how girls fall for it."

"Me neither," I say, chuckling. The cold beer in my hand barely touches my lips before my gaze catches a group walking through the door, their backs to me.

I groan, putting my beer down.

"This can't be good," I say out loud.

"Tonight just got interesting," Landon murmurs, cracking his knuckles.

Oh, fuck.

EIGHTEEN

BAILEY

THE ATMOSPHERE IN THE BAR TURNS tense pretty quickly. I seek out the intrusion, scanning the bar until my gaze lands on a group of people walking in. The one at the back turns towards us, doing a double take before fully facing us, a wide grin spreading across his face.

The rest follow suit when they realise their friend has stopped, distracted by us.

I gasp, utterly flabbergasted by how handsome each and every one is. The one at the back, nearest the bar, steps forward, an intense expression on his face.

Holy mother of Jesus.

I've seen good-looking guys—hell, I design romance covers for a living and see more bare chests than I care to admit—but nothing could have prepared me for the sight in front of me.

Dark, tanned skin, muscles, and tattoos show on his body, but it's his rugged good-looking face that has me under a spell.

Three of the youngest-looking ones must be triplets, because they look exactly the same, including the tattoos inked on their arms.

And they are so goddamn good-looking it should be a crime. I think I whimper out loud—I can't be sure over the buzzing in my ears.

"Family reunion night? Where's the pretty one—Lily?"

"Fuck off, Reid," Maddox snaps from behind him.

"Here I thought I was the pretty one," Liam taunts, knowing Maddox will start something over Lily.

"Ah, Maddox, thought we got lucky and they left you at home," Reid says, letting Maddox pass to sit next to us.

"You never get lucky," Maddox says, smirking.

The guy next to him, the one covered in tattoos and an expression filled with heavy burdens, steps forward. I shuffle closer to Aiden, worried at what may happen. These guys look like they don't fuck around.

"Are they going to fight?" I whisper, so I'm unheard.

Aiden tilts his head slightly towards me. "Nah. Not yet. It will take more than a bit of banter to get us fighting. Plus, Landon's here, and the only one brave enough to fight him is Jaxon, and he tends to keep the peace."

"Which one is Jaxon?"

I feel his sharp gaze on the side of my neck, but I don't look away from the confrontation going on in front of me.

"Why?"

Surprised at his tone, I glance at him. "So I know which one will break it up. If it looks like he's not going to do anything, then I'm hiding under the table."

The laughing lines at the corner of his eyes, crease. "All right. But I don't think they will. It's still early."

"Hey, who's the new girl? Your baby's mum?" The one who looks like he might be a triplet, says.

Aiden tenses beside me. "Isaac, you weren't always the brightest bulb in the pack. And she's fuck-all to do with you."

Well, that definitely answers if they're friends or not. It's confusing. They're not raising their voices, and they aren't been friendly either, but none of them seem to mind each other's company.

So far.

The one they called Isaac glares and speaks up. "Says the person who still needs his shoelaces tied by someone else." His brothers chuckle.

Aiden moves to stand, but I stop him. The guy from earlier—I think I heard someone call Jimmy—walks over, looking between the two families before letting out a haggard sigh.

"I'm too old for this. Boys, if you're gonna fight tonight, take it out back. I lose customers when you start trashing furniture."

The one covered in the most tattoos, smirks. "Jim, I'm pretty sure we bring in extra customers."

"Yeah!" a girl hoots from the back. "Take off a shirt."

"You too, Carter," another girl shouts.

"Which Carter?" Liam shouts back, grinning.

"I don't care. Just take it off."

The old man rubs a hand down his face, looking exhausted and tired. "Just leave a deposit of a hundred with Baz at the bar. Otherwise, you can all get out."

Wide-eyed, I turn to Aiden. "Deposit? Why does it sound like he's demanded this before?"

From the corner of my eye, I watch them all walk off, all but the one with the tattoos and hidden burdens.

"He's just being thorough," Aiden says, but I can hear the lie in his voice. I frown, wondering what it is that was so bad they need to put deposits down.

"You know, I've been wondering: why is it I see you with Lily in other places but never at a bar?" a deep, gravelly voice speaks up from the side of the group that had formed. He's stayed quiet, intent on watching everything play out.

"Careful," Landon warns.

"Don't even look at Lily, Jaxon," Maddox snaps.

Jaxon smirks. "Why? She's the only one worth looking at."

Maddox stands, spilling over his pint. Hayden jumps out of the way before it lands on her. I begin to tremble as everyone moves, including Beau, Faith's fiancé.

"Not tonight, lads. We just came in for a quiet pint," Beau says.

Jaxon holds his hands up as Liam and Landon hold Maddox back. "I'll go. I was just asking an innocent question."

"Then don't ask about Lily, you wanker," Maddox yells.

Jaxon smirks, walking over to his brothers, who are sitting at the bar, drinks in hands.

Once it's all calmed down, I quickly take a gulp of my drink, the cool liquid soothing and cooling down my heated body. Placing the drink down, I wipe my hands down my trousers before clearing my throat. "I'm just going to use the loo."

"You want me to show you where it is?" Aiden asks me, scanning my face.

"I'll show her," Charlotte pipes up happily.

How can she not be affected by what just took place? They were about to get into a fight—and I have no doubt it would have been bloody and messy.

"Thank you," I tell her, standing up after she does. I glance back at Aiden. "Won't be long."

"All right. Don't take ages—it will be Landon coming in to search for you."

I study his face, reading he's serious. I widen my eyes and I quickly look to Landon, who is still watching the men from before.

"Okay."

I let Charlotte lead me to the bathroom. "They're not always like this," Charlotte says. "And don't mind the Hayes brothers; they're harmless really. The guys don't like them because they don't want to admit they have anything in common with them. And the fights never get too out of hand."

"They seemed to hate each other," I comment.

She grins as she pushes the toilet door open and shrugs. "None of the Hayes brothers have really done anything to us. And the reason Maddox hates Jaxon is because he helped Lily out at school. Some girls cornered her after school one day," she tells me, hitting a nerve inside me.

Poor Lily. I know how much that must have scared her.

"Was she okay?" I ask, stopping at the sinks.

"Lily doesn't like people touching her by surprise, so when one of them pulled her arm, she reacted badly. He heard her screaming and came running. He brought her home and Maddox was there. He thought Jaxon had done something to upset her."

"Didn't Lily explain?"

She shakes her head at me, amused. "Have you met the guys in our family? They hit first and ask questions later. He knows; he just doesn't care."

"At least she has people that care," I murmur. How nice that would have been. My mum and dad were stuck in a corner when it came to my bullying. It wasn't like they could do anything without getting in trouble themselves. And my brother was far too young to even understand what was happening to me at school.

"Didn't you need the toilet?" she asks.

"Yeah."

I do my business before washing my hands, ignoring the questioning stare aimed at the side of my face. I don't like talking about my past. Aiden was the first I dared speak to about it.

When we step outside, Landon is standing across the hallway, his arms crossed over his chest. He rolls his eyes when he sees Charlotte's happy face.

"I swear you take forever when you go to the loo," he says.

I hide my smile as I step past them, hearing her answer. "I didn't use the toilet; Bailey did."

"So why did you go?" he asks, sounding baffled.

"Um, girls go in pairs."

I chuckle under my breath, walking into the bar area. The first thing I see is the table filled with the Hayes brothers. Their attention turns to me, making me blush, so I look away.

I'm just nearing our table when I come to a sudden stop.

My nightmare is standing in front of me.

Liam looks uncomfortable as he tries to pry Eva off his lap. Eva, the girl who kicked me repeatedly in the back, who would spit in my dinner and push me into my locker.

I feel the blood drain from my face as Naomi leans against a post nearby, running her finger up and down Maddox's chest.

I close my eyes as the pain of my past strikes, trying to take a breath that won't come. I can feel their fists pounding against my skin, my hair being ripped from my scalp, the spit on my face.

I open my eyes, and my entire body tenses when they land on the ringleader, Marie. She's sitting on the table, her bare legs swinging in front of Aiden.

My mind knows he's trying to ignore her—I can see it in the way he doesn't pay her attention, instead talking to Beau and Faith—but all I can see is my worst enemy, the girl who killed my family, who ruined my childhood.

And she's talking to Aiden.

He smiles at something she says before glancing back at his sister.

Someone bumps into me, and I'm too stunned—too petrified—to make a move or sound. So much so that when I do speak, it comes out as barely a whisper.

"I'm sorry."

Another shove sends me into a hard body. "Hey, watch it, bitch."

A whimper escapes my lips at the hardness in his tone, but when warm arms gently pry me closer to them, I look up.

Jaxon.

His gaze is narrowed on the person who bumped into me, sending a shiver down my spine.

Slowly, I turn to look, scared we've gained the attention of the girls I've been trying to avoid my whole life. But my eyes land on Amy, the last girl in their group who bullied me.

Her lips curl up in a snarl, and I try to take a breath, but my chest won't expand.

"Well, look who it fucking is," Amy snarls, before a cruel smile lights up her face. "Yo, Marie, look who I found."

Marie looks in our direction, and I step further into Jaxon, seeking his warmth.

"Get your fucking hands off Bailey," Aiden snarls, pushing past Marie and storming over to me.

"You know Bailey?" Marie asks, the shock and disgust evident in her tone. The pub quietens as people start watching the commotion.

"Get your hands off her," Aiden snarls again.

He reaches for me, but I whimper, glancing over his shoulder at Marie, who steps forward. She'd be pretty if she didn't act or dress so trashy and slutty. Her bleached-blonde hair needs a break from all the chemicals, and her clothes look like they were made to fit a child. Today, she's wearing a white halter top that stops at her midriff and a short denim skirt with a silver rhino-studded, white belt. Her jewellery stands out, the gold flashing in the lights. She's covered in it; necklaces, bangles, and rings. I always wondered why she dressed like this outside of school, because at school functions, she dressed conservatively in pretty flowered dresses.

I guess her parents didn't want their daughter to bring shame to their name. There's a bitter taste in my mouth as I think of all the money they must have spent to keep her and her friends out of trouble.

"What's wrong?" Aiden asks, his forehead creasing.

"Don't speak to her. She can't hear you," Marie tells him, before cackling like she told the funniest joke.

I step even closer to Jaxon, his one hand sliding to my hip and squeezing. I welcome it. It lets me know this isn't a nightmare, that it's real.

"Bailey?"

"Why are you bothering with the deaf bitch?" Marie asks.

He glares at her. "Shut the fuck up! Never talk about her like that again."

"Are you with her?" she asks, disgust in her tone.

"Yes!" he snaps, before turning back to Jaxon. "Let her go—now."

"No. I don't think she wants me to. And that bitch is probably the reason," Jaxon snaps back.

Aiden looks confused as he glances at Marie, then back to me. "You know each other?"

Marie places her hand on his arm and I gulp, a lump forming in my throat. He shrugs her off, and her pissed off expression aims my way.

"You silly fucking cow. What have you been saying about me?" She steps forward, her arm raised, palm flat, ready to slap me. I close my eyes, waiting for the pain, but Jaxon tugs me behind him.

My eyes snap open when Marie cries out. "Let me go!"

My knees knock together when I see Aiden's arms around her, touching her. Even restraining her, she's getting more of him than I ever have.

Tears run freely down my cheeks, watching silently as his jaw clenches.

"Never raise a hand to her," he growls, before turning back to me. "Bailey, tell me what's wrong."

Finding my voice, I ask, "You know her? Are you friends?"

Marie laughs cattily from his side, her eyes raking seductively down his body. She licks her lips before her eyes narrow into slits. "Oh, we're more than friends, honey. Isn't that right, lover?"

My heart sinks, my breath freezing in my chest as my entire soul is consumed in pain like I've never felt before. Looking into her eyes, I can see the truth there—and the guilt in Aiden's.

"No!" I whisper, gasping for air.

He would be with her, someone so evil and cruel, but not give me the time of day?

I knew he wasn't a saint—he made that clear during our many conversations—but I never expected one of the women of his past to be someone like Marie. Never someone like her.

"It was before I met you," Aiden explains, still looking confused. "How do you know each other?"

"We're old friends, isn't that right, Scaly Bailey," Amy says, giggling. She's probably enjoying this—my discomfort over her using the nickname they called me when I was going through my acne stage.

Aiden looks to Marie, then to each of the other girls, his eyes rounding. "Holy fuck," he breathes out, dropping her like she'd burned him before turning to me. "I didn't know."

"That they made my life hell, killed my family, made me deaf! How could you not see it in them, Aiden? How could you not see how twisted and wrong they are?" I ask in a shrill voice, finding the courage to say the words I've never said out loud in front of people. And I've certainly never said anything to them, afraid it would anger them more.

"You lying bitch," Amy screeches, reaching for me.

I scream, feeling nails dig into my arm, but before she can do any damage, Jaxon lifts me up and carries me through the bar.

"Shh, it's okay. I've got you," he says, and I realise I'm sobbing into his shoulder.

"Bailey!" Aiden roars.

"Aiden, let the cry-baby go. She's lying. Come on, we can go back to your place," Marie says sweetly, before her voice is drowned out by the whispering of others.

"Maddox, keep that fucking bitch away from me."

Cold air hits me in the face when we make it outside. "Come on; I'll take you home."

"I can get a taxi," I whisper, my knees wobbling when he places me on the ground. He reaches out, steadying me.

"You shouldn't—"

"Bailey," Aiden cries out, running out of the bar. "I didn't know. I swear, I didn't."

Jaxon scoffs. "You've seen those bitches in action for years. They bully anyone and everyone who walks into the bar. Don't act fucking surprised that they'd do something like this."

"Stay the fuck out of it," Aiden snaps at him, before turning back to me. He reaches for me, and I pull back, stepping out of reach.

"Don't touch me!" I scream, angry at him and myself. Angry I thought things could change. That I could have something good in my life again.

But he's just like *him*.

Was he using me to get one of them into bed?

My past comes back to haunt me and I try to catch my breath, to breathe through the pain in my chest.

"Bailey, please, talk to me," he begs, taking another step forward.

Jaxon places his hand on Aiden's chest, pushing him back. "She doesn't want you near her."

Aiden turns his angry glare at Jaxon. "And who the fuck are you to tell me what she wants? You don't even know her, Jaxon."

"I know she doesn't want you talking to her."

"Bailey, please."

"I can't. I'm sorry," I tell him, not able to look his way.

When he goes to take another step towards me, Jaxon pushes him again. Aiden makes a sound deep in his chest, before punching Jaxon. I bite my lips to keep in the scream threatening to escape. Instead, I whimper, goose bumps rising on my skin.

Marie and her friends come out of the bar, taking in the chaos before them. They take one look at me and snarl. A cold shiver runs up my spine and I look away, hoping they'll disappear.

Jaxon throws Aiden into the side of a car, but Aiden doesn't even blink. He gets back up and shoves him back. "Fuck off, Jaxon," he growls, punching him in the stomach.

"This is your fault. You're gonna pay, you silly fucking slag," Marie shouts. Maddox blocks their way, saying something to them I can't hear. Her face turns pale, but there's a look in her eyes that promises retribution when she glances around him and directly at me.

Aiden throws Jaxon to the floor and steps over him, wiping blood off his lip as he moves towards me. Blinking back tears, I take two steps back, and I keep going before I turn to run home.

The last thing I see is Jaxon grabbing Aiden's ankle, tripping him to the ground.

———————————

I'M SWEATING AND panting by the time I make it back home, letting myself in like the devil is chasing me. I slam the door shut behind me, gasping for air.

"Bailey? Is that you? You're back early," Gran says as she steps out of the living room.

Seeing her, seeing my comfort, I break, a sob tearing from my throat as my knees buckle beneath me. I land on the floor with a thud, the hardwood floor bruising my skin.

"Bailey," Gran screams, kneeling in front of me. "What's happened? Abel! Abel!"

My granddad's footsteps stomp down the stairs. "Bailey, what on earth?"

I keep on sobbing into my hands but let Gran pull me into her arms.

"Darlin', you need to tell us what happened. Did he hurt you?"

I look up through watery eyes, shaking my head. "H-he—h-he knows them. He's slept with her."

"With who, Bailey? You aren't making sense."

"The girls at school," I get out, hiccupping. "He slept with Marie."

"The ring leader?" Gran asks, looking to Granddad for answers. He shrugs. "What does Aiden have to do with them?"

"I think they were an item. She was there tonight."

"Did she touch you?" Gran asks, sounding angry. "Abel, call the police."

"No!" I yell. "Don't. She just said some nasty stuff."

I wipe at my eyes, angry with myself for being so upset.

"And he slept with Marie? He doesn't seem like the kind of boy to sleep with a girl like that."

I laugh bitterly. "I got back from the loo to see her flirting with him. And they both admitted it. How could he be with someone like that, Gran? How?"

I start crying all over again, the pain in my chest becoming too much. Her warm hand rubs my back.

"If he doesn't know what a good thing he has with you, then he isn't worth it."

"He wouldn't even kiss me, but he's slept with her. What's wrong with me, Gran? What's so horribly wrong with me that the first boy I go out with used me for a dare he agreed to so he could sleep with Amy? He slept with me, took my virginity, and then told the whole school as he showed them pictures of me. Then Aiden won't even kiss me, but h-he—h-he sleeps with her. What do they have that I don't? What is wrong with me?" I cry out, feeling more tears come as I drop my head onto Gran's shoulder.

"There's nothing wrong with you," she whispers, sounding choked up.

"Nothing at all, my darlin' girl. You're a beautiful soul. I'm sure that whatever happened tonight, it was a misunderstanding," Granddad tells me.

I clutch Gran's shirt. "I'm repulsive. I must have done something in my past life that was terribly wrong because I've not done anything that deserves the luck I've had in this one. Nothing at all."

"Oh, baby," Gran soothes, holding me tighter.

Banging starts up on the door and I startle, moving away from Gran. With wide eyes, I turn to her. "I don't want to see him. If it's him—I just can't."

"Go up to your room. Me and Granddad will sort this out."

I give her a quick hug, my chest tightening when I hear Aiden calling my name through the door. I get up from the floor and rush over to the stairs. When I hear my name once more, I reach up and pull the hearing aid from my ear, welcoming the silence.

I know if I hear his pleas, I'll cave and go to him.

And for once, I need to be stronger.

To ignore the pull between us and think of me. Even if it feels like my heart is dying in the process.

NINETEEN

AIDEN

I SLAM THE PLATE DOWN ON THE hot plate harder than I intended to. "Order up," I yell, still feeling grouchy from lack of sleep.

I rub tiredly at my face, glancing at the clock once more before untying my apron. Finally, my day has come to end. With so much on my mind, time has moved slowly.

Not seeing Bailey for the past two weeks has been the cause of it. I miss her. For the short amount of time that I've known her, she's become a huge part of my life.

I've called and text multiple times a day, and even tried to see her. Her grandparents won't let me step even a foot on their front porch. Every time I try to see her, they're out the door and warning me away beforehand.

I even sunk as low as to ask Maddox for help. I wrote her a note—like a thirteen-year-old kid—and asked him to pass it on. He didn't get to see her but handed her gran the note anyway.

LISA HELEN GRAY   178

That night, two weeks ago, I really saw myself for the first time. I knew long before I found out Bailey's story and who was responsible for her pain that Marie and her posse were bad news. Any time women tried to talk to us, or if we tried to chat up another woman, they would interfere. Drinks would be spilled over them or they'd leave the bar after going to the toilet.

Now I know why.

Marie was a mistake. A big one. Had I been coherent or sober, I would never have touched her, and I've never been picky with who I've slept with.

The pickings that night must have been zilch, because I don't even remember going home with her. The second I opened my eyes the next morning, she was lying there, smudged makeup down her face, hair a bird's nest, and drooling as she snored. It was just as unattractive as she is on a normal day.

I'd got out of there as quick as I could, leaving a shoe, my boxers, and socks.

I rip off my uniform, changing into jeans and a T-shirt, still thinking of Bailey's face when I saw her across the bar. She looked like she had seen a ghost. Lily has turned pale a time or two when she's had an episode, but that was nothing compared to how Bailey looked. It was the pain, the torment and anguish in her expression… She reminded me of a little girl in that moment.

But it was nothing to the look she gave me when Marie announced we had hooked up. She had been devastated.

Stepping back into the bar, my eyes catch Maddox, Liam, and Mark, and I give them a mock salute when they wave me over. Stepping up to the bar, I give Mason, who is still working, a chin lift before taking the empty seat next to Mark.

He hands me a Corona. "You look like shit."

"Cheers. I feel it."

"Who's got Sunday if you're drinking?"

"Mum and Dad. They wanted her overnight again."

"You mean your mum did."

I force a grin. "Yep. Dad texted me earlier when I was on my break to warn me I owe him one."

Mason chuckles as he finishes wiping the bar down. "Probably pissed he's not getting any tonight."

"All right, kid hearing over here," Mark snaps.

"Be lucky Max isn't here. He'd go into detail."

I snort, because isn't that the truth.

My phone beeps, then Mark's, Maddox's, and Liam's. We all glance at each other. I pull mine out, seeing a text from Charlotte.

CHARLOTTE: Please don't be mad but the goldfish died LOL, Charlotte.

"Did Charlotte just laugh out loud over the goldfish Landon bought her dying?" Liam asks, sounding amused.

"I don't think she realises it's a group chat," Maddox says.

LILY: Why are you laughing over it?

I chuckle, amused at my sister's reply. If anyone was going to ask, it would be her.

HAYDEN: Did you cook it?

Liam groans at his sister's reply.

LIAM: You did not just say that.

CHARLOTTE: I'm not laughing. I'm crying. I named him Nemo and now he's gone. And how did you guys find out?

LANDON: You sent your message to the group chat, Charlotte. You really need to get a new phone. And why did you put LOL?

MADDOX: Bit disrespectful to the fish if you ask me. At least give it a good send off and fry it.

CHARLOTTE: That's so mean! And I don't understand.

LILY: LOL means laughing out loud, Charlotte.

CHARLOTTE: Oh, my God. I've been learning how to use acronyms.

HAYDEN: What did you think it stood for?

CHARLOTTE: I feel terrible. Nemo's going to think I hate him.

MADDOX: He's dead. I don't think he cares.

LANDON: Maddox, if you don't want to shit out teeth, shut the fuck up.

MADDOX: Yes, sir. Or will you LOL at me too?

CHARLOTTE: I'm a horrible person.

HAYDEN: What did you think it meant? LOL

CHARLOTTE: Lots of love.

LILY: LOL

MADDOX: My girl has jokes.

CHARLOTTE: Landon, can you come over and help me bury him, please?

MARK: Flush it down the loo.

CHARLOTTE: I AM NOT DOING THAT, MARK!

MADDOX: She's using shouty caps, guys. She means business.

LANDON: Fuck off, guys. I'll be there in fifteen, Charlotte.

"He's totally gonna want to flush it down the loo," Liam says, chuckling down at his phone. I put mine away, allowing myself a small laugh.

"If he doesn't eat it. Wouldn't be the first time," I mutter.

"One: that was me. Ashton bet me to eat one when we were at that house party," he says, swallowing. "Went down a treat."

"Didn't you say it wiggled?" Mark asks, straight-faced.

I chuckle, earning a glare from Liam. "Not the point. And two: why are you sitting with us? We aren't talking to you."

"Why?" I ask, wondering what I did this time.

Maddox scoffs and I glower at him, not in the mood for his theatrics.

"We've had to feed ourselves for the past two weeks, all because you're a major fuck-up. She won't even bring us lemonade anymore," he tells me, his voice going high-pitched. "And I smelled some sort of baking going on the other day."

"You've still not seen her?"

He looks at me with disgust. "No, and thanks to you, I won't ever see her again."

"When, exactly, did you sleep with Marie? That girl is nasty," Mark says.

I shove him in the shoulder. "We've all made mistakes—me obviously more than some," I snap, then gesture to Mason.

He walks over, leaning his elbows on the bar. "What?"

"Bring a bottle of whiskey or tequila over," I tell him.

He eyes me warily before sighing and grabbing a bottle. "I'm only doing this because, one time or another, your dad and the rest of us got drunk over the girl we loved."

"I'm not in love with her," I snap, snatching the bottle out of his hand.

Maddox snorts. "Yeah, right. You've been a fucking mess for two weeks. You didn't even blink when you were told you were gonna be a dad. You handled it like a pro," he tells me, taking a swig of the whiskey straight from the bottle (classy) before continuing. "But a girl gets you tied up in knots and you lose your shit. I hate to say it, man, but you've looked better. When was the last time you showered?"

Self-consciously, I smell my armpits. "I've been working in a fucking kitchen all day, jackass."

"Just admit you love her," Liam says, taking the bottle from Maddox. He takes a swig before passing it to me. I take a hefty slug, needing to drown out their voices.

"And soon. It's hard working on an empty stomach," Mark adds.

I snarl at my brother. "Cook your own damn food."

He flashes his teeth. "Why, when she cooks so much better?"

I ignore them, instead choosing to chug down more whiskey, already feeling the effects.

With every swig I keep telling myself she's just another girl; she doesn't mean anything. And with each swig, the lie tastes more and more bitter.

Because she's not some random girl. She's Bailey James, the girl who has somehow wormed her way under my skin.

She's the first thing I think about when I wake up... unless Sunday is crying, then all I think about is her.

Bailey is who I dream of at night. Who I fantasise being with. My heart beats faster whenever I'm around her.

"Holy fuck!" I breathe out, dropping my head onto the bar.

"What?" Mark says, turning his attention away from the conversation he was having with Maddox and Liam.

I lift my head, the realisation hitting me with full force, and I fight to sit up straight.

"I think I love her."

The guys laugh at my expense, Mark slapping me on the back. "And you're only just now figuring that out?"

"What am I gonna do? She hates me."

"Flowers always worked with your aunt Denny," Mason calls across the bar as he serves a beer to an old man.

The old man turns my way, clearly having listened in to our conversation. "Chocolates always worked for my Maisy."

"Are there any shops open now?" I ask, glancing outside to the darkened sky.

"Probably not," the old man says, taking his drink from the bar. "But take my advice: don't waste weeks to do the grovelling. You'll only have to work harder."

With that, he walks off, leaving me feeling more defeated than I did before.

"She's never gonna forgive me," I say, taking a large gulp of whiskey.

"She will. She doesn't seem like the type to hold a grudge," Mark says.

"I dunno. She looked fucking broken at the bar. Those girls must have done a number on her," Liam adds.

"They fucking did. I told you what she told me," I growl at him.

He holds his hands up. "And I told you I spoke to Dad. He asked Liam, Dad's mate, to look into them, see what he could dig up."

"It's not enough," I snap.

"Just go over there," Maddox says.

I glower at him, slamming the bottle on the bar. "I've tried—every goddamn day. I even tried climbing up the side of the house."

"How'd that go?" Mark asks, shuffling his stool away from me. Wise move with the mood I'm in.

My shoulders slump. "It was her grandparent's room."

Maddox laughs, slapping his knee. "Please tell me they were sleeping and not awake."

"Her gran was getting changed for bed," I tell him, loose-lipped from the booze. I hadn't told them how low I had sunk, not wanting them to give me grief over it.

"This is fucking gold," Maddox says, laughing as he pulls his phone out.

I take another swig, swaying in my chair. "You can't tell anyone."

"I won't. I promise," he says, and somewhere inside of me, I know he's lying. I just don't care right now.

"Maybe tonight isn't the best night to see her," Mason says, taking the bottle from me. I look at its nearly empty contents, my eyes widening.

"Who the fuck drank all of that?" I yell, pointing at the bottle.

"You," Mason states dryly.

"No!" I gasp, looking closer.

"Fuck, guys, make sure one of you go home with him."

"I was gonna take a chick back to mine tonight," Maddox replies.

"I don't care," Mason argues.

"Mark, you do it; he's your brother," Maddox says.

"Fine!" Mark sighs. "Come on, bro, let's get you home."

I shove him away. "I don't wanna."

"You're drunk already."

I look up at him, feeling my eyes water. "You know what? Fuck her. I don't care. She can carry on not forgiving me. Why do I care, anyway?"

"Because you love her."

"So?"

He sighs, holding me up by the shoulders when I nearly tip off the chair. "Let's just get you home. You'll regret this tomorrow when Mum drops Sunday off and she starts crying."

"My baby girl. Let's go get my baby. *She* loves me."

"Yeah, we're not gonna do that."

"I know!" I yell, holding my arm up.

Maddox leans around Mark. "We're not in school," he hisses. "Put your fucking arm down."

"Let's go egg Marie's house."

Maddox grins. "And I thought it was gonna be a boring night."

"Maddox," Mark warns.

"Don't be a party pooper," I tell him, smacking him on the shoulder.

Or was it his head?

"Fuck it, I'm in. After hearing what they did, eggs are the least they deserve."

Mark sighs. "I'll get the eggs. If you lot go into the shop, they're gonna know why you want eggs."

"To make an omelette?" I slur.

"No. Last time you accidently egged their car on the way out."

I laugh, letting him help me off the stool and onto my feet.

"I don't remember where Marie lives," I tell them.

Mark looks at Liam, who look at Maddox. Maddox holds his hands up. "Yes, I know. But only because I fucked her neighbour."

"Let's go!" I yell. "Bye, Uncle Mason."

"Get home safe," he warns from the other end of the bar, shaking his head at us. Thankfully he's been talking to another customer for the past fifteen minutes and didn't hear our plans.

"We're going to—"

Maddox slaps his hand over my mouth. "Shut it," he hisses. "He means we're going straight home—to watch some movies."

An old lady and her friend gasp. "Good heavens."

He turns to her, smiling. "We'll be watching Bambi and The Lion King, maybe some Little Mermaid."

"She's so hot for a redhead." Liam grins, earning a smack around the head from Mark.

"Bye!" I yell, waving at everyone in the bar.

"God, please don't let us get arrested tonight," Mark mutters.

TWENTY

BAILEY

CLICKING THE BUTTON ON MY REMOTE, I flick through the movie channels, trying to find something to watch. Trouble is, everything reminds me of him.

First, *Cheaper by The Dozen* came up, reminding me of him and his big family. *Look Who's Talking* was on the next channel, then *Three Men and a Baby*.

Finally, I land on some disaster movie set in Los Angeles.

Movement near my door catches my eye. I sit up in bed, grabbing my hearing aid. I've been keeping it out all week, needing the silence and relief it brings me. The few times I've had it in, he's just happened to turn up at the door. After a few days, Granddad started walking out and meeting him halfway, so I didn't have to hear him. It still didn't help. I felt like he was everywhere—I still do.

I've left my phone off, too afraid to see what he's text me. The first two I did read were him apologising, and I couldn't handle it.

"Hey, Gran, are you going out?" I ask.

She sits down on the edge of the bed, placing her hand over mine. "This isn't good for you, Bailey. You need some fresh air. Staying in bed all day…" She shakes her head sadly. "I'm worried about you."

"Gran, I'm fine. I'm just hurting. I'm sure it will pass," I lie. I don't know whether it will pass, or if the ache in my chest will go. Right now, it feels like my world has ended.

"I don't know, sweetie. It's been two weeks," she says doubtfully.

"Gran," I say, sighing, "I'll be okay."

"Good, because two pretty girls who said they were your friends are outside your door. They've brought you some cookies."

"Oh, God!" I moan, eyes wide.

He's sent his cousin to kill me.

She pats my hand and walks over to the door. "She's descent."

"Thank you, Mrs. Spencer."

"Aw, you two are such sweet girls," she tells them, a hand on each of their cheeks before dropping them and facing me. "Now, have fun. We're off now and won't be back until Monday."

I get out of bed when she walks over. Pulling me into her arms, she holds me tightly.

"Everything will be okay. Have some girl time," she whispers in my ear, before pulling away. "I'll let your granddad know you said goodbye."

"Love you, Gran."

"Love you too," she says, her hand on my cheek. She drops it before leaving us alone.

I feel my cheeks heat when I realise I'm wearing my Buffy pyjamas. I had seen re-runs on the television and got hooked. Now I've got all the merchandise you can get. Including the pyjama set I'm wearing.

"That show gives me the creeps," Charlotte mutters, staring at my shirt.

"I want to be Buffy when I grow up," Lily says wistfully.

My lips twitch into a smile. It feels foreign but so much better than the tears I've shed over the past two weeks.

"You are grown up," I tell her, sitting back down in bed.

They move over, Charlotte sitting in bed with me whilst Lily walks around the other side to jump in too. I'm surprised by them staying and how comfortable they look making themselves at home.

"Buffy is badass, though. She's strong enough that no one can hurt her," Lily says, and when I glance over, a dark look passes across her features.

"You okay?"

She shakes out of her thoughts, forcing a smile. "Yeah. I just think she's great. No one messes with her."

I think about it and have to agree. If I had the strength Buffy had when I was at school, those girls wouldn't have messed with me.

My family would be alive.

"Yeah, I can see why you would want to be her," I say softly. She squeezes my hand.

"Personally, I'd rather be one of the Originals—but be able to have a baby."

"The Originals?" I ask.

Both girls gasp. "You've never watched *The Originals* or *The Vampire Diaries?*"

"Never heard of them," I admit.

"Do you have an Amazon account?" Lily asks, grabbing my remotes.

"I do. Just click on the Fire Stick remote."

She does, and before I know it, she has *The Vampire Diaries* up on my screen.

"You have to start off with this one," she explains.

"Here, we brought you these," Charlotte says.

I gulp, taking the plate of cookies with a sick feeling in my stomach. "Um—"

"Sorry we couldn't bake you anything. It was a spur of the moment thing," Lily says softly, and my entire body relaxes against my pillows.

"You said you wouldn't say anything," Charlotte says, sounding hurt.

Lily giggles. "Sorry," she tells her, before winking at me.

I chuckle as I grab the chocolate goodness and shove one in my mouth, moaning.

"How are you doing?" Charlotte asks suddenly. "We tried to see you, but your gran said you weren't feeling well. We knew it was because of Aiden."

I force the bite of cookie down my throat. "Can we not talk about him?" I whisper.

"I'm sorry. I didn't mean to upset you," she says softly, and instantly I feel guilty.

"They abused me every chance they got; sometimes even going out of their way to find me," I blurt out.

Lily takes my hand in hers. "We've all been through some sort of bullying. Mostly from girls who thought they needed to be jealous of us because of our family. From what Hayden told me, ours was nothing compared to yours."

I let out a dry laugh. "I don't think what they did could even be called bullying, Lily. It wasn't just name-calling or cat fights. They tormented me—tortured me. I've been spat on, beaten within an inch of my life, called names, had rumours spread around school about me, and so much more. I can't prove they killed my family, but I know, with every inch of my heart, it was them."

"Aiden told the lads what happened to your parents. I hope you don't mind, but I told Lily," Charlotte says, her voice quiet and filled with emotion. "Landon told me."

I take the hand she offers, squeezing it, and close my eyes for a second. "I don't mind. It was front-page news everywhere for ages, so it's not like it's a secret. The only thing that wasn't mentioned was me and my grandparents accusing those four of setting the fire intentionally."

"You do know that if Aiden knew it was them, he wouldn't have—you know, don't you?"

"Wouldn't he?" I ask, glancing at her. "In my last year, one of the new guys at school walked up to me. I was so starved of affection, I nearly had a heart attack when he approached.

"We would meet up after school, sometimes go to the cinema, and I started to feel like a normal girl. Back then, the fact those four girls never said a word to him should have been a neon sign that something was wrong. Everyone who tried to talk to me ended up receiving the same treatment as me until they stopped. It wasn't long before everyone just stayed away. When I didn't see

Owen getting the same treatment, I thought… maybe they had stopped. They even gave me a break from the hitting, shoving, and spitting. I didn't need to hide out in the girl's loo or at the back of the school to eat my lunch. They left me alone.

"We started going out as a couple. I thought I loved him. But I think all I loved was the attention, not feeling so alone," I murmur, feeling my throat tighten from digging this all back up.

"We planned a night, when my parents were away at the cottage my grandparents own, to sleep together. He was pushy, and I didn't want to lose him; he was the only friend I had. The first day back at school—after not hearing from him all weekend—I was ridiculed in the halls. Lads were laughing at me; girls were slut-shaming me; and pictures were pinned up on the walls. Of me. Naked in my bed. He took them after I fell asleep. I thought maybe one of the girls who had bullied me had stolen his phone, using that as an excuse as to why he never called me back.

"I went into the breakroom, where I knew he would be, and found Marie sitting in his lap. She grinned at me when I walked in. She held up a voice recording of us together and played it. He didn't even care. He got to fuck a virgin and be with the most popular girl in school," I tell them, wiping under my eyes.

"Aiden isn't Owen, Bailey. He's a lot of things, but he'd never do that to anyone," Lily declares softly.

I look up at her. "She was sitting in front of him. It reminded me of that day at school. The worst thing—the thing that hurt the most—was the fact he won't even kiss me, but he's slept with her. She's ugly inside—and it shines brightly on the outside. How could he not see that?"

"I don't know the full details. I can't even tell you why. But he does care," Charlotte tells me.

"Just not enough," I whisper.

"You're always enough," Lily whispers back.

Charlotte rests her head on my shoulder, her hand still in mine. "You just have to believe."

Lily wraps her arms around me, and like always, I seek the affection offered to me, resting my head on her shoulder as we watch their show.

———————————

YAWNING, I CLEAN UP the last of the mess in the kitchen. When Charlotte had to leave during the third episode, Lily decided to stay and we had a late dinner together.

When I saw it was getting late, I sent her home, not liking the thought of her travelling alone in the dark.

It's been good having them here. Not only for my soul but my sanity. Having friends is a new concept to me, one I like having.

I've noticed Lily doesn't talk about herself too much, preferring to talk about others in her life. She talked about her cats, the children she teaches, but nothing really personal.

I've just finished wiping down the side when there's a noise at the front door. I glance around the doorframe, down the darkened hallway, and frown.

The scuffing noise against the door happens again, so I move closer to investigate.

"You do realise the person who investigates always gets murdered," I hiss to myself, my entire body shaking.

I glance through the peephole, but don't see anything, wishing I hadn't left my mobile upstairs. If this is Marie and her friends, there is no one here to witness what may happen, or help me. I quickly run back down the hallway, into the kitchen and through the conservatory, to make sure the backdoor is locked. I sag with relief when I find it is, before moving back into the kitchen, locking that door too.

A loud band against the front door has a squeak falling past my lips. I rush back down hallway, sweat beading at the back of my neck.

I glance through the peephole again and gasp at the sight of a large form bending over. I push away from the door when Aiden pops his head up, like he heard me.

What is he doing here?

He knocks on the door, and I weigh my options. I could ignore him and hope he goes home. But as I look through the peephole once more, my chest hurting at seeing his face for the first time in weeks, I can see something is wrong. He's swaying on his feet, reaching for something on the ground.

Ignoring my better judgement, I open the door.

"Aiden?"

He quickly grabs something from the ground and my eyes widen at the sight of one of the plant pots my gran placed at the bottom of our path. She said it would make it look presentable until we have the gardening company come in next week to lay the fresh grass and plant new flowers in the flower beds. To me, they just looked out of place, but she's not a woman you argue with.

Why Aiden has one has baffled me.

"I brought you flowers," he slurs, wobbling towards me.

"They're from my garden," I tell him, confused by his behaviour. Why is he turning up here drunk? Did something happen? Where is Sunday? They're all questions I have no right to ask, or receive answers to, but I can't help but want to know.

I miss him. So much.

"The shop was closed," he tells me. At least that's what I think he was trying to say; it didn't come out right.

He goes to hand me the flowers, but before I can reach it, the pot slips from his fingers and smashes on the doorstep. Dirt and broken pottery cover my feet, and I wince.

"Who moved the table?"

"Aiden, there wasn't a table," I groan, moving into the house. When I hear him step in behind me, I turn back around. "Stay there. Do not walk dirt into my gran's house."

He salutes me. "I want to talk to you, Bailey."

"Let me get a dustpan and brush," I tell him, moving quickly through the kitchen and into the laundry room. I grab the dustpan and brush, and a black bag, before walking back down to Aiden, finding him sitting against the door, his head flopping forward.

Sighing, I sweep up as much as I can get and drop the bag of dirt and pottery just outside the house.

Stepping back inside, I lock the door behind me and bend down so I'm face to face with Aiden. it hurts to look at him. He has dark circles under his eyes, and it doesn't look like he's shaved for a few days.

"Need to tell her," he mumbles.

I go to help him up, but my hand is met with something slick and wet. I pull my hand back, revulsed as I look down at the gooey mess. "Um, Aiden, why do you have egg all over you?"

He looks up at me, his boyish smile popping out as laughs. "I accidently threw them on myself," he says, before his faces scrunches up. "That's what Maddox said anyway. I think he threw them at me."

"He threw them at you?"

He nods, smiling wide. "You're here."

He reaches out to touch my face, but I grab his wrist before he can. "Yes, but I want to know why you're here."

"I needed to see you," he says, his expression turning sad.

"We've got nothing to say to each other," I whisper painfully.

"I love you, Bailey. I'm sorry—I'm sorry for everything."

My breath freezes in my lungs at hearing him say those three words to me. I've dreamt, over and over for the past two weeks that he would tell me he loved me. Not like this though. Not drunk.

My eyes fill with tears, and I try hard to keep the emotion out of my voice when I answer.

"Let's talk about this when you're sober."

Or never.

"No. I need to tell you. You need to forgive me," he slurs, grabbing my arms. I nearly topple over but manage to stay upright.

"Let's get you home."

"I don't want to go home," he tells me, before pulling me against him. I fall on top of him, my face meeting a gooey surface, and cringe. "You smell so good."

"I smell like eggs now," I mutter unhappily.

"Hmm, I could eat an egg sandwich," he hums, squeezing me.

I pry myself out of his hold and take his face in my hands, trying to get him to look at me. When it's clear he's in no fit state to go home, I realise I have a choice to make.

He either goes home and chokes on his own vomit, or he stays here— where I can keep an eye on him.

I already know what the answer is, but the war inside my heart still rages on. It's so hard to be in front of him, especially when he's telling me things I've desperately wanted to hear.

"Come on; you can stay here," I tell him, helping him to his feet.

"I love you, Bailey."

A sharp pain shoots through me once more, but I fight through it, helping him over to the sofa. His weight bares down on me, and my legs threaten to give out more than once before we reach the sofa.

He flops down, closing his eyes. "Stop spinning the damn room," he chokes out.

I lie him down. "The room isn't spinning; it's you."

"You make my world spin," he says, his eyes opening and landing on me. Trapped in his intense gaze, I don't see his hand reaching for my face until it's too late. He cups my cheek, running his thumb smoothly over it. I close my eyes, willing the emotions running through me to disappear. They don't. And when I open them, his gaze burns through me. "Soft," he murmurs. "I love you, Bailey. And I need you to forgive me. You've wormed your way under my skin and I can't forget about you. I've tried. I've tried so goddamn hard."

"Right back at ya," I mutter under my breath so he doesn't hear me.

"Why do you have egg on your face? Is it a new face mask?" He yawns, his eyes drooping.

I wipe the disgusting egg yolk from my face and glare at him. "No, it isn't."

"Do you forgive me?"

I ignore him—as painful as it may be—and get up. "I'm going to get you a bowl, a glass of water, and some paracetamol. You're going to need it."

"I only need you. Just you. I didn't know what I was missing until you came into my life. You and Sunday," he says, slowly drifting off. "You and Sunday. You." He yawns. "Make my life." He sighs. "Complete."

With one last yawn, he drifts off, and I finally let the tears fall. I get up and head to the kitchen for supplies, before returning to him with a bowl of warm water. He's still lying at an awkward angle, so I grab his legs and lift them onto the sofa, then take off his trainers. He mutters my name under his breath, and the tears fall harder.

He isn't making this easy on me. It was already hard for me to get over someone I never really had, but to have him come here and tell me he loves me… He's made it impossible.

After removing his shoes, I grab the cloth from the bowl and start cleaning down his face.

Wait, is that a tyre mark on the side of his face?

At first glance, it looks like dirt, but on closer inspection… it's definitely a tyre mark.

"What the hell did you do tonight?" I muse out loud.

I wipe it off the best I can before moving onto the egg on his clothes. It would be better if I could take his jacket off, but he's dead to the world. I'd need a crane to move him right now.

A puff of air escapes his plump lips, and my eyes are immediately drawn to them. He looks so peaceful right now, no longer bleary-eyed and drunk.

Finishing up, I place the cloth back in the bowl before drying him the best I can with the tea towel.

I run my fingers through his hair, and before I can stop myself, I lean forward, placing a gentle kiss on his forehead. I close my eyes against the array of emotions running through me, unable to handle them. They're consuming me, just like my love for the guy in front of me.

He says I've wormed my way under his skin, that I complete his world, but he's so off balance and so utterly wrong. It's he who makes *my* world complete.

He fills it with family, friends, and love. He brought me laughter when I didn't have a reason to laugh. He fills my heart with hope. He brought me a future I felt was worth living.

He brought me peace.

"I love you too," I whisper back, tears running down my cheeks and landing on his face.

Heaven help me, I think I can forget he slept with the enemy. He didn't need my forgiveness. There was nothing to forgive.

And tomorrow, when he wakes up, I will tell him that. Because if the last two weeks have taught me anything, it's that my life is dull and gloomy without him in it.

I just hope he makes it through the night without choking on his own vomit.

TWENTY-ONE

AIDEN

WITH BLEARY EYES, I SIT UP, clutching my head. I groan, feeling like someone's taken a sledgehammer to my brain.

How much did I drink last night?

And why can I smell eggs? I sniff myself and gag. Standing up, I go to rush to the loo but realise I'm not even in my apartment.

How did I get to Bailey's?

With no time to ask questions, I grab the vase from the side table, throw the flowers out, and vomit. Whiskey burns as it rises up my throat.

Fuck! It tastes just as bad coming up as it did going down.

Memories from the night before assault me. I remember throwing an egg towards Marie's house but hitting Maddox in the head. I think he was trying to let down her tyres—I'm not sure. The whole scene is blurry. I do remember him getting pissed and throwing eggs at me. And I think I dropped one on myself.

I heave again, fluid pouring out my mouth.

Oh, God, someone kill me.

I sit back down on the couch, a wave of dizziness hitting me.

"Do you have something against my gran's flowers?" Bailey's sweet voice calls as she walks in.

I look up at her, wincing at how bright it is in here. She looks tired. I inwardly smile. Does that mean she's missed me as much as I've missed her?

"Are you going to keep staring at me or answer?" she asks, handing me a cup of coffee. I put the vase down, greedily taking it from her. I moan in appreciation when the strong coffee burns my tongue. If I'm going to survive today, I need caffeine.

My voice is hoarse when I speak. "What did you ask?"

"The flowers," she muses, glancing down at the floor. I wince when I see the flowers I dumped there, and the clear vase filled with brown liquid.

"I'm sorry. It was either the vase or the floor."

"You also smashed my gran's flower pot outside."

I cringe. "I'm so fucking sorry. How did I get here? Did I do or say something stupid?"

She flinches like I just slapped her. *What the hell?*

"Nothing that matters. Did you want some breakfast before you have to go?"

She's letting me stay?

Wait! Go! That means she's just being polite about breakfast and wants me gone.

"Bailey, I'm really fucking sorry for what happened. I really am. Marie…" I grimace; even her name tastes bitter on my tongue, making me want to vomit all over again. "It's no excuse, and it's a lame one at that, but it's the truth—"

"You don't have to talk about her," she rushes out, sitting on the arm of the sofa opposite.

Rubbing the back of my neck, I shrug. "I need to. It was only one time— one time I don't even remember." I let out a bitter laugh. "God, that makes me sound even more of a jerk," I tell her, feeling hopeless. I feel like I've already lost her. "I was so drunk that night. Her and her friends have always tried it on with me and my family, but we've never given them the time of day. I don't know why; it was just something about them. I just need you to know I would never have given her the time of day had I not been drunk to the point the whole night was a blur."

"You don't have to explain anything to me, Aiden. I overreacted. My past with them isn't exactly pretty. I shouldn't have taken it out on you. Seeing her next to you brought back some painful memories."

"What do you mean?" I ask, focusing her.

I listen to her as she explains what happened in school—the lad called Owen. Anger boils through me as she replays everything he did to her.

I want to kill him.

"Now you know," she whispers, looking ashamed.

I get up from the sofa, my footing unsteady at first. Her eyes are round as I walk towards her. I cup her face, relishing in the way her eyes close and she leans into my touch.

"I'm so fucking sorry," I painfully choke out. "So, so fucking sorry."

She stands, her cheeks bright red. "I'm really sorry for the way I reacted. And that you got hurt," she says, her fingers running over the fading bruise on my cheek.

"Don't be. It kept me from hitting a girl for the first time in my life. After I realised who they were, I wanted to strangle them."

Most girls would be repulsed, but if anything, her gaze softens as she chuckles softly. "It might make me a bad person saying this, but they would have deserved it."

I lean forward, ready to kiss her for the first time. There's no hesitation inside me, no what ifs. Bailey is what I want.

She ducks out of the way, and my ego takes a massive hit. She looks at me with disgust. "You stink of vomit and rotten eggs."

I get a whiff of what she's smelling and wince. "Shit! Yeah, um… sorry."

She giggles. "Just so you know, I would have kissed you back."

I grin, staring into her ocean-blue eyes. "You would?"

She nods. "Totally."

"I've missed you."

Her expression saddens. "I've missed you too."

"Bailey, I—"

She presses her finger against my lips, stopping me from telling her I love her.

"Don't say anything—not yet," she whispers, her eyes misty. "Go home and shower first, at least."

She's not giving up on me.

My chest expands with hope. "I need to get Sunday from Mum and I want you to come with me. After, we can take her to the park before dropping her back off. 'Cause tonight, I'm cooking you dinner."

"You are?" she asks, her voice teasing.

I'd pull her against me, but I really do stink. She's brave being as close as she is; I smell like Maddox's feet.

And they reek.

"I am. So, will you spend the day with me and Sunday and your night with me cooking and us watching a movie?"

She grins. "I'd love to."

"Good."

I hand her back the coffee cup and make my way towards the front door. Standing on the threshold, I turn back to her, finding her still watching me with a cute, goofy smile on her face.

I smirk, raking my eyes up and down her body. "By the way, cute pyjamas."

I laugh at her expression and step through the door. My feet crunch on something below my feet, and I frown, staring down at layer of dirt and small pieces of broken pottery.

I pop my head back inside. "And you really should clean this up. You'll have people traipsing dirt through your house."

"You did that!" she snaps.

"I did?"

"Yes, now go—before I change my mind."

"Not before you explain how I did this," I demand playfully. I look around to see what could have done it, but there's nothing but a black bag out here.

Maybe she just thinks it was me because of the whole smelling of egg thing.

She throws a pair of trainers at me, and they look a lot like mine. I duck before they can hit me and glance down at my feet, realising they are, in fact, my trainers. I laugh, picking them up. "Okay, okay; I'm going."

"Bye," she calls out as I make my way across the garden, walking backwards so I'm facing her. She's standing in the doorway, clutching the doorframe.

"Be ready in thirty minutes," I tell her.

"Why? You take an hour just to do your hair."

I chuckle. "Ah, girl has jokes."

"Not a joke if it's the truth," she sasses back.

I smirk, blowing her a kiss before rushing up the stairs, self-consciously touching my hair. Bits of it are rock-hard.

Just how many times did Maddox egg me?

I step inside my apartment and hear my phone ringing from the sofa. I quickly grab it, answering the call.

"Hello?"

"Good, you're alive. I've been worried sick about you all morning. Did you know Maddox got dropped off at Lily's by the police last night? I thought something had happened to you when I couldn't get in touch," my mum rants.

"He did?" I ask, thinking back to the two bottles of vodka we bought when we picked up the eggs.

"Yes. He was half-naked and swimming in the outdoor pool."

Huh. "What outdoor pool?"

"The one at the leisure park."

"Isn't that a fifteen-minute drive?"

Mum sighs. "Yes. Evidently, your brother told the taxi driver that address as a prank. He just couldn't remember if you were still in the taxi with Maddox or not, so they've been looking for you all morning."

"Wait, so Mark gave the taxi driver the leisure centre's address?" I ask, then burst out laughing. "Why the hell did Maddox go in there?"

"He was drunk, Aiden, so who knows."

"I'm gonna ring him," I tell her, still chuckling.

"Okay. I just wanted to make sure you were safe and well."

"Is Sunday okay?" I ask before she ends the call.

"She's fine, Aiden," Mum muses. "But her dad sounds rough."

I chuckle. "I feel it." I admit. "I'll be by soon to pick up Sunday. Are you still okay to have her again tonight?"

"Of course I am. I've loved having her here."

"I love you, Mum. Won't be long."

"Love you too, son."

We end the call, and instead of getting in the shower, I dial Maddox, a smile on my face, laughter ready burst free.

"What the fuck do you want?" he grouches.

"Morning, sunshine," I cheer into the phone, enjoying his pained groan that follows.

"You're a bastard."

"Mum and Dad were married before they conceived me, so technically, I'm not bastard," I rattle off, moving into my bedroom. I put him on loudspeaker, dropping my phone on the bed so I can strip out of my top.

"Twat!" he groans, and I hear shuffling through the phone. "I'm gonna kill Mark when I see him."

"Where did Liam go?"

"It gets foggy after the first bottle of vodka, but he left to get more eggs. I spoke to him this morning."

"And he didn't return?"

Maddox lets out a throaty chuckle. "No. He was breaking into Charlotte's house 'cause the shop was closed. He knew she has them stocked like the world is gonna end tomorrow."

I laugh. "What happened?"

"Landon happened. He was halfway through the kitchen window when Landon pulled him through by his T-shirt and started beating him up. He's a little sore this morning."

I sit on the edge of my bed in my boxers, clutching my stomach as I laugh. It reminds me of the time he snuck back home after leaving to go to his mates' in the middle of the night. He got drunk, and on his way back in, he bumped into the dishes drying on the draining board, smashing a few plates in the process. My uncle Max thought someone was trying to rob him and sprayed him in the face with hairspray. He never snuck out again.

"Mum said you went swimming. Why the fuck did you go inside?"

He groans. "I don't even remember. The last thing I recall is Mark calling a taxi, and then the police taking me home."

"Wish we could have recorded you doing this."

"Fuck you. And I bet you did something stupid last night."

I grin. "Nope. Unless you count crashing on Bailey's couch stupid—which I don't—then no."

"And you didn't say anything or do anything?" he asks, like he doesn't believe me.

"Maddox, trust me; I can handle my drink way better than you. I didn't do shit. She would have said something," I tell him.

"Yeah right. Anyway, I'm off to sleep. I need to get rid of this hangover," he says. "Is it a hangover if you're still pissed?"

"I dunno," I admit. "I'll speak to you later. I'm going to get ready. I've got a date with Bailey."

"What? She forgave you?"

I feel lighter than I have in weeks when I answer him. "Yes."

"If you say so. Be careful; women fight dirty. She's probably waiting for you to lower your guard before she cuts your dick off."

"Bailey isn't like that," I snap.

Is she?

She wouldn't do that to me, right?

"No one thought Hayden was like that but look how sweet she is before she turns into a piranha."

"That's Hayden. If lads fall for her bullshit, that's their fault. Bailey isn't like that."

"All women are like that. Remember Charlotte—Charlotte, who wouldn't kill a fly, but we caught shoving muffins down that bloke's throat?"

Thinking about the guy who fucked Faith over makes my blood boil.

"I wasn't there, remember?"

"Oh shit! You were making Sunday," he muses. "Well, you should have been there. I thought she was going to suffocate him with her muffins."

"That sounds so wrong," I tell him.

"It does if you haven't tasted one of her muffins," he grouches. "Now fuck off, I need my beauty sleep."

"You need more than sleep to make your ugly mug beautiful."

"Screw you, dickhead. Speak to you tomorrow—or next week."

I laugh into the phone. "Bye."

Before the call ends, he mutters, "Fucking morning people."

TWENTY-TWO

BAILEY

MEETING AIDEN'S PARENTS FORMALLY for the first time wasn't as hard as I thought it would it be. His mum was as lovely as I remembered her to be. The day she laid me down in Aiden's bed to rest, she treated me as if I was a part of the family. It was nice.

His dad, although scarily intimidating with his tattoos and brooding expression, wasn't actually as grouchy as he came across, either. I could see he loved his son and granddaughter. I also got to meet another one of his cousins—Ciara. She seemed down to earth, just like the rest of his family.

Walking along the path in the park, I struggle with what to say to Aiden. It wasn't uncomfortable this morning when he woke up, so I'm not understanding why it is now. Everything had seemed fine when he left to shower and change.

It wasn't until he picked me up that the conversation felt forced. He jumped every time I moved or spoke, and I'm worried that throwing his shoes at him has scared him somehow.

It's like dealing with a traumatised kid.

I'd spent most of the night watching him sleep, making sure he didn't choke on his vomit. Not having enough sleep has affected my mood, which isn't helping my paranoia. I'm tired and cranky and won't have time for a nap since he's planned to spend the whole day with me. And there is no way I'm going to risk him changing his mind, just so I can sleep. Sleep can wait until tonight.

But I can't take the awkward silence anymore. It's killing me. I've been surrounded by silence for years, and he filled it with laughter and noise. There have even been moments over the last two weeks when I've taken my hearing aid out and still silently longed to hear his voice. Now, I'm getting nothing. Not a word. Just awkward glances and a wide berth.

"Your mum is really amazing," I tell Aiden. He pulls the pushchair to a stop in front of a pond scattered with ducks and swans.

"She is," he says, sitting down on the bench.

Inwardly groaning, I sit down next him, seeing him glance at me warily from the corner of his eye and shift along the bench.

That's it. I need to know what the fuck is going on. Because I know for a fact I don't stink. I checked when he got out of the car.

"Have I done something to upset you?"

He jumps, grimacing. "Shit!" he whispers. "Sorry. It's just Maddox and something he said."

"Something he said?"

Turning his body towards me, his face is filled with worry. "Do you really forgive me? Are we really okay?"

"Of course, we're okay," I say a little loudly, wondering what has brought this on. *Has he changed his mind and only wants to be friends now?* "And I told you there was nothing to forgive you for. You didn't sleep with her whilst knowing who she was, and even if you did, it's no business of mine to tell you what to do."

"And you mean it? You aren't lying so that you can chop my balls off in my sleep or something?"

Eyebrows raised, I reply. "Um, no. Why would I lie to you?"

Did I miss a conversation we had or something? Because this has come out of nowhere.

"Fucking Maddox," he groans, scrubbing his face.

"Maddox? What does Maddox have to do with this?"

"Nothing. Just filling my head with crap," he says, closing his eyes briefly.

"Tell me what he said."

His eyes meet mine. "He's just being Maddox. I don't even know why I listened to him," he says, then explains what Maddox said.

"You really think I'm that vindictive?"

"No. But he has a way of making you believe what he says," he explains, looking ashamed.

I grin. "So, if he told you a leopard was on the loose, you'd believe him?"

He chuckles, nodding. "Don't mock me. Just wait until he does it to you. He gets so animated—so excited over what he's saying you have no reason not to believe him."

"Oh, I can believe it."

"I'm sorry. I'm an idiot. I'm new to all of this and I royally fucked up," he says, a little red-faced.

I place my hand over his, resting between us on the bench, and gently squeeze. "It's fine," I tell him, fighting back a sigh. "Can we just forget about that night at the pub, please?"

"Why?" he asks, looking up from our joined hands sharply.

"Because I don't want you to keep having to say you're sorry. I let all the hurt they've caused—the stuff they *did*—boil up inside me, and I took it out on you."

"Mum always says you hurt the ones you love the most," he whispers.

Our eyes lock in an intense stare, neither of us fighting to look away.

"So they say," I whisper back.

A bird flies low, shooting between us, squawking and breaking our connection. Aiden shakes his head before reaching under the pushchair for the bag of bread his mum put in for him. It brings a smile to my face when I think of her handing it to him, saying she had already ripped the bread up. Aiden had blushed like a little boy whilst his dad laughed and teased him, offering to cut his crusts off his sandwich.

"Do you want to feed some ducks?"

Finally feeling like things are good between us again, I nod. "Why don't you take Sunday a little closer. When the ducks come, I'll take a photo for you. You should have a keepsake for her first day in the park."

He grins. "I never even thought of doing that. I've been filling out the baby book Mum and Dad bought me, but she's not old enough for most of it yet."

"At least you can add this one to the album; her first day at the park," I tell him.

He smiles back at me as he pushes the pushchair closer to the pond, before throwing bread around the front of the pushchair.

"Not that close," I shriek in warning, my hand ready with the camera.

But it's too late.

I snap a picture just as birds, ducks, and swans flock around him, his mouth agape and his eyes filled with horror.

"Aiden," I cry out, taking a step towards him, but a bird nearly hitting me stops me in my tracks.

He screeches like a banshee when one of the pigeon's land on top of the pushchair. Frantically, he tries to knock it off, but the stubborn bird isn't having it. None of them are. "Shoo, you fucking vermin."

A swan pecks his leg and he howls, his wide, panicked eyes finding mine. My mouth is agape, wondering who fed them steroids and speed. They're all acting insane, like they haven't been fed in weeks.

"Get her out of here," he yells as the bag of bread tears a little.

All at once, they gravitate towards him and the bread, moving slowly away from Sunday. Rushing over, I reach for her pushchair and pull her away from the herd of crazy-ass birds.

Aiden's arms start failing around, trying to fend them off, but it's no use. He has something they want, and it doesn't look like they're going to stop until they get it.

I place my hand over my mouth to smother the roaring laughter escaping my chest. He screams louder, tripping over a massive swan, who doesn't like not being fed and starts pecking Aiden relentlessly.

"Run!" he screams before, turning back to a swan. "Get off me!"

I watch as he tries to fight them off, but more come from the water and head directly for him. I can barely see Aiden as they jump all over him, only hearing his screeches of pain.

"Aiden," I warn when he crawls closer to the water.

I shouldn't laugh, but it's hard not to.

The bag of bread in his hand catches my eye. "Oh, my God, throw the bread!"

He looks up at me through the flock of birds before he tilts his head up, his gaze landing on the bag of bread above his head, still clutched tightly in his fist. Most of the bag has ripped, and when he throws it, bread lands all over the place.

They all move away, assaulting the bread like they've never been fed. I find Aiden getting back up, wiping down his jeans and blowing out a breath. I'm just about to tell him there's a piece of bread on his shoulder when two swans lunge for him.

He screams, stepping backwards and holding his hand out like he's trying to tame them. But it's no use. There's no stopping them, and I see the second he realises that when his eyes widen and his skin pales, panic clearly setting in.

"Aiden," I scream, ready to rush over, but it's too late. His gaze meets mine as he falls, his arms flapping around in wide circles—like that's going to stop him from falling. He lands on his back in the water, the loud slap making me wince. "Holy shit!"

He comes up spluttering, wiping water from his face and hair. I quickly snap another picture, laughter bursting free.

"It's not funny," he growls, trying to get out of the water. He gets halfway out before slipping back in, and a disgruntled growl escapes him.

"Oh, it really is," I tell him, laughing even harder when ducks begin swimming over to him. His face is a picture, only making the entire incident funnier.

He looks out at the water, his eyes wide at seeing more ducks coming for him. I've never seen anyone move as quickly as he does then, scrabbling to get out of the water and out of the line of fire.

He rushes over to us, grabbing the handles of the pushchair in one hand and taking my hand in his other.

"You're making this worse by laughing, you know," he mutters as we rush back down the path, water squishing around in his trainers. They squeak, and I struggle to breathe through my giggling. It's so funny.

"I'm sorry," I say. "But you just got attacked by ducks."

He stops at the gates, facing me, his entire face bright red. Tiny little marks cover his face, neck, and arms, and his shirt is ripped on the shoulder in two places. "Did you see the size of that swan? And when he spread its wings out at me? He was going to eat me," he screeches, glancing towards the pond as if he's afraid they can hear him. "I'm calling the council. They have psycho birds and it's not safe for kids."

I look down at Sunday, sleeping soundly. "She's fine."

He glares at me. "*I'm* fucking not."

"Aww, poor baby."

His glare intensifies. "Not a word of this to anyone."

"How are you going to explain being soaked to your mum?"

"I'll tell her I was getting something for Sunday?"

"What? A fish?"

His eyes narrow into slits. "Yes—no—I don't know! I'll think of something when we get there. I'll have to borrow some of Dad's clothes."

I lean in a little, sniffing him. "And take a shower, 'cause you smell worse than the eggs this morning."

He groans. "Can we forget about all of this? We can start over and do something else," he says, sounding pitiful. "Just not at this park," he quickly adds.

"I heard the ducks are bigger in Hetsford."

His head swivels slowly to face me, his mouth agape and eyes round in terror. "Never, and I mean never, mention ducks again. I'll be surprised if I can have more kids after today." He storms off, his clothes dripping a trail of water behind him. I giggle and take another photo.

I'm totally showing his mum and dad.

I might even send it to Lily and Charlotte.

"What do you mean?" I ask, running to catch up with him.

We head towards his mum's, and he sticks his nose up at any people who dare to stare at him. He waits until no one is around before leaning down, his eyes filled with sadness and pain. "One of them kept going for my dick. I swear, it was like that Woody the Woodpecker toy that pecks all the way down the tree until it reaches the bottom. But instead of it moving, it stayed in one place. That shit hurt, even with jeans on."

He looks around with wide eyes, a pink tinge to his cheeks. I stop walking to hold onto the wall when laughter bubbles free. I laugh so hard my side hurts and I have to bend down on my knees to stop myself from peeing my pants.

He walks back until he's beside me. "Will you get up? You're drawing attention to us," he hisses out.

Say's the person still dripping water everywhere.

I look up, blinking away the drop of water from his T-shirt that lands in my eye, and laugh harder.

"Oh, my God," I gasp out. "I can't breathe." I wipe away the tears on my cheeks, trying hard not to picture his face when the birds attacked. But I do, and it only gets harder to stop laughing.

"Fucks sake," he growls, before bending down and picking me up. I lean against him for support. "I go through a traumatic experience and you're laughing. My remains would have been fish food."

I look up through tears of laughter. "Fish food?"

He rolls his eyes before walking off. More composed than before, I follow him, but as people stare, it's hard not to be reminded of what just happened.

"Jump on my back," he calls back to me. I'm still laughing like a hyena, and that comment has me sobering, looking at his back in bewilderment.

"What? Why?"

He stops to look back at me. "Because my boxers are chafing my balls and you're taking your sweet-ass time."

"Then I'll be wet," I tell him, wiping my cheeks.

His eyes dilate, darkening with hunger. "Really?"

I roll my eyes. "I promise to behave."

"No way in hell. Get on my back or I'm carrying you over my shoulder."

"You wouldn't."

"Try me," he warns, smirking. "If you don't, I'll make a big scene out of it."

"You've got Sunday," I remind him.

"I'm a mum *and* dad now. I can multitask like a pro."

A step back and he charges, bending at the waist and lifting me over his shoulder. I scream.

"Put me down!"

He slaps my arse. "Stop asking me to spank you," he yells. "There are children present."

I can feel my face redden, and it's not from hanging upside down. "Aiden!"

"Gonna jump on my back?" When I don't answer, he smacks me again. "Stop feeling me up in public. You can wait for S.E.X. later tonight when the baby is sleeping."

I look up and see an old couple weeding their garden. They narrow their eyes in disgust, shaking their heads. A man walking away from his van just grins at us.

"Okay. You win. I'll get on your back."

He lets go of the pushchair and slides me down his body. A shiver of desire runs through me. I swallow past the lump in my throat, but never break eye contact.

When he cups the side of my face, I sigh, longing to close my eyes but also not wanting to break the moment.

"I can't wait to get you alone."

"Let's go, then," I tell him, sounding breathless. I move around him, and without wasting time, place my hands on his shoulders and jump. I wrap my legs around him, squealing when he bounces me higher up his back.

"This position will be fun later," he flirts.

My core heats. I bring my mouth to his ear. "Got to get me home first," I whisper.

I laugh when he picks up speed, every so often stopping to lift me back up from where I've slid down.

I've not fought my attraction towards him. I'm not one to play games—I was never taught or shown how. And even if I had grown up differently, I still truly believe I'd crave him just as much as I do now.

To some people, that might make me sound easy. But I'm not. I trusted him the very first moment I saw him. It helped that he says what he thinks. He doesn't sugar-coat things.

It feels like I've waited a long time to have him.

And tonight, I will.

TWENTY-THREE

AIDEN

I FINISH DISHING UP THE MEATBALLS and spaghetti before heading into the
front room. I'd left Bailey to set up the surround sound for the latest
Jurassic Park movie. When I walk in, she's typing away on her phone,
giggling quietly.

"Who's texting you?"

She jumps, dropping her phone on the sofa. "Shit. You scared me."

Just then, my phone vibrates, then beeps in my jeans. I glare at her, gasping
in shock. "You didn't!"

She bites her bottom lip. "Didn't what?"

I set the plates down on the table before pulling my phone out. Two pictures
come through; one is of me, right before I plunged into the pond.

It took me a shower at Mum's and a shower at home before I got all the
grime and slime off me.

I think I even swallowed some of the water. I shudder as I look at the picture, flashbacks happening.

And if that wasn't humiliating enough, the next picture is of an innocent-looking duck.

This duck is wanted for questioning over an incident that happened at The Pond park earlier today. He is known to be violent, so please do not approach. Man is said to be in critical condition.

MADDOX: Charlotte posted this on Facebook. I called Aunt Teagan; she verified this is true. I'm laughing so hard right now.

LANDON: LMFAO. This made me laugh.

ME: ARSEHOLES! And you don't know how to laugh—stop lying. And the picture was taken out of context.

MADDOX: She has another picture of the epic fall into the pond. Ask Bailey to record it next time.

I look up from my phone and glare at Bailey. She happily ignores me. "I'm going to get a glass of wine. I'll grab you a beer."

I sit down on the sofa, wondering how I'm going to get out of this one.

LANDON: I think he's crying.

MARK: Mum said he had tears running down his face when he got back.

ME: It was fucking water!!!

ME: And those birds were on fucking speed and steroids. They attacked me.

LANDON: You gonna file a report?

ME: FUCK YOU! And when the fuck did Charlotte get Facebook?

LANDON: She wanted to make sure people knew how violent the ducks were, so started up an account.

MADDOX: And a group to make people aware.

ME: Please tell me you're not serious!

MARK: She'll be adding you soon. She's trying to figure out how to work it.

LANDON: On my way to help her.

ME: I don't believe you.

Mark sends a link through. I click on it and it directs me to a group on Facebook. Over four thousand people are already members. The group's name has me groaning. *Dangerous Ducks Attack Local.* I scroll down to the description, and in detail is the entire ordeal.

I'm going to kill Bailey.

My phone continues to blast with messages, so I quickly flick it on vibrate.

She walks in, humming to herself. I grab my plate of food, sulking.

"You okay?"

My fork pauses midway to my mouth at her words. I place it down on my plate, turning to look at her. She sucks a string of spaghetti into her mouth, moaning.

I lick my lips, shifting on the sofa.

I forget about the whole Facebook dilemma and concentrate on those lips and the sounds escaping her.

"This is so good," she mumbles, moaning again.

My dick tightens in my pants.

I clear my throat. "By any chance did you send Charlotte a picture from today?"

She blinks innocently. "Yeah, she wanted to see Sunday's first day at the park."

"Really?" I comment dryly.

Her face brightens. "Yeah. I told her about the bird incident, too. Why?"

"And who made the graphics out of those pictures?" She loses her composure and starts giggling. Then it clicks. "Wait, that was what you were doing in your office while I showered?"

She wipes under her eyes, straightening herself up. "Sorry, but I couldn't pass up the opportunity."

"She's put it all over Facebook," I yell, hurt by her laughter. "And set up a group. Did you tell her to put it on Facebook?"

She chuckles. "No. I was just hoping she'd send it to your family."

I raise my eyebrow at her. "She did."

"How many friends does she have?" she asks, her eyes lit with amusement.

"I don't know. She didn't have it before today. Our parents were strict on the girls not using social media because of cyberbullying and that. When they left school, all of them opened accounts but Lily and Charlotte. She's gonna read that, *What's on your mind?* status every day and actually write what is on her mind."

"Can't be that bad," she mutters, taking another bite of food. I watch, trying not to get distracted.

"She woke her mum and dad up once because she kept thinking about the twins. Maddox was born first and Maddison was born after midnight. She wondered if they were still classed as twins since they were born on different days—"

"Are they?" she interrupts, looking interested.

I roll my eyes. "Fuck if I know. They share a birthday still as she was only born two minutes after."

"Never even thought about that," she mutters.

"Anyway, point of the story is thanks for making me trend on Facebook," I say dryly when she doesn't seem to care.

"Don't you trend on Twitter?"

My eyes widen, hoping like fuck Charlotte doesn't have Twitter too.

I smirk. "I'm Aiden Carter; I trend anywhere."

"Are you going to answer your phone?"

I glance over to the table where my phone is vibrating, then look at her like she's lost her mind. "To listen to them call me a pussy? No thanks."

She groans. "I don't get that saying. They're basically saying pussies are weak. But if you think about it, men only get tapped in the groin area and it's like watching a football player trying to get a penalty. You act like you just got hit by a two-by-four. You don't see girls doing that."

I chuckle, leaning back on the sofa. "I'll text them later and tell them to call me a dick instead."

"Nah, chicken seems fitting."

I narrow my eyes at her. "Funny."

"Quack, quack!"

I chuckle at her sense of humour before finishing off the rest of my food.

WE'RE NOT EVEN twenty minutes into the movie and Bailey is sobbing into my T-shirt. I'm all for her clinging to me, but the tears, even over a movie, tighten my chest. I lay back on the sofa, kicking my feet up and lying her directly on top of me.

"Hey, what are you doing?" she mumbles against my chest, still sniffling.

"Getting comfy."

She looks up at me, her eyes glistening with tears. Even upset she has to be the most beautiful girl I've ever laid eyes on.

"Oh," she whispers, before glancing back at the television.

As she shifts her body around to get more comfortable, her pussy rubs against my dick, causing me to groan when I feel myself stiffen.

"Did I hurt you?" she asks, looking back up at me with those big round eyes.

"No," I choke out, my voice husky.

Our gazes lock, neither of us looking away. Not that I want to; I could watch her all day.

I gently push back the hair clinging to her wet cheek, and her lips part.

Feeling this is the moment, I slide her up my body until her face is level with mine. Her breathing is heavy, her breasts pressed up against my chest. I graze my nose against hers, and her chest lifts with a small gasp.

When I pull back, I have to fight not to look away. The way she's looking at me... always like I'm front and centre. No other girl has been able to do that to me; make me feel like I stand out from the rest of my family. We're all good-looking guys, and girls fight over us, but given the chance, they would jump from one bed to the next, just to say they've had us all.

"Why is it that when you look at me, it's like you can read my mind?" I whisper huskily, rubbing my thumb up and down her cheek.

"I was just thinking something similar. It's almost like you can read me—like you see who I am, inside and out."

"Only because you let me," I admit. The trust she hands over freely to me is humbling, especially knowing about her past and how many times she's been fucked over. Thinking of everything she told me this morning feels like a lifetime ago.

I got drunk the night before, thinking what we shared was over. I took something else in my life for granted, always trusting it would be there. Then she was gone because I fucked up. I didn't see a way back for us.

And now I'm here, with her in my arms, and I'll never take it for granted again.

"Because you make it easy to," she suddenly says. She blinks slowly, like she didn't mean to let that out in the open.

A grin teases the corner of my mouth and I pull her further up, so she has to lean over me, her face directly above mine.

Her hair falls like a curtain, covering us. I raise my hands and cup her face, my thumbs resting on her cheeks, and then I bring her face down to mine.

I close my eyes, not fighting back the groan that escapes when her lips meet mine. She's so close. She's everywhere. Her hands roam up my chest, her body relaxes on top of mine, and I can't fight back the desire.

It's powerful and all-consuming.

I pull back to catch my breath, the taste of her still in my mouth. And I crave more—I crave her.

Her eyes are cloudy with desire, and before I can suggest we take it slow, she grabs my face in her own hands, keeping me still before slamming her lips back down on mine.

I moan into her mouth, now gripping her arse in the palm of my hands. Satisfaction surges through me when she lets out a breathless moan of her own, rubbing herself against me.

Unable to handle it any longer and needing to be inside her, I grip her arse tightly and shoot to the edge of the sofa. She squeals in surprise, pulling back to stare down at me.

She's just as effected as I am—if not more, and something flares inside me. "I need you," I tell her, desire thick in my voice.

Not even caring that I don't know where I'm going, I lift us both from the couch, heading towards the stairs.

She kisses the side of my mouth, moving along my jaw and down my neck, then licking a trail up towards my ear.

Fuck it.

I slam her against her the wall, and distantly, I hear a picture frame fall to the floor. Neither of us looks or even cares as we continue to assault one another's mouths. She grips the hair at the bottom of my neck, using it to control the kiss. I try to slow it down, wanting to do this properly, all romantic and shit, but something surges through her with a shudder, and she kisses me like she can't breathe without me.

Fire explodes inside me when her nails claw at my back, trying to lift my shirt. Dropping her to floor, she sways towards me, drunk on lust. I hold her up whilst using one hand to remove my shirt. Her tongue flicks her top lip, her eyes hungrily raking over me.

"Your turn," I bite out huskily, barely holding on by a thread. I've never been so hard in my life, and the need I feel to have her is compelling. She is addictive.

I pull her T-shirt over her head, trying to be as gentle as I can, not wanting to scare her. She doesn't seem to mind, her hands going behind her back to unsnap her bra.

The second her dark rose nipples flash, I'm on her, lifting her back up the wall and taking one in my mouth.

She cries out, gripping my shoulders as she arches her back to give me more.

Always giving me more.

I show the same affection to the other.

We need a bed before I fuck her right here—hard—against the wall. She protests when I pull away, trying to bring me closer. I chuckle against her nipple and they tighten. I grin, looking up at her.

"Bed?"

"Upstairs, first corridor to the left, last door on the right," she rushes out, surging forward.

I chuckle against her lips and kiss her back, and in a haze, I make my way upstairs, knocking over some pictures and another vase on my way.

In the corridor, near the door she mentioned, we stop, neither of us taking a breath as we grab at one another, undoing each other's jeans. She slides my zipper down, but before she can pull my trousers off, I grab hers by the belt and drop to my knees, ripping them down her legs. I kiss the inside of her thigh, and a throaty moan escapes her. I look up, mesmerised as she throws her head back. I lick my way up until I reach the waistband of her knickers, enjoying the way her breath hitches. When I don't go any further, she looks down, her eyes wide with wonder and her chest heaving.

I tap the back of her leg, a silent request to step out of her jeans. She does, and before I know it she's standing in front of me in nothing but a pair of black, lacey knickers.

I kiss her just below her belly button before standing up and pressing a brief kiss to her nipple. Pulling her into my arms, I carry her the rest of the way to the bedroom, enjoying her naked body pressed against me.

I don't bother to take in her room, or to kick the door shut behind me. I lay her down on the bed, nuzzling her thighs open. She spreads them eagerly and looks down at me with so much trust and love.

I ache for her to touch me, but I know if she does I'll explode, and it will be over too soon.

"Please," she whines when I continue to watch her.

Smirking, I slide my finger down her stomach, before swiping my tongue against the inside of her thigh again. Her stomach rises off the bed as she arches her back, and I use the opportunity to remove her knickers. Her breathe hitches as I slide my tongue higher.

Groaning at the throb between my legs, I quickly remove my jeans.

She tastes sweet, and the first swipe of my tongue has her entire body shuddering. I open her up to me, licking along her slit and loving the way she cries out my name.

"Aiden, please—I need you inside me."

"Not yet," I groan out, wondering how long I'm going to last if she keeps begging.

"Please," she pleads, closing her legs, though arching her pussy towards me. Growling, I kiss my way up her body. I've never seen anything so fucking perfect in my life.

Teasing her nipple, I flick my tongue over it before taking her mouth in a hard, punishing kiss.

"Condom," she breathes out, reaching over to her bedside drawer.

"What?" I snarl, wondering why she has them. She said she hasn't had a boyfriend before—unless you count that prick who fucked her over big time, and I don't want to think about him with her right now.

"My gran keeps them there," she assures me, rushing to open it. Her expression becomes unsure, and she bites her bottom lip. "I don't know how to put it on. I've never done it before."

I groan, feeling myself leak at her words. "I'll show you next time. Right now, I just want to be inside you."

She grins, nodding. I pull back, resting up on my knees, and slide the condom down my dick. I look up to find her mouth agape, before looking at me with fear in her eyes.

"Do not ask me if it's going to fit," I tell her quickly, leaning over her.

"But—"

"Trust me," I whisper, brushing my lips against hers. "You were made for me. I'll fit."

She gasps as my dick pushes against her entrance, her nipples brushing against my chest. A guttural groan escapes me when my fingers run through her wetness, teasing her before lining my dick up. She tenses briefly, but a quick flick of my tongue against hers has her softening. In one thrust, I enter her slowly, and her breath catches.

"Oh, my God," she chokes out.

"You okay?"

"Please fuck me—I need you," she rushes out. Her legs clamp around my waist, pushing me further inside her. I groan, closing my eyes through the pleasure. "Please."

I brush a piece of hair out of her face and move in and out of her, slowly at first, until her body is undulating beneath mine. Her nails dig into the muscles of my back, and with each thrust, I watch her. I watch her pleasure-filled expression and thrust harder—*harder*.

Our eyes lock as I stretch her arms above her head, raising her breasts. I take one in my mouth, sucking and flicking it with my tongue.

Her nails dig into my hands.

I drive myself into her; harder, rougher, going as far inside of her as her body will allow. She cries out with every stroke, sweat beading on her forehead.

"More," she pants, her hips moving in rhythm with mine.

I groan, feeling my climax building, driving me wild. The heels of her feet dig into my arse suddenly, slamming me so hard inside her my climax rips through me. She cries out when her own orgasm strikes, her walls clamping so tightly around my dick, milking me, that I swear I could climax again.

I crush my mouth against hers, drowning out the sound so I can taste it instead. Her body trembles, her pussy spasming around me, making my now semi-hard cock twitch—grow harder.

Her eyes open when the shudders subside, and a look so tender and loving passes between us.

"I love you," I rasp, never looking away.

Her gaze holds mine, and her eyes begin to water as her hand reaches up to brush a lock of wet hair from my face.

"I love you too, Aiden," she tells me, and I relax above her. I hadn't realised how badly I needed to hear those words until she said them. I didn't even realise I was afraid she didn't feel the same way.

"Ready to learn how to put a condom on?"

She giggles, her eyes shining with happiness as she nods. We don't waste any time, both of us determined to examine and memorise each and every part of the other's body.

TWENTY-FOUR

BAILEY

R OLLING OVER, I LOOK DOWN AT the floor, smiling to myself when I see three more condoms have joined the first one.

Last night had been mind-blowing. I didn't know sex could be like that. I guess a part of me never wanted it to be, not after what Owen did to me. Aiden had proved over and over, though, that sex could be special.

And boy was it special—*he* was special.

I ached in all the right places.

Aiden's hand on my hip slowly tenses against me when I reach over to put my hearing aid back in. My breath catches, and he lets out a throaty chuckle. He slides his hands over my stomach, roaming up until he's cupping my breast. I wiggle my arse into him, feeling he's already hard.

He leans forward, kissing my shoulder. "How can I want you again already? I didn't think my dick would ever work again after the last time."

I chuckle. "If I have another orgasm, I'm scared I might die."

He kisses my shoulder again. "Death by orgasm is the best way to go."

A yawn escapes me. "God, I think I could sleep all day."

He chuckles against my shoulder, his fingers pulling and twisting my nipple in delicious torture. "I'm just that good."

I roll onto my back, and he moves over to give me room. My breasts are bare to him, and he licks his lips as he eyes them.

"Or I'm that good," I tease.

Our gazes meet, and he grins. "Oh, you were *good*. You rode me hard."

I feel my cheeks redden, and he laughs quietly under his breath, tucking a piece of hair behind my ear.

"I fucked you every way imaginable, licked and touched every inch of your body, and you still manage to get all shy, still manage to blush."

Warmth and desire surge through me. I lean up to kiss him, but his phone ringing somewhere on the bedroom floor startles me.

He frowns. "I shouldn't have put that on loud. I'm going to go apeshit if it's Maddox ringing to wind me up."

I giggle, bringing the blanket up to cover my breasts. He smirks before shaking his head and jumping from the bed, gloriously naked. A tingle shoots through me at the sight. He's not ashamed of his body—he has no reason to be.

But seeing him in the morning light… I'm speechless.

"Hey, Mum. What? Um… yeah. I'll be right over. Yeah, love you too," he says, losing his happy glow. He ends the call, looking at me with sorrow in his eyes. "That was my mum."

I sit up straighter, worry twisting my stomach. "Is everything okay? Is Sunday okay?"

He sits down on the end of the bed, and I crawl down with the sheet still over me and hug him from behind, resting my chin on his shoulder.

"Yeah. She finally got word back from the funeral directors. We've got permission to bury Casey."

"Sunday's mum?" I ask.

We've only talked about her briefly. He feels terrible for not being there. She had known the risks of carrying Sunday to term. She knew there was a chance she wouldn't live to hold her baby. But she did because she wanted her more than anything.

He holds guilt for that—for not being with her when she needed someone the most.

"Yeah."

"This is good, right?" I ask, kissing his shoulder.

"It just feels final. Sunday won't ever know her. And the worst of it is, we only have her provisional driving license as a form of photo. We have nothing else. She didn't have Facebook, and we don't even know if she had any friends because the address on her licence now has new tenants. She was in hospital for the last two months of her pregnancy."

That must have been lonely for her. I don't say that out loud though, not wanting him to hurt any more than he already does.

"Sunday is going to know her mum loved her, Aiden. She sacrificed her life for her. I can't think of anything more beautiful than that. She gave her life. Now you get to say goodbye and give Sunday a place to visit. You won't be alone, either. I'll be with you every step of the way."

I avert my attention at the weight of his gaze, looking at me with so much emotion that I can't read it. A part of me feels like I've stepped out of line. He probably doesn't want me involved. But he surprises me when he grabs me under the arms, and pulls me onto his lap. I wrap my arms around his neck.

I can't tell if he's mad or not.

"I love you so fucking much, Bailey. Being with a single dad isn't something you probably wished for in a relationship. But those words... those words are what I needed to hear. I love you. And it might be selfish of me to need you with me, but I don't care. I don't think I can do this without you."

I run my fingers through his black, spikey hair. "I think you're wrong. You can do anything, Aiden Carter. Look at how you're raising Sunday. I've never known such a devoted and loving father. Not a single one, anyway. Give yourself some credit—this is new to you," I tell him, kissing the corner of his mouth before pulling back. "But if it helps any, I love you too."

"I'm so fucking lucky to have you," he says.

Needing to lighten the mood, I shrug and tilt my head. "Yeah, you kind of are."

He chuckles, and a squeal escapes me when he stands up with me still in his arms. "Mum needs me to get over there, but I think I have time to fuck you if we take a shower at the same time."

I grin, resting my forehead against his. "You won't hear me complaining."

As we step out of the taxi, something occurs to me. "Why don't you drive?" I ask him, taking his offered hand. He links our fingers together, and butterflies swarm in my stomach.

"I've got to do my driving test again," he admits, looking away from me.

Wait, again?

And what was that look that passed across his face?

"You failed?"

His eyes meet mine briefly before looking away, and he curses under his breath. "Something like that."

"Nu-uh, out with it, mister."

"You can't get mad at me," he says, but it comes out almost like a question.

I grin. "Okay. Pinky swear."

"I tried it on with my instructor."

"You're gay?" I screech loudly.

Harlow, his lovely aunt I met yesterday, walks up behind me, tapping my shoulder as she passes. "We always thought so."

I giggle but turn to Aiden for answers.

"Aunt Harlow, that's unfair. I'm a freaking stud."

She turns, walking backwards with a grin on her face. "Ah, to be young and naïve again."

Laughing, we watch her step inside the house, not bothering to knock. I nudge Aiden with my hip as we reach the doorstep.

"It was a female instructor and she kept wearing these tight skirts. I asked her out, leaned in to kiss her, and she slapped me. Failed me right there before we even drove off."

Clutching my stomach as laughter rips through me, I glance up at him through watery eyes. "Epic!" My laughter fades into chuckles. "When's your next test?"

"First week of next month. I've had to wait five weeks since the waiting list for the next nearest driving centre—which is an hour away—is long."

His mum bursts through the open doorway. "You're here. Come on, I'll talk you through everything," she says, ending our conversation. Slowly, she scans our bodies, her eyebrows scrunched up, as if she can't figure something out. Then her eyes widen, resting on our linked hands. She looks up, beaming at us. "You're finally together?"

I look to Aiden, not knowing how to answer. I can feel a blush rising to my cheeks. I'm not worried if she approves or not, because his mum is lovely.

Aiden's cheeks redden. "Yeah, Mum—but don't make a big deal of it."

"Big deal of what?" his dad, Maverick, asks, coming down the stairs.

Teagan spins around, her hair whipping through the air. "They're together. As in together—as a *couple*."

His dad grins, giving his son a chin lift before facing me. "You might want to take your hearing aid out when he's around. He whines like a girl."

I laugh. "Noted."

Teagan's eyes go round as she slaps her husband. "Maverick, you can't say that."

He looks down at her, the skin between his eyes creasing. "Why not?"

"It's disrespectful."

Aiden groans, squeezing my hand. "Please don't change your mind."

"Change her mind about what?"

Aiden groans louder. "I always think a situation can't get any worse, but then you happen," he says.

I remember the man in front of me from the day they were all fighting outside my house. He grins at Aiden, flashing his white teeth.

"I make everything better. You need some Uncle Max lovin'?"

Ah, so this is the uncle Max I've heard Aiden and the others talk about. I can see why they would call him nuts.

He holds his arms out to Aiden, ready to hug him, but he steps back when Aiden says, "Come on, Bailey. I want to give Sunday some cuddles."

"Wait, are they together?"

"Yes," his mum answers proudly, making my heart swell.

"No sex before marriage!" his uncle shouts.

His aunt Harlow looks up from the sofa where she's holding Sunday. She moans, her eyes narrowing. "Bloody Max. I told him to stall you a bit longer. I wanted time with my great niece."

"You set me up?" Aiden asks, sounding affronted.

I turn my head to the side, trying to hide my smile.

"You never let anyone hold her," she mutters, getting up. "Want a cup of tea?"

When I realise she's talking to me, I nod. "I'd love a coffee, if you're offering. Milk with two sugars."

She nods her approval. "I'd need all the coffee in the world if I had to listen to him all day."

"You love me," Aiden teases, taking Sunday from her arms. He coos down at her, his face shining with love. "Doesn't she, Sunday? They all love me. I'm their favourite."

"I lived with Max, and you remind me so much of him. He wasn't my favourite, either," she teases, winking at me when he looks away.

"Hey! I take offence to that, woman," Max yells as he walks in. He startles Sunday, and she starts crying. "Christ! I'm sorry."

"She's due a bottle anyway," Teagan says softly. "I'll go make it up."

Aiden glares at him before handing her over to me. "I've got it, Mum," he tells her, before looking up at me. "Can you change her whilst I make her one? Her stuff is in that box."

"Sure," I tell him, and drop down in front of the fireplace and pull her box towards me. I take out her mat and blanket and lay them on the floor.

"Hey, stop crying, baby girl, otherwise Daddy will have a stroke."

She quietens down, and it's then I realise the entire room is silent. I glance up as I lay her down, shuddering when all eyes are on me. Teagan's mouth opens and closes before she turns to her husband, her expression miffed.

"Did I do something wrong?" I ask, scanning Sunday to make sure.

"He gave her to you willingly," Teagan suddenly blurts out.

I look up, surprised by her comment. "He does all the time. Should he not?" Do they think I'm trying to be her mum?

Teagan must sense the fear in my words because she settles down on her knees next to me, placing her hand on my shoulder.

"It's nothing bad. We just have to fight to hold her. I'm surprised he let me have her all weekend. Last weekend he came and got her early."

"Really?" I ask.

Harlow scoffs. "I asked if I could take her to a baby show up in Easton and he gave me a list of things that could happen. He spent thirty minutes telling me no."

"I thought everyone held her," I mutter, feeling warmth seep through my chest.

Teagan removes her hand, and when I look to her, she's smiling. "Don't worry, we all get our cuddle time in when he's at work."

"If she's anything like her dad when she hits two, he'll hand her over to a stranger," Maverick mutters.

"I did," Max agrees.

"Didn't you sit Liam next to another family in McDonalds because he was playing up?"

Max grins. "Lake killed me when she came back from taking Hayden to the loo," he says, then goes on to explain what Maverick meant. "I kept getting funny looks off people—and I was hungover."

Teagan scoffs. "I still can't believe you did that."

He shrugs carelessly. "It wasn't like I was gonna leave them. Plus, they all kept giving me snotty looks, and then the mum ordered one of the workers to get the manager because of the noise he was making. It didn't help when he put his hand, covered in tomato sauce, all over her white blouse."

Maverick laughs, nodding like he remembers. "That was it… The manager came out to have a word with the woman, but you quickly sat Liam next to them."

Max chuckles, his eyes lit with amusement. "Yeah, then walked up to the manager and hissed that their kid was making too much noise."

"What happened?" I ask, awed by the craziness.

He turns to me, smirking. "He went over to her, and it got heated when she denied Liam was hers. But Liam was at the age when he liked to call every fucker 'Mum'—including me. The manager saw him destroying their property and asked her to leave. She didn't like his attitude, so stormed out. The manager went to pick Liam up, panicking and thinking a woman had just abandoned her kid, when Lake came out and starting screaming, saying he was trying to kidnap her baby."

"No way?" I breathe out, eyes wide.

Teagan giggles. "Yeah. She was pissed at him for weeks."

Aiden walks in but pauses when he notices us all laughing. "What's going on?"

I answer as I change Sunday. "They were just telling me some stories."

He looks at his parents warily. "None about me I hope?"

"If you're talking about the time you took a shit in the model bathroom at B&Q, then, nah, we weren't," Maverick says, grinning at his son.

Looking at Aiden, my eyes widen, before laughter spills free. "Please tell me you were two."

His cheeks redden and his uncle answers for him. "Six or seven, wasn't it, Aiden?"

Aiden glares at him before turning to me and explaining. "He," he growls out, pointing his thumb over his shoulder at Max, "fed me some Mexican food he bought from a burger van outside the store. It didn't even have a food licence or hygiene certificate, but we didn't know that until after. And I was hungry. Anyway, ten minutes into looking for new tiles with my dad, Max, and Malik, I needed to go. I couldn't see where the toilets were, then saw the models."

"He even closed the door," Max laughs.

I finish buttoning Sunday's dress as I laugh. "You surprise me every day."

Aiden groans. "I've lost my man card when it comes to you." He sulks as he sits down on the other side of me.

I pick up Sunday and take the bottle from his hand, smirking at him. "Did you have one to begin with?"

"I like her!" Max booms, laughing as he heads into the kitchen.

"I love your family," I tell him.

He gives me a dry look, but then his eyes light up. "Then next weekend you can come cheer me on at Family of The Year."

"What's that?" I ask.

A lazily smirk lifts at the corners of his mouth. "You'll see, Bailey James. You'll see."

I shake my head, grinning wide at his behaviour.

God, I've never felt this happy.

And if he wants me at Family of The Year, then I'll be there, cheering him on. Because whether he knows it or not, I'd walk through fire for him.

TWENTY-FIVE

AIDEN

I BOUNCE ON THE BALLS OF MY FEET, giddy with excitement. I live all year for this day. The day we get to rub it in the Hayes brothers' faces that we're better than them. Last year's win on their side was a one off. We made a mistake in underestimating them. This year is different. We've turned up early to make sure they can't fuck up our list. We have until twenty minutes before the games begin to make sure they don't change anything.

"Son, I'm going to head over to Teagan and Hope's stall. They're advertising Maddison's new vegetable garden and selling some arrangements."

"That's fine, Mum," I tell her, leaning down to kiss her cheek. I pull Bailey against my side as I say, "Just remember she needs feeding in an hour."

Mum rolls her eyes but looks at Bailey when she answers. "He acts like I didn't raise four kids."

Bailey giggles, however remains quiet. I know she's nervous about being out with us. It's a town event and everyone turns up.

"See you later, Mum."

"Be safe. No getting into fights with the Hayes brothers."

"Like I would," I scoff.

She pauses to look at me over her shoulder. "You said that last year and then they won. Three of you ended up in hospital. No getting into trouble, Aiden. I mean it."

Shit, she used the 'mum voice'. I gulp, nodding. "Yes, Mum!"

Bailey leans into me, whispering, "Did you just piss yourself?"

I clear my throat. "Yep, just a little."

"Who's the family of the year?" Maddox shouts, jumping between us, which pulls us apart. He wraps his arm around our shoulders, grinning like a mad man. "We're gonna fucking destroy them. Sorry, little one, but you need to be a Carter to join in. We tried to get Beau in on the fun. He rocked the assault course we did while camping not long ago."

"It didn't work?" I ask surprised, and a little disappointed.

"Nah. Even Landon tried intimidating them, but then they only went and made it worse by saying once Faith marries Beau, we won't be able to use her, either," Maddox replies.

"Who the fuck is gonna bake? She's the best."

We both glance at Bailey and I lick my lips at the thought of her baked goods.

"We're not married, remember," she reminds me, her face flushed.

"Yeah, but by the time Beau and Faith get married, you two will tie the knot."

I pause when not one bit of dread or fear passes through me. Not one single thing. I mean, it makes sense. I love her and don't see that ever changing.

"I—I—" she looks to me for help "Aiden?"

I shake out of it and glance at her. I shrug and say, "Man has a point. Do you want to be with someone else?"

"No!"

Hearing that, a wide smile spreads across my face. "Well, then. We'll wait a while though—until Sunday is walking. She can throw shit at people."

"Not actual shit, right?" Maddox asks, scrunching his nose up.

I do wonder about him sometimes.

"No. You know what I mean. When they walk down with the bride."

"Flower girl is the word you're looking for," Bailey comments sounding choked up, her eyes round. In fact, she looks kind of pale and tense.

Probably picturing what her wedding will be like now. I heard all women go bridezilla for their wedding.

"That's the one."

"Guys, you coming to sign in?" Mark yells from across the park.

I shield my eyes from the sun and wave back at him. I take Bailey's hand as we walk over to the rest of them.

My eyes are immediately drawn to Lily. She looks pale and is clutching her stomach. "Lily, are you okay?"

Her eyes meet mine, and I see the anxiety and fear in them. I step forward, but Maddox beats me to it, pulling her into his arms.

"What's happened?"

He looks to Mark, who curses. "They put up a fucking beer tent this year. We walked by it and there's already a group of lads drunk and messing around."

Lily whimpers and Maddox pulls her closer. "Come on, we can go home."

"B—but, it's Family of The Year," she says, her body trembling. "But I don't think I can do anything today. Do you mind if I don't participate?"

He glances down her lovingly. "We don't mind if you want to leave."

She grips his hand, shaking her head. "No. I don't want you guys to do that. Please don't, I'm begging," she says, and the heat in her voice even has me choking up. She looks close to tears, and I know it's because she thinks she'll ruin something for us.

She wouldn't. We'd all die for her with a smile on our faces. That's how much we love her.

"You can stay with Bailey so she's not on her own," I quickly butt in, watching her relax.

She smiles at Bailey, who smiles back. "I'd love the company. I hate been around big crowds."

"Me too," Lily whispers, looking at Bailey in a new light.

"Come on; let's go sign in. The quicker we beat these fuckers, the quicker we can all go home and celebrate," Maddox tells Lily.

We head over to the sign in tent. Maddox walks up to us with Lily still in his arms, taking the assigned sheet and our numbers from the bloke there. We stand behind him, waiting.

"New rules this year, boys. We assigned you to each post. You can't change it," the bloke in charge says.

I frown when Maddox turns pale. "Um, they put Charlotte in the bake off."

Charlotte starts jumping up and down, clapping her hands. She snatches her number off Maddox gleefully. "I'd better get going over to the tent, then," she excitedly yells. She walks off but stops and turns to us with a bright smile. "Go kick some butt!"

We all quickly move to the bloke at the tent. He looks up, startled when we overshadow him. He swallows deeply, and I swear I hear him whimper.

"You can't do this," Maddox growls.

"She's going to kill people," Mark hisses.

"I'm not eating it—I wouldn't even make the Hayes brothers eat her cakes," I snap.

He holds his hands up. "Guys, I'm sorry, but this is out of my hands."

"Do something," Jacob, Charlotte's only sibling, squeaks out. "She makes me eat them. All of them. And I can't say no."

The bloke behind the table winces. "Look, I'm sorry. If it makes you feel any better, the others assigned to that contest probably won't do much better either. She's up against Isaac Hayes, if that helps."

"That does not help," Landon snaps.

"I'm sorry," he yells, throwing his hands up. He turns away from us, looking over at another family coming to sign up.

"I can't believe I put the last of my pocket money in to contribute to this. Instead of gloating over our win, I'll be throwing up in the toilets."

"It will be okay," Lily tells him, patting his head.

We all turn to head over to the first round. I take the piece of paper, grinning when I see my name. "Holy shit, they've got an inflatable adult course for the first round."

"Who's doing that?" Maddox asks, his eyes lit up.

I smirk. "Me, Hayden, and Liam."

"Bullshit!" he explodes. "Please tell me I got something like the heavy lifting, or even the bike race?"

"You got the egg and spoon race," Bailey tells him happily, looking at the sheet of paper.

"Aw, little bitty Maddox has to hold up a spoon and run," Isaac Hayes taunts, stepping up to us with his brothers.

"How'd you get that?" Jaxon asks, grinning.

"Fuck you," Maddox spits out, going to step forward. Liam quickly jumps in front of him, blocking his path to Isaac.

"I don't know why you're grinning, Isaac; you're cooking, like a good little wife," I tell him, grinning. His eyes widen, fists clenching as he takes a step forward. I take one too, daring him to throw the first punch.

Bailey pulls me back and I stare Isaac down, not looking away when Jaxon steps in, pushing him back.

"Come on, your mum said no fights," Bailey whispers, but it's enough for Reid to hear. He starts laughing.

"Aw, Mummy going to spank you if you get your arse whipped?"

I grit my teeth, letting Bailey pull me back.

Luke, the last triplet, smirks. "I wouldn't mind spanking his mum. She's hot."

I surge forward, my fist already raised. I can hear the groans around me as my fist comes down. Suddenly, I'm pushed backwards, my body tucked against another as they carry me away.

"Wait until after," Landon hisses. "You cause a fight in front of kids, we'll never be able to compete against them again."

I point at Luke, glaring. "I won't forget."

"Well, I am unforgettable," Luke taunts back, still grinning.

"Um, Maddox… he has Luke in the first round," Lily says softly.

Maddox bounces on his feet. "Today is going to be fucking awesome."

I roll my eyes, following behind the rest as they head over to the inflatable obstacle course. A pudgy older man walks up to us, a relieved look on his face.

"You're here. That's great. We need to open this to the public soon, so we need to get the race started," he explains, before frowning down at his clipboard. 'Wait, there should be another group." He looks over our shoulder, nodding once again. "Great, you're all here. Right, I need an Aiden Carter and Luke Hayes to head over to the starting line over there," he says, pointing to where the inflatable course is.

I grin and rub my hands together, before pulling Bailey into my arms. "You going to cheer me on?"

Her face lights up. "Of course. Enjoy yourself."

"Ready to get bested?" Luke says, jumping up and down.

I narrow my gaze on him. "Keep bragging, it will help with the gloating later when we kick your arse."

"Pretty sure Hayden is up against Reid, so you've got no fucking chance."

His smirk slips when Hayden walks up behind him and slaps the back of his head. "At the end of this, I'm going to make you eat dirt, dipshit. When will you fuckers learn? I kicked Eli's arse last year on the bike trail."

"You kicked his back tyre," Reid growls.

Hayden looks over at Reid, blinking seductively at him as she points a finger to her chest. "Who, me?"

"Yeah, *you*," Eli growls, joining the group.

Hayden swings her gaze over to him, smirking. "And you punctured my tyre before the race, and I still won."

"I don't know what is going on, young men," the pudgy bloke starts, gulping when Hayden turns her fierce gaze to him, making me chuckle. "— and ladies, but we need to get this race started."

I glance away from the bickering between Hayden and the Hayes brothers and squeeze Bailey to get her attention. She looks up at me in wonder. "I love your family."

"I love *you*. I'll see you at the end?"

She nods, melting against me. "I'll be here."

I grin, liking the sound of her words. "See you at the finish line," I tell her, and head off. I spin around, walking backwards with my arms in the air. "I'll be the one people are congratulating."

"Fuck you, Carter, and hurry up and get over here," Luke yells from the starting line.

I wink at Bailey before turning to Luke. "Stop being a demanding little—"

"Children present!" the pudgy bloke yells.

I grimace. "Sorry."

He sighs, rubbing his beard. "Just get into position."

Luke is to the right of me as I step up to the inflatable obstacle course. Following him are three more contenders, and behind us the rest wait for the signal to go.

The first one is pretty easy; we just have to climb up the wall and go down a slide.

My eyes lock with Luke as the pudgy guy shouts to get ready. Everyone begins to yell encouraging things to their families.

"Ready, steady, go!"

I jump up, reaching half way up the wall before grabbing onto the rope. Luke has done the same, so I pull myself up faster.

I am not going to let that fucker win.

Reaching the top, I don't bother sliding down, not wanting to waste time, so instead, I jump into the blow-up forest, smacking the plastic trees out of the way as I move through them. The course will get smaller soon, only allowing two to go through at a time.

I want my opponent to be Luke—to give him a first-class view of my winning moment. He's just behind me now, so towards the end, I pull the tree branches back, letting it swing free once I've pulled it hard enough.

I hear him curse behind me and laugh, moving ahead, diving through the small rolling pins.

Crawling out, I head up another ramp, grinning like a mad man when I see three large inflatable balls for us to run over.

"I heard your mum is good in bed and loves giving head," Luke taunts as I hit the first ball, feet planted firmly. I wobble, snapping my head to him.

"Fuck you."

"Might go see her later," he says, grinning at me.

"Yeah? I heard Paisley's tight. Like, really fucking tight," I taunt back, hating to use Paisley in our pissing match.

He trips, yelling, "Wanker."

I'm grinning like a fool by the time I reach the next obstacle. My thighs are burning already, but that's what I get for not being in better shape. But having a baby really tires you out. I can't even have a piss in peace, let alone work out.

My feet wobble on the first of the rotating rollers. A smug smirk twitches at the corners of my mouth when I land on the second one.

Then everything happens. Two hands push me sideways and horror washes through me. I can see the grass and brace my body, ready for the fall. It hurts like a bitch. I groan, hearing Bailey cry out my name.

"Don't talk shit about my fucking sister, dickhead," Luke yells, before continuing on.

My head snaps up and I see his smug salute, before he rushes off. I jump to my feet, more determined than ever to win this. It's fucking personal now. Fucker hit me whilst my back was turned.

Pussy.

He's ahead of me, his brothers racing alongside of him on the grass, cheering him on. I run over the rings, push through the tubes, jump across more balls and go down another slide. I'm closing in on him, and he can hear me, his entire body tensing. I chuckle under my breath as we push through the spikes in the cave and run out the other side.

Seeing the last part—the maze—I quickly step through the inflatable tyre rings, and at the last second, shove Luke with all my strength, falling in the process.

"You dickhead," Reid yells from the side-lines, running over help his brother. I get up, shrugging, and move through the maze.

"Go!" Jaxon yells.

I laugh, hearing Maddox yell, "Run, Forest, run."

"You're a fucking knob," Luke growls behind me. I push forward, laughing hysterically now, and jump out of the maze, signalling for Hayden to go. She's off, and seconds later, Luke rushes out, winded and signalling for Reid to go.

Luke pushes me, his face red. "Why the fuck did you push me?"

I push him back, my own anger spiking. "You fucking pushed me first."

"Now, girls, calm down," Maddox says, chuckling.

"Luke," Jaxon snaps. Luke stares at me for a beat longer.

I don't even blink, staring right back. "Run along."

He shoots forward, but Jaxon steps in, grabbing him around the waist. "That's enough, both of you," he snaps. "There are children here." He looks to Landon. "Sort your cousin out, Landon, or I will."

"Don't threaten me," Landon warns, his tone deadly.

"You won," is screamed behind me, and I turn, just in time to catch Bailey in my arms. I smirk down at her. "Did you have any doubt?"

She shakes her head, laughing. "No."

"Come on; let's watch Hayden kick some arse," I say giddily, a rush of adrenaline shooting through me.

I can't wait to get back home and fuck my girlfriend.

TWENTY-SIX

BAILEY

WHO KNEW FAMILY OF THE YEAR could be so competitive. After watching Mark race off on his bike, Lily and I left, leaving them with the next challenges. We browsed the little stalls set up, selling handcraft items, and we popped in to say hello to Teagan, Madison, and Sunday. We didn't stay long as they were busy, so leaving them behind, we go to see Charlotte.

"I think she's forgotten she's surrounded by people," I murmur to Lily.

She giggles, linking her arm through mine. "She probably has. She loves baking, and although that cake will look like a masterpiece by the end of it, it will be disastrous to eat. It's one of her favourite hobbies."

"Her favourite?" I ask, whilst watching in amazement as she places tiny iced flowers on a three-tiered cake.

"She likes animals too, but they don't last long in her house, which is why

Faith stopped giving them to her. Landon thought giving her something simple would ease her into it, but her goldfish died a few weeks ago."

"How long did she have it?"

Lily sucks in her bottom lip while she thinks about it. "I think she had it that morning, or the morning before."

I chuckle. "She's amazing."

"She is. You know, she got bullied like you and me," Lily says quietly.

I turn to face her. When I don't see any pity, I relax. "She told me about you the night I went out with them to the bar. She didn't say anything about being bullied herself."

She sighs. "She wouldn't. Charlotte only sees the good in people. Half the time, I don't think she realised she was being bullied. She had Maddox and Imogen at school with her though. Imogen is our cousin, who was a year above those two."

I start to see Charlotte in a new light. To be laughed at behind your back… or not understanding that they're not simply teasing… I don't know if that's worse than being confronted or not.

"I'm glad she had them," I whisper.

"Me too."

"I wonder what the boys are up to," I say.

She giggles. "I need to go the toilet, but after, we'll go and find them."

"Come on, then. I saw some Portaloo's near the back."

She pulls on my arm to go the other way. "They have a toilet block this way. I'd rather use those. I don't like being in those confined spaces."

"That's fine with me. Lead the way; I've never been here," I tell her.

I can see the toilet block she was talking about a few minutes later. Lily startles me suddenly when she calls out, "Paisley, is that you?"

The girl a few feet in front us turns around. She's beautiful, even in the baggy jeans and long-sleeved T-shirt she's wearing that looks too big for her. I glance down at her feet, seeing dirty trainers. And even with all that, she still works her outfit. She makes it look trendy.

Her hair is a dark brown towards the top, but falls into a lighter brown towards the bottom, ending midway down her back. Her bright hazel eyes have flecks of gold in them, her long black lashes making them pop. Rosy cheeks and pink, full lips stand out on her pale-skinned face.

Seeming wobbly on her feet, Lily and I both rush forward. Lily takes her arm, steadying her. "Paisley, are you okay?"

"Hi, Lily," she says, her voice shaky. She forces a smile as she glances at us. "I'm good. I just need to use the bathroom."

Lily doesn't look convinced; me neither. The girl is lying. She looks ready to pass out. "We're heading that way too. We'll walk with you."

"I didn't see you at the egg and spoon race."

Lily winces. "How badly did it end?"

Paisley giggles. "It ended up in an egging match. Both Maddox and Eli are covered."

I laugh. "I can't believe we missed that. What is it with them and eggs?" I say, then look to Paisley when she glances my way. "I'm Bailey, by the way. I'm Aiden's girlfriend."

Her lips twist in thought. "Ah, I think Jaxon mentioned something about you."

"Well, looky fucking here," a voice from my nightmares bites out.

Everything around me stops. I stop hearing kids laughing and screaming, stop hearing parents chatting or shouting, stop hearing the noise of the crowd nearby. Instead, I focus on the girls and guy in front of me.

All four are dressed like they're ready to burgle a house, opting for black clothing with a hooded jumper. If I wasn't so petrified, I would laugh and ask if they had their names on the back too.

My stomach drops as Marie, the ring leader, steps forward, her hands hung loose beside her, but I know that means nothing. She's here to hurt me. Like she's done a thousand times before. I can see it in the curl of her lip, the feral look in her eyes.

"We don't want any trouble," Lily says gently, taking my arm. Her hand is cold and trembling, and I hate that I've put her in this situation. They can't hurt her too. Something I've seen in Lily's eyes time and time again tells me she's been hurt one too many times before. She understands the meaning of pure pain.

"What's this?" the guy says, looking down at Marie warily.

Her expression turns fake as she glances up at him, fluttering her eyelashes. "I told you, Jasper. Payback."

"Aiden isn't here," he says, looking around.

She runs her finger down his chest. "I said you could get payback. These little bitches are payback. That one," she says, pointing to me. "Is his girlfriend. Fuck her and it will destroy him." My stomach sinks at her cruel words, then her top lip curls when she eyes Lily. "And that freak is his sister. They're protective of her. But it's Bailey you want to hurt. Lily is just a bonus."

"Um…" Paisley says shakily, looking at the other three girls as they begin to surround us.

"What are you doing, Marie?" I ask, trying to remain calm.

She glares at me. "Shut the fuck up, you little slag."

I take a step back, but stop when I see Naomi move closer, shaking her head.

"I didn't sign up for this. He fucked my mum. I wanted to punch him, not fuck his girlfriend, who, by the way, wouldn't be willing," Jasper growls out. He's skinny and extremely tall, but looks like he's barely out of high school.

"Does it matter?" she asks sweetly, but I can see the hardness behind her eyes.

He looks down at her with disgust. "Yeah, it fucking does. And not being funny, but I go to school with Colton and Theo Hayes. I don't want them as enemies. Fuck this, I'm out."

He goes to walk off, but she stops him, pulling on his arm. "But what about the promise we made you?"

He shakes her arm off, scoffing. "Yeah, no fucking orgy is worth doing what you want me to do. You lied to me about this whole thing. You said if I turned up with you on my arm, Aiden would get pissed. I wanted him to pay for fucking my mum and breaking up their marriage, not rape someone."

"Fucking pussy," she sneers, shoving him away. He walks off but stops to look backward. "If you knew what was good for you, you'd run. You don't want to mess with those families. I've heard of the Carter's; they don't care about anyone but family. They rip people like you apart. And the Hayes? They'll bury you alive for messing with their sister."

"Fuck you. You don't know what you're talking about," she yells back, but I can see a little bit of doubt behind her eyes.

He laughs like he's humouring her. "Yeah, you tell yourself that. But watch your back. I heard the Hayes attack when you least expect it."

Once he's gone, her sneer turns my way and she takes a step closer. "You've been a pain in my arse for years."

"I've never done anything to you, Marie, ever. You made it your mission to bully me," I snap, finding courage.

She grins. "You still don't know, do you?"

My face scrunches up. "Know what?"

The other two beside me are quiet, but I can feel the fear coming from them in waves. I know the feeling well, accustomed to it all throughout school.

"Your granddad fired my dad. He lost his job. We nearly lost our home."

"What?"

My grandparents would have said something to me. She laughs like she heard the funniest joke in the world. "Yeah, my dad worked for your granddad at some firm. If he hadn't had fired him after the first time we hit you, we'd have stopped. We wouldn't have carried on. But you had to fuck it up. We nearly lost our home."

I gulp, my nails digging into my palms until I can feel blood. "Are you telling me you did all that stuff because your dad lost his job?"

She screams. "My mum left him! She left us! After she found out he didn't have any money, she left."

I take a step back. "I didn't know. I had nothing to do with that."

"Yeah? Then what about now? My dad started over, started his own business using the contacts he made working for your granddad, and now he's been arrested. Your fucking boyfriend called the dogs on him. They've frozen all his accounts—*my* accounts. We have nothing."

I hold my hands up, not understanding a word of what she's saying. "I didn't do anything."

"I'm going to fucking ruin you," she sneers.

I see movement to the side of me, next to where Lily is standing, and watch as Eva grabs her. Lily's eyes flash, and the look in them will haunt me forever. She screams, and the sound tears through me like a shard of glass. She screams again, this time falling to her knees, sounding desperate—terrified. I take a step towards her, watching the blood drain from her face. Paisley goes to do the same, but Amy grabs me by my arms, pulling them behind me.

"Let me go. I have to help her!" I scream, kicking my legs out. She grunts, holding me tighter.

"We won't stop this time," Amy whispers in my ear, and dread sears through me.

She drags me backwards as I scream for help, more for Lily than myself. Seeing her broken on the floor, writhing in pure agony as she clutches her head, is heart breaking. It's like she's reliving some kind of nightmare.

Eva pushes Paisley to the floor, kicking her in the stomach before moving towards me. I'm dragged into the toilets, the smell of urine and dirt hitting my nostrils, and just as the three other girls step in front of me, I'm comforted by Paisley crawling over to Lily, pulling her head into her lap. The last thing I see is her looking up at me, terror shining in her eyes.

Lily will be okay; Paisley will get help.

The door closes shut behind the three girls, and Amy drops my arms. I stagger to the side, my stomach plummeting when they all circle around me.

"Stop this!" I yell, holding my hands up.

"No, this is payback, you fucking slut," Marie yells, stepping closer. I scan the room, finding no way out other than the door they just locked. I glance at it, and with only a second to spare, I duck under Eva's arm, diving for the lock. My hand reaches for it, but as the tips of my fingers touch the lock, I'm pulled back by my hair. My scalp burns as I'm thrown backwards, landing against the row of sinks.

One grabs for my T-shirt, pulling me towards them, and in doing so, they rip the fabric and I lose my footing, falling into them.

"Please, stop," I beg, knowing I won't survive this time. I can read it in their expressions. They are going to beat me to death this time.

"Please, stop," Marie mimics, her voice mockingly high-pitched. She punches me in the face as Eva holds me. I cry out, grabbing my cheek.

Everything comes flooding back to me.

The spit in my hair.

My head thrown into a toilet.

The kicks.

The taunts.

Owen.

My family.

Everything they've ever done floods back in like a tidal wave, hitting me full force. Months ago, I wouldn't have had anything to lose. My grandparents were untouchable. My granddad was basically a celebrity in the business world. These girls, they were nothing. They'd be a spider he squashed under his shoe, and I think they know that. I think it's why they've never gone after them. Why they targeted me.

They've taken so much from me. At one time, I believed they took my spirit, my soul, but they didn't. I know that now because Aiden owns it. He holds it in the palm of his hand and cherishes it.

And for him, I won't go down without a fight.

I underestimated the lengths they would go to when they killed my family. I never thought they'd go that far. I wasn't prepared. I am now.

They just didn't count on Aiden—on my love for him. And for him, I will fight. He's given me so much to fight for.

With no more thinking, I push Eva out of the way. I get a split second to read their surprise faces before I rush into a toilet.

I try to slam the door shut behind me, but it's pushed open and smacks me in the face.

"Get here, you silly bitch," Naomi shouts, Marie and Amy standing behind her. As she grabs for me, I push her, but she's expecting it. She dodges my outstretched arms and digs her fingers into them, pulling me out of the stall.

I fall forward, lose my balance, and land once again against the sinks with a thud.

I turn my head, still bent over, and kick out at Marie, who is coming for me. She grunts when I hit her. I shiver at the dangerous glint in her eyes just before she charges at me.

I cry out when she grabs me, my T-shirt tearing again, showing off my pale pink bra. She throws me to the floor, and I can't even think of the shit I've fallen in as wetness soaks into my jeans. I try to push to my feet when my eyes land on the door, hearing banging on the other side.

Hope.

I'm dragged backwards roughly when they hear it.

"Come on; we need to get this done," Marie snaps, and I can hear the panic in her voice.

"We shouldn't have left those two outside," Amy says as she helps turn me, a sneer of her face.

"Let me go!" I scream, still fighting, clawing at her face when they all start hitting me, their punches winding and choking me.

I turn, struggling to get free as the hits keep coming, and manage to twist my body back so I'm lying on my stomach, when something hard hits my back. I cry out, my spine arching at the force, feeling like a bat has been taken to me.

"Get it done," Marie screeches.

They don't stop punching me, even though my body is weak and tired. I'm scared to let myself feel everything. I'm afraid that if I let the pain in, then they will have won. And as long as I'm conscious, I'm going to fight.

I see Marie's feet in my vision. My fingers twitch, wanting to fight back, but everything hurts and is starting to go hazy.

Her foot rises, and I know it's going to be bad. I cry out a little when I try to move, to avoid what is about to happen.

They kick me. They don't even take turns like they did back in the day. Instead, they kick me all at once; my hips, my ribs, my face and jaw. My hands move, clutching my head to try and ward off their attack. I knock out my ear piece and everything becomes silent.

I don't hear their taunts, their threats, or their promises to kill me. I don't hear Marie laughing, telling them to kick me harder.

I can't fight them. I never could.

The silence is welcome as I fight to stay awake, jolting every few seconds when one of them kicks me. The pain is crippling. No matter how hard I try to shut it out, I can feel it. I can feel it so badly, I beg for them to kill me.

I see muddy footprints all over the floor, toilet paper balled up and scattered, or unravelled from the holder.

And this is how I'm going to die. In a dirty bathroom, lying in piss and dirt.

I close my eyes and shut it out. Instead, I picture Aiden and Sunday. I imagine them sitting in bed with me, Aiden bouncing her on his lap.

I smile at the sound of her laughter.

Her smile is the last thing I see before darkness overcomes me.

TWENTY-SEVEN

JAXON
(Yes, you read that right)

I SHAKE MY HEAD AS I WATCH WYATT argue back and forth with Ashton Carter. They're putting elastic bands across a watermelon; the one with the most bands before it bursts, wins. But the way they're acting, you'd think they were defusing a bomb.

The entire competition is stupid, and not something we'd compete in if it weren't for the Carter's. Anything to stick it to them, though.

For as long as I can remember we've had a war with them. Everything somehow turning into a competition.

And I don't mind. Some of them are too cocky for their own good and need putting in their place.

My eyes lock on the back of Landon's head and my gaze narrows. I went to school with Lily, so he was only a kid when we first met. But at nineteen, he's a force to be reckoned with. No one messes with him. And I can see why. He can fight—I've seen him. He holds back when he's with us, unless he's fighting me, but The Circle he's involved in are bad news and you need to know what you are doing to stay alive. The people running them are lethal. And I don't think he's ever met the main boss, only the lackey who organises them.

I nudge Reid to get his attention. "Yeah?"

"I'm going to grab a beer. Could you not get into any fights?"

He grins at me. "Want us wait for you to come back?"

I roll my eyes, sighing. I'm too old for this. I run a moving company, and my mum's farm. Getting into fights, then arrested, is something I don't have time for.

"Just don't cause shit while I'm gone."

"I'll come with ya," he says.

I shrug, not caring. Isaac hears us and steps closer. "I need one too. I need to wash this cake down," he says, still looking green in the face.

"I can't believe they made you eat it," I say, chuckling as we walk off.

He grunts, clutching his stomach. "We had to try each other's. I swear, she was trying to kill off the competition."

I chuckle under my breath. "Didn't you go to school with her?"

He frowns. "Yeah. The girl is nuts. She's happy all the goddamn time."

My mind wanders to Lily, who is the opposite. She always holds a sadness in her eyes and in the way she holds herself.

I shake myself out of it when a skinny kid walks up to us. The other two haven't noticed, too busy whistling at a group of girls walking past.

"Call me," Isaac yells.

My eyes don't leave the kid in front of me, and when the others realise I'm not walking, they stop, turning around and looking at the lad with arched eyebrows.

"Did you want something?" I growl.

He shifts, twisting his hands together nervously.

"Um, yeah, I—I—" he stutters, annoying the shit out of me.

I step forward, bending down a little so we're eye level. "If you keep pissing me off, I'm going to remove you myself. Now, what the fuck is it you want?"

Isaac stands beside him, crossing him arms over his chest while Reid mimics his brother, staring the guy down.

If they keep on, he's going to piss himself. I scrub a hand down my face and move around him, but I stop when he says her name.

"Paisley."

I grab the front of his hoody and pull him against me so our faces are an inch away from each other. "Why the fuck are you talking about my sister?"

Fuck, she went to take her injections a while ago. She should have been back by now.

"Marie and her friends?"

I drop him, dread filling my bones. If they hurt her in any way, I will destroy them, girls or not. "Where are they?"

"I didn't know. Aiden slept with my mum a few months back. He told her he was still a minor," he says, scoffing. "Probably to get her out his bed—I've heard the rumours. My dad left her. I wanted payback."

I shake him, getting further in his face. "What does this have to do with Paisley? Where is she?"

"She was with his girlfriend and the sister. I think they said her name was Lily? They're going to do something bad. Really bad."

I can feel the two next to me tense even more.

"Where the fuck is our sister, dickhead?" Reid growls, stepping closer.

The guy panics, looking ready to shit himself, and points behind us. "They're by the toilet blocks."

I drop him, and he falls to the floor. "Go and find one of the Carter's and tell them what you just told me," I snap, moving ahead to find my sister.

And Lily.

"I'm not fucking crazy," he yells.

I don't stop, but Reid does. "If you don't, I'm going to break every bone in your fucking body, then send it to your mum," he snaps.

"Okay, okay," he yells, his voice trembling.

"Call the others," I yell to Isaac, but when I look back, he's already on his phone.

It takes us seconds to get to the toilets. A small crowd has formed outside, but then I see my sister on the floor.

"Paisley," I yell, running up to her.

She looks up, her shoulders sagging in relief, and I can see she's about to have an episode. "Fuck! Isaac, give Paisley her medication," I say, just as she falls on Lily, who is unconscious, laying on the grass.

Holy fuck.

Her entire body is writhing on the floor, like she's fighting someone in her sleep. I rush over just as I hear crashing coming from inside the toilets. "What happened?" I ask Paisley, throwing her medical bag to Isaac.

"She just started screaming when the girl touched her," she gets out shakily, reaching for me. I take her hand and lift her chin so she's facing me.

"Who hit you?"

She points to the bathroom, tears streaming down her face. "All four of them have Bailey inside. No one is doing anything."

I glance at the bathroom, hearing a scream followed by a scoff of disgust, and people just stand and listen, not doing one damn thing about it.

Fucking cowards.

I look up at Isaac, and his gaze meets mine. "Don't leave her."

I get up and grab the handle of the door, but it's locked. I bang on it, pressing my ear against it, and hear Marie tell the others to "get it done".

Fuck!

I push the door with my shoulder, but it doesn't budge.

"Lily!" Maddox Carter screams, and in this moment, I'm glad they're here.

"Where's Bailey?" Aiden asks, his voice filled with panic and fear.

Isaac must have told him because in seconds, he's next to me, screaming at the door.

"It won't open," I tell him, still trying to push it. "Move back."

I don't give him another warning as I step back and kick the door. He does the same, and we both attack the door until the wood splinters and hangs off.

The scene we find makes me sick to my stomach. And I don't give a fuck that they're girls. I charge in, ripping Marie away by her hair and dragging her off the broken woman lying on the floor.

Fucking Carter's and their shit.

More of us file into the bathroom, Reid grabbing another girl around her waist and flinging her over to the other side of the room.

"Call the police!" a girl in the background yells. And I pray it's for the girls and not us.

We drag the girls outside, leaving Aiden and Charlotte with Bailey. Marie bites me on the arm, and I drop her.

"Fucking bitch," I hiss, reaching for her again. As she struggles, her hoody slides down her arms, and she shrugs the rest off. I notice something fall to the floor and go to pick it up. She takes that window to run, grabbing her friends in the process. No one tries to stop them, because after today, they won't get far. Even if the police don't deal with them, we will.

Clicking the menu button, I grin when I see the phone isn't password protected. I click through files, and one has my stomach rolling.

I open it up and find the menu for pictures and videos. Thousands of them. I click on a random video, turning the sound down when it draws too much attention.

Isaac steps up beside me, Paisley in his arms. "We need to get her to the hospital. Her glucose level is really high," he tells me, but then glances down at what I'm watching. "Did they just say what I think they said? Wait, are they really doing that?"

I look up at him, feeling my hand clench around the phone. "You mean them torching Bailey's house and laughing at the sounds of screams? Then yeah." I pause, running a hand through my hair. "Wait, isn't Bailey's last name James?"

He swallows. "Holy shit. I remember that fire now. Didn't it kill a little boy and his parents?"

I remember it too. I didn't know it had been Aiden's Bailey. The papers never mentioned her name, just that she was in hospital, but I do remember them talking about the rest of the James family. I'm sure my mum said she used to attend the same play group as the woman who had died in the fire.

"Yeah."

"Fuck!"

"What are you going to do?" Paisley asks, her voice shaky.

"Let's follow these to the hospital. They need to see this, too, before we hand it over to the police."

I tuck the phone into my pocket and take Paisley from my brother. Before we do anything, she needs to get checked out. Her medication is working less and less lately.

"Come on; let's go," Reid tells us.

We walk past a devasted family, all of them weeping or cursing up a storm. We might not get along with the Carter's, but one thing I do respect is their loyalty to family.

Because like us, they'd die for one another.

TWENTY-EIGHT

AIDEN

B AILEY'S GRANDPARENTS CALLED THE hospital, giving them permission to let me and my mum in her room. They were on their way back from their new cottage and should be arriving any minute.

It doesn't matter; she still hasn't woken up.

I glance down at her bed, feeling hollow. If it wasn't for the fact I can sense her, feel her, I wouldn't even recognise her. Her face is one big bruise, with thousands of others on top.

Her left eyelid is cut, swollen so beyond belief that it looks like a golf ball has been tucked underneath. The doctors are unsure at this stage if any damage had been done to her sight. And it won't be until the swelling goes down and she's gained consciousness that we will find out.

She has bruising everywhere.

"Son, sit down," Dad says, his voice soothing.

I pull at my hair, facing him. I know I have tears running down my face. I know I look and am acting like a mess.

"Look at her, Dad. Fucking *look* at her. She's got to have surgery soon. Fucking *surgery*. I shouldn't have made her come with me. My stupid ego wanted to show off in front of her. And it could have gotten her killed."

"You saved her life," a soft voice says.

My attention shoots to the doorway, finding Bella, Bailey's gran. "What?"

Her eyes fill with tears as she rushes to her granddaughter's bed. "She has been a prisoner in her own mind—her own house—for years. Since our return, we've seen a change in her. She glows. We've never seen her this happy, not even when her parents and brother were alive. She tried so hard to keep what was happening hidden, but we could see the turmoil it was having her."

"Why didn't you do anything?" I bite out, then grimace, instantly feeling guilty. Bailey didn't blame them for anything—rightly so—so I shouldn't either. "Sorry."

She forces a smile, wiping her cheeks, but it's Abel, her granddad, who answers. "We tried, but we didn't have proof."

"They can't get away with it this time," I declare, reaching my mum's side, where she sits by Bailey. "Look at her."

"We know. We've just been informed who the ring leader's dad is. We didn't know it at the time. We had no clue."

I spin my gaze his way. "What are you talking about?"

"Marie's dad. He ran my accounting department. We found out he was embezzling funds from our companies, so I had him fired. We got the money back—we have contingency plans in place for when things like that happen. But it wasn't until the young lady outside in the waiting room told us that we realised who his daughter is. She told us that Marie's mum left them after he was fired, and she took her anger about that out on Bailey."

"We're taking her up to surgery now," a doctor announces as he walks in.

"Surgery?" Bella asks, panic all over her face.

"You must be her grandparents." The doctor approaches, shaking their hands. "Your granddaughter has a ruptured spleen," he explains, before going over the procedure one more time.

I feel sick listening to it. They'll cut into her. She's already hurting so much—too much.

A whimper escapes my throat, and my mum gets up from her chair and pulls me into her arms. "Oh, Aiden," she whispers, clutching my head against her shoulder.

I cling to her, a sob bursting forth. "Mum."

"We're ready," I hear said, and pull back from my mum, wiping my eyes with the sleeve of my shirt.

"Wait!" They all pause just as they're about to wheel her out of the door. I lean over her prone, broken body and kiss her head, hating the thought that my lips on her might be causing her pain. But there's not any skin on her that isn't bruised. "I'll see you in a little bit. Don't leave me, please. I just found you. If you go, you'll be taking me with you," I whisper, and I hear Mum cry out as she listens to my words. I clench my eyes shut. "Come back to me. Whatever happens next, we'll get through this. I promise. I'll promise you the world if it means you'll come back to me. I'll go to war to give it to you. I love you, Bailey James. To the moon."

I step back, nodding to the doctor. I turn to find Mum in Dad's arms and Bella in Abel's. It hurts. They have their other half. Mine just got wheeled out on a bed, being taken for surgery.

"I need to get some fresh air," I tell Mum, who nods at me.

"I'll wait here in case there's any news."

Numbly, I walk out and head down the hall, but come to a stop when I reach the visiting lounge. The room is filled to bursting with a majority of my family, but it's not them who's snagged my attention. It's the Hayes'.

I don't know what comes over me. My mind registers that Jaxon helped me back at the park, but the anger I feel inside me needs to lash out, and when my eyes land on him, he's the target.

"What the fuck are you doing here? Did you come to gloat?"

His eyes widen with surprise before he stands up. "I get that you're fucking hurting but watch how you speak to me. I'm the one who helped get her out of there."

"What are you doing here?" I ask, not bothering to apologise—he'd only laugh at me anyway.

"We're actually waiting for the police. They said they'd be along to take our statement."

"The police have been here?" I ask, just as Faith and Beau step up next to me.

"Yeah, Aiden. They've taken a few statements, but Jaxon was with his sister downstairs."

"Paisley?" Landon asks, stepping to the right of me. His gaze sweeps straight over me and finds her. "Are you ok?"

Jaxon narrows his eyes at Landon. "Fuck off, Landon."

Landon steps forward, his fist ready to swing, but Beau walks in front of him, blocking his way. "Go outside and cool the fuck off. You've been a raging mess since they brought Lily in."

"Lily?" I ask, my eyes widening in horror. *What happened to Lily?*

"I'm fine," Lily says, and I spin around, finding her sitting next to Maddox, who's half asleep on her shoulder.

When my gaze flicks to Maddox, he shakes his head in warning.

Right. The Hayes brothers. There's no way we're spilling Lily's problems in front of them. Message clear, I turn back to Jaxon.

"I'm going. I'll be back in a bit," Landon snaps, pushing Beau off him.

Liam stands up, but Hayden's hand on his chest stops him. "Leave him. He needs to cool off."

He nods and sits back down. Jaxon sighs, pulling his phone out of his pocket.

"I don't want your number. Just because you helped save my woman doesn't mean we're best friends," I snap.

A guttural growl escapes his throat. "I swear to God… Could your ego get any bigger? This isn't my phone, wanker. It's Marie's. And there's shit on here the police need to see—if they hurry the fuck up," he snaps, directing the last bit at Beau.

Beau nods, reading the message clear, and pulls out his own phone, leaving the room for privacy.

"What's on it?"

Paisley steps forward. "I'm going to get a taxi and head home. I can't watch or hear that again," she says softly.

"I'll come with you," Reid says, looking just as pale as his sister.

My stomach coils and I clutch it, knowing it's going to be bad. Nothing bothers these brothers—I've seen the shit they've done to guys who've tried to mess with them.

She places a hand on Reid's arm. "No. I'll be fine. I promise. Mum is waiting for me and you need to give your statement. I can do mine another day."

"We can't leave you alone," Reid says, giving her a pointed look.

She sighs. "Please. I just need to get out of here. I hate this place and you know it."

I watch in amazement as his eyes soften in understanding. "All right but call us when the taxi gets here—and when you get home."

"I will. I think Wyatt is downstairs still getting treated, anyway. I'll see how he is and check if he's ready before I go."

"What happened to Wyatt?" Maddox asks with keen interest.

It doesn't look like anyone's going to answer, but then Ashton speaks up, sounding bored. "His watermelon burst and bits of it got into his eye."

"He's had to have it flushed out," Paisley explains.

I'd laugh, but I feel dead inside. And I will until I know Bailey is okay and out of surgery.

Paisley leaves and Jaxon takes a seat. I frown, looking at Beau, who walks back in before turning to Jaxon. "Are you going to show us?"

He looks up, his eyes haunted. "No!"

My hands tighten into fists. "What the fuck do you mean, *no*?"

"I'm not doing this to be a dickhead, Aiden. I'm really fucking not. But there's shit on here you shouldn't see. Not just for your sake, but for your girl's. It will haunt the both of you."

"What the fuck is on it, Jaxon?"

Reid stands up, crossing his arms over his chest. "Look, we get you're hurting, we do. But tone it the fuck down. When Jaxon says you don't need to watch it, you really don't. It's not Cartoon fucking Network. What is on there is sick. If you want to listen to a little boy scream while he's being burned alive, have at it. If you want to watch video after video of the shit they did to your girl, see the enjoyment on their faces while they did it, then go ahead. If you want to listen to her virginity being taken, then a whole school laughing at her while it's played for them, go for it. But I'm telling you; you can't erase it. We've been trying to for the last two hours and nothing is working. So, shut the fuck up and sit down."

I stagger backwards, my eyes widening at the phone. I clutch my chest, feeling it tighten. I can't breathe. It has everything on it.

Everything.

Beau steadies me, but I push him away from me, scanning the room until my gaze lands on Hayden. "You!"

"Me?" she asks, pointing at her chest.

I reach over, pulling her up. "You're coming with me. I need you to kick some arse."

Her eyes turn hard. "I'd be happy to."

"I'll come too," Hope says, and even though the girl can't fight, I know she'd do it for me.

"Me too, although I'll probably get my arse handed to me," Charlotte says, standing up.

"Family outing, then," Ciara pipes in.

"I'd stop them before they could hit you back. I just can't hit them," I say, even though I desperately want to strangle the life out of them. But I'm afraid if I go alone, that's exactly what I'll do.

They can't get away with this.

"Aiden, you can't," Beau says, trying to block me.

I square up to him, shoving him, but he doesn't budge. "Don't fucking stop me, Beau. You heard what they did to her from them," I say, pointing to the Hayes brothers before thumping my chest. "I've heard first-hand what she went through, and she still played it down. They aren't getting away with this.

They aren't going to sit in a cosy fucking prison cell and not feel what it's like to get hit back."

He pushes me back, his face reddening in anger. "I'm a fucking copper, Aiden. You need to remember that before you say that shit to me."

"We've been sat with a police officer all this time and you didn't fucking say anything?" Isaac hisses.

Beau and I aim our glares at him. "Shut the fuck up!"

He holds his hands up, sitting back down. "Alrighty then."

I narrow my eyes at Beau. "Have you seen her?"

He looks puzzled by my question. "Who?"

"Bailey."

His expression changes, pity shining in his eyes. "No, I haven't."

"Then you don't understand," I whisper, feeling tears well. "She is bruised all over. There's not an inch of skin that isn't black and blue. She's lucky— really fucking lucky. She has two fractured ribs and a ruptured spleen. The rest, as they've said, is superficial. It will heal. But it doesn't change the fact that they did that to her. They probably would have left her alone if it hadn't been for me getting Liam to look into her and her family. I wanted to destroy her, take everything she holds dear. And look where it got us." I growl, feeling restless. "If we hadn't discovered her dad skimming money from his new company and fixing his taxes, then he wouldn't have been arrested and she wouldn't have done what she did. I *need* to do something."

He places his hand on my shoulder, fixing me with a level gaze. I don't flinch or shrug him away. "I know this is hard, trust me," he says, and his eyes briefly meet Faith's over my shoulder. "But going to find those girls is not going to help Bailey one single bit. They could use anything you do to get out of charges or get a lesser sentence. Trust me. And believe me when I tell you it will not help that girl lying in a hospital bed. This isn't anyone's fault but there's. It's that simple. They chose to react that way, not you."

"And you have Sunday to think about," Faith says, coming up beside me.

I scrub my face, feeling defeated. "They can't get away with this."

"And they won't," Beau assures me.

"Who's fucking arse are we kicking?" Uncle Max booms from the doorway. We all groan, everyone going their seats.

And people wonder why I'm the way I am.

Four hours later and the door to the waiting area bursts open. I'd gone back in to see Bailey after surgery, and by then, the police had come and gone for more statements and to fill us in. When Mum said Harlow had brought Sunday to see me, I came back out into the waiting area.

I put Sunday back into her pushchair and look up to find Mum out of breath. She chose to stay by Bailey's side in case there was any news.

"She's awake. She's awake!"

I rush over to the door, nearly tripping over my over feet to get to her. I don't stop for Mum, only shout a request for someone to take care of Sunday. I push past her and down the hallway to Bailey's room.

Her eyes meet mine when I walk in, and a single tear rolls down her battered cheek. I notice her gran has placed her hearing aid in. I know they were worried about further injuries to her ears, but most of the damage is on her face and body.

"Bailey," I croak out hoarsely.

I walk over to her, and Bella rises from the chair. "We'll give you two a moment."

I don't pay them any attention. I only have eyes for my woman.

"You're awake." She goes to open her mouth but winces in pain. I take her hand gently, not applying any pressure in case I hurt her. "Shush, the doctor explained you might not be able to talk for a while because of the swelling to your jaw. It should go down in a few days." She blinks up at me, her eyes watering before more tears drop down her cheeks. I want to brush them away, but fear stops me. "They got them, Bailey. They got them."

Her eye with the least amount of swelling widens slightly, and her fingers clench around my hand. I chuckle, but it's forced. "We found some evidence—

well, Jaxon Hayes did. They handed it to the police," I explain, rubbing the back of my neck. "But they reopened all investigations and charged them an hour ago with everything they did to you. They filled us in on everything."

Her eye twitches, and I can tell she's surprised. I've been unsure whether to tell her the rest until she's better. But I know if it was me, I would want to know. I also know Bailey, and news like this… she'd want to know about it. She'd never forgive me for keeping it from her.

Her hand twitches in mine. "There's something else," I tell her, watching as she becomes more focused. "They're being charged with the murder of your mum, dad, and brother. They found video footage. They were all picked up trying to leave town two hours ago. The police have them, baby. It's over."

Her eyes clench shut as she struggles to control her emotions. It doesn't work. Her face crumples with despair as a sob tears through her chest. The animalistic sound she makes as she cries for her parents, for the long-awaited justice, is my undoing. I can't hold back anymore. Hearing the broken sounds coming from her body is gut-wrenching, and it tears my soul apart, so I move forward, doing my best to comfort her without hurting her further.

I hold her head in my hands, bringing my lips to her ear. "Shh, it's over, Bailey. I've got you. I love you. I love you so goddamn much."

Her hands find my waist, and, using all her strength, she clings to me, soaking up my comfort as tremors rake through her body. I let the anguish roll through her, knowing she has to get it out. I also know this must be hurting her physically. And as hard as she tries to restrain herself, the sobs break out harder every minute.

She lets it all out, and I take it from her. It's now mine to bear, and mine to destroy.

Nothing and no one will hurt her again.

I won't let them.

They'll have to kill me first.

And a Carter is hard to take down. Trust me, many people have tried— and failed.

TWENTY-NINE

MY HAND SEEKS OUT AIDEN'S WHEN everyone begins to file back into the courtroom. It won't be long until they bring in Marie, Eva, Naomi and Amy from the detention cells beneath the courts. Beau had explained the whole process in detail, including what would happen during the court proceedings; the evidence, the testimonies, and then today—the sentencing.

It didn't make any of this any easier to deal with. Nothing could have prepared me for it.

Seeing them again after the attack made it all come flooding back. The bathroom, thinking I was going to die, the sheer terror I felt. Memories of waking up in the hospital bed, seeing my grandparents and Teagan, the agony

I felt when it registered what had happened to me and that every inch of my body hurt.

It was suffocating. I couldn't breathe, and I hated being so close to them—even if they did have guards. Whether those guards were to keep them safe or us safe, it was left unsaid. I know Aiden had to be restrained himself by Maddox and Landon the first time whilst his dad calmed him down.

In the brief glance I made their way, I felt fear, then anger, and then finally relief at seeing them where they belonged.

I scan the room as everyone takes their seats. My heart fills with warmth at the Carter's and my grandparents surrounding me, here to show their love and support. I was even shocked to find some of the Hayes brothers here. After they had given their testimonies, I presumed that would be the last of it. I hadn't yet had the chance to thank them for saving me that day. I'm hoping today I can catch them before they disappear.

My eyes water at the memory of how hard the past six weeks had been. I'm still recovering now, but at the beginning it had been incredibly difficult. A week of my stay in hospital, I had found out that although I didn't suffer any more damage to my hearing, I was no longer eligible for the operation due to the all swelling both internally and externally. I could wait, get my hopes up one more time, or live with my disability. I'm choosing to live with my hearing aid. It no longer bothers me, and I'd rather have it than lose my hearing altogether, which could happen if I went ahead with the procedure now.

Aiden and his family have been there for me since day one. Not only had his mum not left my side for the first four days, but she continued to visit every day until I was released. I really enjoyed my time with her, getting to know her better without her son stopping conversations when they got to be embarrassing—on his part. In some ways it felt like my mum was there with me. She had treated me as if I was her own daughter.

Aiden had been overbearing at times, refusing to the leave the hospital altogether. I think the nurses felt pity for what happened to me. In the end, they caved and got me my own room, so he could stay with me without disturbing anyone or making the other patients uncomfortable.

By the time he got out his brooding faze, the other patients on my floor loved him. We even heard the nurses fighting over who was going to attend to me, just so they could see him.

It would be pathetic, yet… I couldn't blame them.

He wasn't quite back to his cheerful, fun-loving self, but he was healing too. I could see the toll from what happened was playing on his mind, no matter how hard he tried to play it off.

My grandparents smothered me like always; this time going further than they ever had before. While I was in hospital for two weeks, they had completely renovated the upstairs bedrooms and moved Aiden in.

Yes, they moved him in. He seemed gleeful and smug about the whole thing, saying it would be pointless keeping his apartment next door when he wasn't leaving me again, anyway. He didn't leave room for argument.

Not that I wanted to argue. I found I liked having him and Sunday around. It was peaceful.

I returned home to my bedroom having a new fixture. It was like Narnia had landed in there. They had knocked through the wall, fitting a door that lead to the guest room. A guest room which is now a nursery. A beautiful, bright pink, sparkly nursery with thousands of fairies and stars hanging all over the place.

Sunday was going to be a spoiled child. When Maggie had found out what they were doing, she started to contribute, buying everything her eyes landed on. Then, not wanting to be outdone, Maverick and Teagan started taking stuff over, giving the nursery a little touch from them. The room had everything a child would need until she reached her teens. They had thought of everything.

I was never alone once when I returned home, for which I was grateful. Even though I knew those girls were in prison pending trial, every noise made me jumpy.

I was still processing everything I had been told. I hadn't been convinced anything would be done, and a part of me fears they'll still get away with it, but then Beau started making some calls. He got the trial pushed forward, so I would settle back into a routine. Turned out, he knew a judge, who knew another a judge, and together, we had a date set.

The past few days have been emotionally draining, not only on me but everyone around me. I haven't slept much and eating just made me want to vomit.

The worst day was when they started screening the evidence, playing the videos and showing the pictures to the jury. The second Marie's evil laughter echoed through the room, I bolted. I knew the first video they were showing was going to be the day they murdered my family. Staying would have broken me all over again, and already, I was barely hanging on. Deep down, I knew they started that fire, but a part of me never wanted to believe it. The guilt that it had been my fault consumed me. It wasn't even five seconds into the video before I ran. I had known I would never sleep again if I watched it. The court seemed to understand and didn't question my reasons for rushing from the room.

Today, I'm not leaving. Today, I want to look into their eyes and watch as their lives gets taken away from them, just like they stole my parent's and brother's lives from them. I want to watch when they realise their rich families have no chance of getting them off. Although none of their family are here, it doesn't mean they haven't been given the best representation they could get. I have no idea why their families didn't make it—I don't really care. They deserve to stand there alone for what they did. Maybe now they'll have an inkling of what it felt like to be me when I was alone and afraid.

I squeeze Aiden's hand tighter when I feel them walk into the room. I don't even have to look their way to know they're approaching the defendant box. I can sense their hatred and anger; it's rolling off them in waves. But I ignore them, leaning closer to Aiden, who had tensed at the sight of them, too.

"It won't be long now, baby. I promise," he whispers from the corner of his mouth.

"I'm scared," I admit. My gran, hearing me, takes my free hand in hers, holding on for dear life.

"No need to be scared; we've got you."

Maddox leans forward, resting his arms on the back of my chair. "Want me to cheer you up? I could flash the judge; he needs to crack a smile."

Even with the distressing ache inside of me, I manage to crack a smile. He's been doing this a lot. It was worse at beginning because he didn't know how to deal with his emotions—or so I'd guessed. He used comedy as a shield to mask what he was really feeling, which was anger.

Now, I just think he likes winding Aiden up.

"Shut the fuck up, Maddox," Aiden grouches on a resigned sigh.

Maddox tsks at Aiden. "You're no fun anymore, Aiden. Such a pity," he says mockingly, before I feel his gaze on me. "He's jealous because you think I'm hotter," he whispers loudly. "When you need me, call me." He pauses, and I can sense him grinning. "Hey, isn't that a song?"

Aiden quickly turns around in his chair, knocking Maddox back. The usher glances over at us with a curious eye. I begin to fret over being kicked out, but after a few moments, he turns back to the front of the room.

"If you don't shut the fuck up, I'm going to get you kicked out," Aiden hisses, leaning back in his chair.

Maddox gasps. "You wouldn't?"

Aiden smirks. "Try me," he says, then his attention flicks to the door at the back of the room, the one in which the judge is now stepping out of. "Behave."

With that warning, Maddox sighs, but not before whispering, "Call me when he's gone home."

He holds his hands up in surrender when Aiden turns his furious gaze at him, silently warning him not to push any further.

My lips twitch, but all amusement vanishes when the judge stands up. I flinch in my seat, and Aiden takes my hand, kissing it.

Feeling my gaze on him, he looks at me, his expression softening in understanding. My eyes begin to water. I'm trembling, fearing what the outcome will be. Even with the damning evidence, I've been petrified that they'll get away with what they've done. Again. Aiden knows that, having held me after each and every one of my nightmares.

"Has the jury reached a decision?"

The foreman acting as a spokesman for the jury stands, straightening down his tie as he nods. "We have reached a unanimous decision, Your Honour."

This is it, this is the moment I've been waiting for. Gran leans in closer, wrapping a supportive arm around my waist. A part of my heart breaks at the sound of her hitched breath. Sometimes I forget I'm not the only one who lost them. My grandparents lost a daughter, a grandson, and son-in-law. And it wasn't until this moment that I realised how selfish I've been.

My attention turns back to the judge, listening to the rest of the charges he's listing off, even charges from previous years where there wasn't enough evidence for it to go to court.

"On the charge, S.18 grievous bodily harm, do you find the defendants guilty, or not guilty."

I hold my breath, sitting on the edge of my seat.

"We, the jury, find the defendants guilty."

"What?"

"No!"

"You can't do this!"

I notice Marie's voice doesn't carry through the courtroom, and against my better judgement, I glance in her direction. The coldness in her eyes sends a shiver down my spine. I never understood the saying, 'if looks could kill' until this very moment. It's like everything that made someone human skipped her altogether. There is so much darkness in her. I move closer to Aiden as the judge reprimands the others for speaking out in court.

He lists off other offences, all of which they are found guilty, but it's not them I'm panicking over.

When it comes to the one I most care about, the one I've been losing sleep over, I gaze back at him, giving him my full attention. I also know that if they find them guilty of this offence, they will all get 'life' in prison. It didn't even matter who lit the match, they were treating the offence as a 'joint enterprise' for murder. They will automatically be sentenced for sixteen years. The most we can hope for with the smaller charges is twenty to twenty-two years. I'm hoping they agree with my thoughts about longer the better.

The question slips smoothly from the judge's mouth, but my eyes are focussed on the foreman. Sweat begins to drip down my temples and the back of my neck. My entire body tenses as his lips part.

I squeeze Aiden's hand tighter.

My gran squeezes me harder, and hands of comfort reach for my shoulders. I inhale, trying not to pass out.

"We, the jury, find the defendants…" I can't breathe. I gasp, the urge to run filtering through me. "Guilty."

I fly back in my seat, my eyes wide as shock shoots through my system. Cheers of joy surround me, but all I can do is stare at the foreman.

"Hey, don't cry, baby. You won—you *won*."

I glance at Aiden, feeling completely numb. It isn't until he wipes under my eyes that I realise I'm crying. I rest my forehead against his, clutching his arms as he grasps my face in the palm of his hands.

"It's really over," I whisper hoarsely.

"Yeah, it is," Aiden agrees, pulling me against his chest.

"I therefore sentence you to twenty years in prison before you're eligible for parole."

Gasps are heard around the courtroom, and a tingling sensation—the one I got through school—runs up my spine. I don't know what brings the feeling on, I just know I should be on alert, like a sixth sense.

Slowly, I turn to Marie, knowing without a doubt this is her. My gaze catches on the other three, all weeping into each other's shoulders as the guards begin to escort them out.

But Marie stands there, watching me, her entire body trembling with rage like I've never seen from her before.

I blink as it happens. She tries jumping over the box they are seated in to get to me. I yelp—even though she isn't close to any of us—and bump into Aiden. He grips me around the waist and places me in his chair, before standing protectively in front of me, even though she can't reach us.

"I'm going to fucking kill you, you silly fucking slag. You'll die for this!" she screeches as the security guards subdue her.

Peeking around Aiden, I watch with satisfaction as he slams her head into the wooden bench in front of him, pinning her down so she can't attack. It doesn't mean she doesn't try, fighting and screaming profusely.

"Let's get out of here," Gran says, taking my hand.

Aiden moves to the side, walking behind me as we leave. We pass Granddad and shake hands with our lawyer before coming directly side by side with Marie. It only angers her more, spit flying from her mouth as she yells and curses.

Our eyes meet, and pure hatred rolls off her. There is no doubt in my mind she would kill me given half the chance. I can see it—feel it.

Her eyes narrow. I pause, meeting her gaze head-on, knowing this will be the last time I will ever see her. Her eyes flash with undeniable anger, but I feel nothing. Not wanting to waste another second around garbage, I give her a bright smile before walking away.

I hear her desperate struggles as I walk off, my back now to her. "I'll kill you. Mark my words, I will fucking kill you," she screams.

I don't look back as Aiden ushers me out of the courtroom and outside into the fresh air. The second the cool wind hits my face, I feel like I can breathe again.

Aiden steps up behind me as our families begin to celebrate. He brings his lips down to my ear, his breath warm. I shiver.

"That was badass," he whispers.

"What was?" I ask, wishing we didn't have to wait another three weeks before we can have sex. Doctors' orders and all that.

"Smiling at her. That must have been worse than a beating for her—you smiling at her," he says, before chuckling and nibbling my ear. "It was sexy as fuck."

"You're turned on right now, aren't you?"

His chuckle vibrates down my spine, making me smile. "Yeah."

Just as I'm about to say 'fuck the doctors', I see a group walking down the stairs ahead of us. Aiden tenses, but I ignore him. He won't admit it, but he's secretly grateful to the Hayes brothers for what they did.

"Jaxon," I call out, making the small group stop and the Carter's and my grandparents pause.

"What are you doing?" Aiden asks, a warning in his tone.

I glance over my shoulder briefly. "Something I should have done weeks ago: thanking them."

I walk off and he lets me go, knowing this is something I need to do.

"Hi," I greet when I get to Jaxon. A flash of confusion flashes across his expression before he turns aloof.

"I'm glad today went well," he says.

"I want to say thank you for helping me that day in the park. The others told me there were other people outside, not doing one darn thing to stop it."

He looks uncomfortable for a moment, before shrugging. "It was no bother. Anyone would have done the same."

"But they didn't," I point out, before doing something I've wanted to do since I found out he and Aiden stormed into those toilets. I step forward, push up on my tiptoes, and hug him. He stiffens under me, but I don't care. "Thank you."

"Yeah, I'm feeling a little uncomfortable with this," Aiden whispers behind me, before I feel his hands at my waist. He pulls me back and I roll my eyes at Jaxon, as if to say, 'what can I do'.

"Aiden," I whine, letting him pull him into my arms.

"I'll let you guys celebrate," Jaxon says, before walking over to his brother.

"Remember, this doesn't make us friends," Aiden calls out to him.

Jaxon turns around, smirking. "You're right, it doesn't. Just don't hate me, because I *won't* be friends with you. See you at the next Family of the year."

Aiden's body tenses. "We would have won that, and you know it."

Jaxon shrugs carelessly. "Whatever you say."

"You're the one who dropped out," Aiden points out.

Another shrug. "Yeah, but it would have been no fun annihilating anyone else but you."

"Ah, you love us," Aiden cheers.

"In your dreams, Carter."

"Always," Aiden sings sarcastically, before turning his back on him. Jaxon chuckles, catching up to the rest of his siblings.

Aiden pulls me against him gently—always so gentle, like he's afraid he'll break me.

"You're mine; don't ever hug another dude in front of me again."

I raise my eyebrow at his warning, finding it amusing. "And you're mine. But I was going to thank him either way. He helped me. He helped *you* to get to me."

He frowns, an annoyed look on his face because he knows I'm right. "Still don't like it."

"So, you don't want what I have in mind to say thank you to you, then?"

He eyes light up with mischief. "Oh, yeah? And what would that be?"

I shrug, a teasing smile curving my lips "Well, it involves you being naked. And me being naked…" I say, trailing off.

He grins. "I can be down with that."

"Of course you can," I tell him.

"I still don't like you touching other men, though."

I rise up on my toes, giving him a brief kiss. It wipes the frown off his face, and he melts against me. "I love you, so you don't have anything to worry about."

He gives me a 'duh' look. "Of course you do; I'm sexy as fuck."

I giggle whilst shaking my head. "But that isn't why I love you."

"Well duh; I'm fucking awesome." He pauses, losing his playful expression. "But just so you know, no one could possibly love you as much as I do. I didn't believe there was someone out there for everyone. I really didn't. But you, Bailey James, were made for me. I love you, and I truly believe our love is everlasting," he says smoothly. I soften at his words, falling harder and harder for the man in front of me.

"Ah, Aiden. You really have no idea how much that means to me. You helped me believe again—to hope, to love. I love you."

His eyes dilate, lust burning through them as he brings his lips down to mine. A growl rumbles from his chest as he deepens the kiss.

My body tingles, from my lips to my toes, and I press further against him. I can't wait to have him. To feel him inside of me. The only thing stopping me is Aiden. He won't touch me sexually until the doctor gives me the all clear.

We pull away, breathing hard, and he rests his forehead against mine.

"I love you so fucking much it drives me crazy," he rasps.

"Right back at ya."

"Come on; let's go celebrate. Uncle Mason has organised some food and drink at the restaurant. Today was a good day."

I look up at his stark features, palming his cheek. "Thank you for standing by me the whole time, for being my rock. I don't know what I would have done without you."

He scoffs. "Bailey, you're one of the strongest people I know. People like you, who overcome something so horrific, so tragic, and still walk out on the other side intact, are admirable. They may have beat you, but they didn't break you. They didn't break your soul. It takes someone fucking strong to go through that. So even if I wasn't here, you'd have gotten through this," he says fiercely. "I'll always be here for you. Always. So, don't ever thank me."

How the hell did I get so lucky?

My eyes water as I pull him close for a hug. "I love you, Aiden Carter."

"Guys, come on; I'm hungry," Liam whines.

We pull apart, and a watery laugh slips free when I see Liam's pout.

"You can make googly eyes at each other later," Maddox yells in agreement. "I need food."

"And we need to celebrate those bitches getting sent down," Hayden whoops.

"Language, Hayden," Lake, Hayden's mum, says, but sighs, like it's a losing battle.

"Ready?" Aiden asks, a big grin on his face.

Looking up at him through my eyelashes, I flirtatiously run my finger down his chest, to the lining of his trousers. He gulps, his heated stare burning into me.

"Don't you know? I'd follow you anywhere," I tell him with a sultry voice. I move forward, my lips a breath away, before pulling back. He sways forward, like an invisible string is forcing him, and it makes me grin inwardly.

I walk away, leaving him to watch me as I go. I grin when I hear him run to catch up.

"That's so unfair. You left me hanging," he whines.

Life with Aiden is never going to be boring, that's for sure.

But I couldn't picture my life without him—without any of them.

EPILOGUE

BAILEY
THREE WEEKS LATER

S ITTING BACK IN THE CHAIR THE KIND nurse offered me, I smirk up at a
pacing Aiden before looking over at a happy Sunday in a hospital cot.
Her legs and feet are going crazy, the tiny mobile hanging above her
making her excited. I don't even think she realised or even cares where she is.
She's just a happy baby.

I glance back up at Aiden when he begins to huff and puff once more.

"She's fine," I remind him. Although, she was fine before he rushed us all
here.

He turns to me, his hands still gripping his hair. "She hasn't cried for over
a day, Bailey. Babies are meant to cry. That's what Mum kept telling me when
she was always crying the first few weeks she was home."

I chuckle under my breath at the hysteria in his voice. "Sunday is fine. Just because she hasn't cried, it doesn't mean something is wrong."

I'd pinch her toes to prove it to him, but it will only set him off. And, I don't want to hurt poor Sunday. She's probably already traumatised by her dad's reactions to everything she does.

The doctor walks down the hall, not looking too pleased at being called once again to Sunday's bedside, especially when there are sick children on the ward who actually need his attention.

"Sunday Carter?"

Aiden spins on the heels of his feet, his shoulders sagging in relief. "You need to look her over."

"She's fine, Mr. Carter."

Not happy with that answer, Aiden growls. "She cried when I left the room. She cried when I went to the toilet. She even cried once when I turned the boxing over to football. But she hasn't cried now, sir, in over twenty-four hours. Something is terribly wrong with my daughter."

The doctor sighs. "If your daughter was screaming the hospital down, or in any kind of pain or distress, I'd be worried. They have a way of letting you know when something's wrong. All Sunday is doing right now is showing you she is happy, that she feels loved."

Aiden looks dubious, his eyes going back to Sunday. I can see the corners of his mouth lift and his chest puff out. "You really think so?"

The doctor shakes his head. "Yes, Mr. Carter, I do. Now, if you don't mind, I have other mini people to see."

Aiden waves him on, no longer listening to him. The goof is still stuck on Sunday being happy. He leans over her cot, running his finger down her chubby cheek. Her hair has gotten darker over the past few weeks, her character coming out more and more.

And I thought the day she first smiled couldn't be trumped. It was beautiful. So was Aiden. Seeing him proudly show it off to everyone made me love him even more.

But the day she laughed? The day she laughed I will treasure forever. He had spilt orange juice all down his T-shirt, then tripped over the new table Gran had put in the hallway with the new flower pot that sat on top. Sunday was in her chair and saw the whole thing. Then she giggled. His eyes sparked with wonder, like he was hearing sound for the first time. Then he continued to do everything and anything to make her laugh, recording it on his phone, sending it to everyone, including me—who was in the room when it all happened—then video called his mum and dad.

"Bailey?" he calls, his voice loud, and I look away from watching him trail his finger down Sunday's cheek.

"I'm sorry, did you say something?"

He smirks. "Yeah, I asked if you think the doctor was telling the truth," he whispers, before leaning in closer. He looks around, watching the nurse nearby warily. "He looked too old to be doing this job. What if he's forgotten the symptoms of a really sick baby?"

And I've lost him again.

"Aiden, you're wasting their time. While they're running around after you, they could be treating a sick baby. What if it was Sunday and some overprotective parents were hogging up all the doctors' time?"

He narrows his eyes. "I'm not overprotective."

I roll mine, amused. "Aiden, the other day you surrounded her with pillows and blankets even though she was strapped into her bouncer."

"That thing bounces," he mutters.

"I know—you were still bouncing it an hour after I put her to bed."

He grins, but then it vanishes. "It's a habit, like lifting your leg when you fart."

Ew.

I scrunch my face up. "That's just gross," I mumble.

He chuckles, grabbing her little knitted cardigan Maggie made. "Come on; let's go. I'll have Mum check her out."

I groan. "Your mum will say the same thing."

Just then his phone starts ringing. He looks down at it, his eyes wide. "Oh, my God."

"What?" I ask, worried.

"I have magical powers," he informs me, holding his phone out so I can see the screen. I roll my eyes as he answers his mum.

"Hi, Mum. How did you know I was at the hospital? What about Landon? What?"

His body language changes, his entire body tensing. His head jerks to the side, and the tension surrounding him doubles. He drops the arm holding his phone to his side, and I can still hear his mum on the line. Carefully taking it from him, I lift it to my ear.

"It's Bailey, is everything okay?"

AIDEN

It's like I'm on autopilot as I barge through the doors of the floor Mum said Landon had been taken to.

The corridor is already filled with family, all clinging and weeping together. I don't care. I just need to see for myself. To see if Mum was right. If someone has hurt Landon, then it hadn't been a fair fight. He has taken three blokes on at a time and not broken a sweat. For him to be hurt as badly as Mum described... I dread to think what they used on him.

This isn't right. They had to have got it wrong.

Taking two more steps—Bailey right behind me, carrying Sunday—I reach Mum, who's holding Hayden. I struggle to take a breath at the sight of her crying, looking vulnerable for the first time in her life. Liam isn't doing much better. His palms are resting on the glass window of the room he's looking inside of, pain clear on his face. I can see he's struggling to hold it in. I can't even imagine what they're going through right now. He's their triplet, the eldest. They were the only kids their parents had so it made them even closer, even if they didn't have their weird triplet bond thing.

Anger flares inside me when I step next to Liam and look into the room.

Doctors and nurses rush around, trying to stabilise him. Max and Lake are inside, refusing to leave when the nurse asks them to.

I'm too scared to ask what happened, to cut through the silence, knowing people are processing just as much as me.

Footsteps rushing down the hall have me turning. Dad's face is a mask of thunder and pain. "Where is he?" he asks, and I don't think he's asking about Landon.

I'm right when Mum answers. "He won't leave the room. Neither of them will."

Dad nods before barging into Landon's room. Uncle Max crumbles at the sight of him. The hallway suddenly stills, all of us watching as my uncle falls into Dad's arms, his sobs breaking through the silence.

Dad pulls Lake against him when she crumbles too, her gaze never wavering from her son lying on the hospital bed.

I can see from here that it's bad. His stomach is pooling with blood, and his face is deformed. His nose is broken in more than one place, and his jaw looks like it's been knocked out of place. His ear is torn.

My view is obstructed when a nurse steps in front of him, but my attention goes back down the hall when I hear more footsteps.

Fuck!

Charlotte's face is red with tears as she flies down the corridor.

"It's not true, is it, Hayden?" she yells, her voice hitching.

Hayden looks up from Mum's shoulders, her eyes swollen and red. She nods, not saying anything, then all of a sudden, both her and Liam gasp.

I watch as they share a look of horror, before she rushes over to her brother next the window.

"No!" she sobs, just as we hear machines blaring from the room.

"What's happened?" Max yells, panic in his voice.

"He's coding. We're losing him," a doctor yells.

"No!" Lake wails. I watch, glued to the spot as she collapses to the floor. It doesn't feel real as I watch the medical staff move around in a blur of motion.

"We need you to leave the room," a nurse tells them gently. Dad tries—really tries—but it's like they're all frozen in place.

My lungs freeze as I watch them attach pads to his chest, and I feel Bailey come up beside me. I take her hand and squeeze, feeling tears building in the back of my eyes and a lump forming in my throat.

Charlotte, seeming to come unglued, runs into the room screaming at Landon.

"You'd better wake up, Landon. Wake up!" she screams. Myles, with a tortured expression, clutches her around the stomach, pulling her back out of the room. But she cries and kicks and screams.

"Wake up, Landon. Wake up! Don't leave me!"

"No," a soft voice cries, and I turn my head at the new sound, surprised to find Paisley here. A nurse rushes up to her from behind, like she's been looking for her, and my eyebrows draw together. "No!" she sobs one more time, before her eyes cross and she falls to the floor.

I take a step towards her when I notice a slash down her arm, but more nurses rush over to help. I look up and down the hospital corridor and feel my world implode.

My knees lock together when I hear them shout, "Clear."

"Still no pulse," a male voice booms.

We're never going to recover from this.

As I look around, watching my family break apart and fall to pieces, I vow to make whoever did this pay.

Maddox meets my hard stare and nods, as if reading my mind, his jaw hard and his throat working—struggling not let his emotions take over.

Mark meets my gaze next, his chin lifting, telling me he's in too.

Whoever the guys were that did this will wish they had never been born.

We want retribution—revenge—even if it means stepping over a line we've never crossed.

And a Carter never makes threats he doesn't keep.

And we always get what we want.

AUTHOR'S NOTE

I bet you're wondering whose book is next, right? I bet you're all cursing me for leaving you with such a traumatic cliff-hanger. I'd say I'm sorry, but I'm not. LOL. I really do love torturing you all.

As for the next book in the series… I'll never tell.

What I can reveal—and I'm happy to announce for the first time—is the Hayes brothers will be getting their own series!

Yes, you heard that right.

If you loved meeting Jaxon and the rest of his wild siblings, then please do let me know by leaving a review on Amazon, Goodreads, Nook, or Kobo. I'll enjoy reading what you guys think—as always.

The same goes for Aiden. If you loved his book as much as I loved writing it, please, please, please leave a review.

I want to thank every reader out there who reads my books and falls in love with the characters as much as I do.

Your support means more to me than you will ever know.

Please, keep reading and keep sharing.

You guys are awesome.

Stephanie Farrant, thank you so much for always being there when I need you, for guiding me when I'm a little lost.

As always, you rock.

You may be small, but you are mighty.

OTHER TITLES BY LISA HELEN GRAY

FORGIVEN SERIES
Better Left Forgotten
Obsession
Forgiven

CARTER BROTHERS SERIES
Malik
Mason
Myles
Evan
Max
Maverick

A NEXT GENERATION CARTER NOVEL SERIES
Faith
Aiden – Out Now

WHITHALL UNIVERSITY SERIES
Foul Play
Game Over - Out Now
Almost Free - Out now

I WISH SERIES
If I Could I'd Wish It All Away
Wishing For A Happily Ever After
Wishing For A Dream Come True - Coming Soon

ABOUT THE AUTHOR

Lisa Helen Gray is Amazon's best-selling author of the Forgotten Series and the Carter Brothers series.

She loves hanging out, but most of all, curling up with a good book or watching movies. When she's not being a mum, she's a writer and a blogger.

She loves writing romance novels with a HEA and has a thing for alpha males.

I mean, who doesn't!

Just an ordinary girl surrounded by extraordinary books.

Printed in Great Britain
by Amazon

41497034R00162